CLEOPATRA'S
SISTER

Books by Penelope Lively

fiction

THE ROAD TO LICHFIELD
NOTHING MISSING BUT THE SAMOVAR
TREASURES OF TIME
JUDGEMENT DAY
NEXT TO NATURE, ART
PERFECT HAPPINESS
CORRUPTION
ACCORDING TO MARK
PACK OF CARDS
MOON TIGER
PASSING ON
CITY OF THE MIND
CLEOPATRA'S SISTER

for children

ASTERCOTE
THE WHISPERING KNIGHTS
THE WILD HUNT OF HAGWORTHY
THE DRIFTWAY
THE GHOST OF THOMAS KEMPE
THE HOUSE IN NORHAM GARDENS
GOING BACK
BOY WITHOUT A NAME
THE STAINED GLASS WINDOW
A STITCH IN TIME
FANNY'S SISTER
THE VOYAGE OF QV66
FANNY AND THE MONSTERS
FANNY AND THE BATTLE OF POTTER'S PIECE
THE REVENGE OF SAMUEL STOKES
UNINVITED GHOSTS AND OTHER STORIES
DRAGON TROUBLE
A HOUSE INSIDE OUT

nonfiction

THE PRESENCE OF THE PAST:
    AN INTRODUCTION TO LANDSCAPE HISTORY

PENELOPE LIVELY

CLEOPATRA'S SISTER

A NOVEL

HarperPerennial
A Division of HarperCollinsPublishers

A hardcover edition of this book was published in 1993 by HarperCollins
Publishers.

CLEOPATRA'S SISTER. Copyright © 1993 by Penelope Lively. All rights
reserved. Printed in the United States of America. No part of this book
may be used or reproduced in any manner whatsoever without written permission except in the case of brief quotations embodied in critical articles
and reviews. For information address HarperCollins Publishers, Inc., 10
East 53rd Street, New York, NY 10022.

HarperCollins books may be purchased for educational, business, or sales
promotional use. For information please write: Special Markets
Department, HarperCollins Publishers, Inc., 10 East 53rd Street, New
York, NY 10022.

First HarperPerennial edition published 1994.

LIBRARY OF CONGRESS CATALOG CARD NUMBER 92-54424

ISBN 0-06-092217-6 (pbk.)

94 95 96 97 98 RRD 10 9 8 7 6 5 4 3 2 1

For Jack

Part One

1

Howard

Howard Beamish became a palaeontologist because of a rise in the interest rate when he was six years old. His father, a cautious man with a large mortgage, announced that the projected family holiday to the Costa Brava was no longer feasible. A chalet was rented on the north Somerset coast instead and thus, on a dank August afternoon, Howard picked up an ammonite on Blue Anchor Beach.

He presented it to his parents. 'What's this?'

'It's a stone,' said his father, who was listening to the test match.

'No, it isn't,' retorted Howard, an observant child.

'It's a fossil, dear,' said his mother. 'That's a very old sort of stone.'

'Why?' persisted Howard, after a few moments. The single word embraced in fact a vast range of query, for which he did not have the language.

His mother, too, paused to consider and was also defeated, though for different reasons. She evaded the issue by offering Howard a tomato sandwich, which he accepted with enthusiasm while continuing to pore over the ammonite. During the rest of the afternoon, he collected five more fossil fragments, including one embedded in a slab of rock weighing several pounds.

His parents expostulated. There were already the picnic basket, the folding chairs, the radio, the beach bag, the ball, the cricket stumps. 'Any of those stones you want to take back you're carrying yourself, do you understand?' instructed his father.

'They're not stones,' the child protested. And staggered up the cliff path with the fruits of his first field trip wrapped in his jersey and slung over his shoulder. Thirty years later, the large chunk displaying *Psiloceras planorbis* was to do duty as a doorstop in his office in the Department of Biology at Tavistock College.

There were of course a number of other children on Blue Anchor Beach that August afternoon, several of whom picked up fossils, but not one of whom was to become a palaeontologist. And Howard, during the hours spent there, had also enjoyed a game of beach cricket with his father and listened with interest to a young man strumming on a guitar, but he never showed the slightest inclination to become a sportsman or to play a musical instrument. Choice and contingency form a delicate partnership. Howard became a palaeontologist because he was endowed with a particular intellect and a particular direction of interest. Nevertheless, the economic climate of the time and the action of the Chancellor of the Exchequer must be given their due.

Howard did not revisit Blue Anchor Beach until he was thirty-eight, and the trip was indeed intended as some kind of pilgrimage and nostalgic celebration. He had just been made a Senior Lecturer, and had recently published a book which had been received with some acclaim. But he was now accompanied by the woman with whom he was rapidly falling out of love and the whole afternoon went sour. Vivien complained about the steep and slippery path down to the beach and when she got

4

to the bottom she looked around her with distaste. 'There's no sand. And the sea's the colour of *mud*. I don't see anywhere we can sit, either – the whole place is nothing but pebbles.'

'It's not the sort of beach you sit on,' said Howard. 'It's the sort of beach you wander about on, looking for things. And there is sand when the tide goes out. I have played cricket on that very sand.'

Vivien cheered up a little when he found her a chunk of rose-coloured alabaster. She decided to take it home for the sitting-room mantelpiece. This inspired Howard to talk about the *Psiloceras* doorstop, a fatal move since it led with awful inevitability to a mention of the departmental secretary, a jolly girl with whom Vivien suspected Howard of carrying on some sort of liaison. Vivien was pathologically jealous.

'And why precisely were *you* moving the filing cabinet for Carol? Surely she could have got one of the students to do that?'

'There wasn't anyone else around at that moment. The point of the story is that I thought I'd lost the thing, but it turned up again, not the whys and wherefores of the moving of the filing cabinet, for God's sake. I'm fond of that ammonite and I was sad it had gone missing, Vivien.'

But by now the scene was set. Vivien fell silent; her face took on that familiar pinched look indicating a combination of pain and anger and which was designed to make Howard feel guilty and uncomfortable. She dropped behind him. He could hear the stones grinding under her feet, the sound becoming fainter as he drew further ahead of her. He strode along the beach. When he turned to look back he saw that Vivien was now seated on an outcrop of rock, glaring at the wastes of the Bristol Channel. Howard too sat, and began an automatic survey of the surrounding section of beach. He saw layer upon layer of pebbles worn into eggs, spheres and ovals by time and tide, softly grey and darkly blue, seamed and banded. Behind him, the cliffs too were seamed with alabaster and the sea in front rose in delicate strata of dun and grey to melt imperceptibly into the great pewter dome of the sky. It was a sombre landscape, entirely appropriate to his mood.

He turned over a pebble with his foot, and exposed another in which hung the neat curl of a small ammonite. He considered offering this to Vivien as a reconciliation present, and decided not to. Instead, he covered it up again and sat thinking not of her but of that other afternoon whose imprint hung here also, imbued with the anarchic and inquiring spirit of his own six-year-old self and the rejuvenated presences of his mother and father, setting out chairs and picnic things, no longer diminished and slightly querulous in retirement at Deal but with all the vigour and authority of young parenthood, omniscient and omnipotent.

Except that they had failed him over the matter of the ammonite. Perhaps the further significance of that day had been his own perception that adults do not know everything and that an interpretation of the world cannot be had from any single person. No wonder this place was so filled with resonances. And these, at that precise moment, interested him rather more than the matter of the tiff with Vivien, which would have to be resolved, or not, as the case might be. He sat there, in melancholy contemplation, while two hundred yards away Vivien rehearsed the acid speech she would later make in the car on the way home and which would accelerate the disintegration of their relationship.

Howard rehearsed no speech – that would not have been in

6

character – but homed in upon that other August day. He saw in it the seed of his present self, subsumed within that small boy, and saw suddenly, alarmingly, a whole sequence of tendencies and likelihoods, lurking there like a mirage around the innocent and unknowing family group. His mother's arthritic hip; his father's deteriorating temper. His own hay fever, his objectivity, his agnosticism. Even Vivien shimmered there; he had been doomed to Vivien from the start, or someone very like her.

But he was already embarked upon the process of detaching himself from Vivien, and knew this, though he shrank from the thought of the travails yet to come. Vivien was receding even now, just as she had appropriately receded to a threatening blob of royal blue anorak further along the beach. What occupied him most at this moment was the vision of the entire direction of a life latent at any single moment, implicit in the scheme of things, as though a silent refrain from the future were woven into the narrative, if only you knew how to pick up the frequency.

Mercifully, it is impossible. The wisdoms of foresight are given only to fortune tellers and writers of fiction. Howard, who had little patience with either activity, rose abruptly to his feet, turned to his left and waved to Vivien, who did not wave back, though the set of her shoulders made it quite clear that she had noticed. He sighed, and set off along the beach towards her.

That childhood holiday in the chalet on the cliff-top campsite was not repeated, there or elsewhere. It had been a success, as these things go, but Howard's parents had a mild taste for travel and when the interest rate recovered, and his father was promoted to branch manager of the bank for which he worked, they headed for Europe once more. The afternoon at Blue Anchor was overlaid by many other afternoons in France, Italy, Spain, Greece – encamped upon other beaches, or staring from a car window at the cinematic scenery, or slumped upon a bed in the package hotel or the low-rent apartment, reading or making lists.

He had developed, by then, a passion for classification. He barely noticed the wonders of Corfu, or the Algarve, or the Côte-d'Or, locked as he was in the identification and description of species. Plants, birds, shells, whatever offered itself. It was the orderliness he liked, the symmetries. The fact that everything belongs somewhere, that nothing is unidentifiable. Surprising that he had not become a taxonomist. In the last resort, though, it was not so much the process of classification that entranced him, as the perceived elegance of design that lay beyond it. There was an aesthetic pleasure, repeated in the patterns and structures of mathematics, which also fascinated him. He loved equations, and would cover sheets of paper with those inverted cones which diminished so satisfactorily to a pair of single complementary figures. He led the frenetic interior life of the only child, which both worried and gratified his parents. They saw that he was intelligent but feared for his social skills. They urged him to fraternize with other children, pointing out likely targets: 'Now there's a boy just your age, I'd say' and 'Look, Howard, that's an English family'. In Brittany, they deposited him for a morning at a Club des Enfants, a large mesh enclosure in which a milling throng of children was herded into forms of competitive sport by a few hearty students in red shorts, hired for the purpose. Howard spent the time cowering against the perimeter fence. The experiment was not repeated.

In fact, Howard had no particular objection to other children,

8

and was quite gregarious by disposition. It was simply that he had other uses for his time. It was difficult for him to explain this satisfactorily to his parents – he usually ended up being seen as uncooperative or unappreciative. He was to run up against the problem years later with Vivien; it is always perceived as offensive to prefer to read a book than to talk to someone.

Moreover, he never read stories. He read Junior Encyclopaedias and glossily illustrated Wonder Books of this and that, progressing from these to textbooks, car manuals and closely worded instructions for the installation of cookers or washing machines. He liked language to be technical, complex and (to his ears) innovative. He liked words he didn't understand but whose meaning he could eventually deduce from a context. His parents watched with respect verging on awe, and a tinge of concern.

'Howard, you've never even looked at *The Book of Legends* Grandma gave you for Christmas. And it's got the most beautiful illustrations.'

'I did look at it. I just didn't like it all that much.'

'But why not, dear? Some of the stories are very exciting.'

'They couldn't happen, could they?' said Howard after a moment.

'Well . . . no. But that's not supposed to matter.'

His mother, valiantly, tried a new approach, thinking she had put her finger on the problem. She visited the local library and brought back an armful of good red-blooded realism – adventure, crime and derring-do. Howard dutifully had a go, and was unimpressed.

'Somebody made it up, didn't they? It's not true, so what's the point of it?'

In the fullness of time Howard would come to mitigate this harsh judgement, and to read novels, though never with great relish. He recognized the significance of allegory and the power of narrative but would always prefer accuracies of a different kind. From time to time he read poetry and looked at paintings, because he saw reflections there of transcendent moments in his own experience, and was duly enriched. He may appear a tiresomely literal-minded child, but should be seen rather as one whose intense engagement with the world forced him to subject it to rigorous scrutiny. He could not, at that point, cope with the further dimension of fantasy.

He came early to scepticism. His parents were not overtly religious. His father, if pressed, would probably have come clean and said he didn't believe in anything very much. His mother liked to go to church at Christmas and Easter and, more furtively, at moments of stress. She had no difficulty about putting 'C. of E.' in reply to that nagging query on forms, and would probably have agreed that she was a Christian, albeit a somewhat passive one. She was surprised when Howard, at the age of ten, said that he would rather not go with her to the Christmas service in the church down the road.

'But there'll be carols, dear. And the crib and all the decorations.'

Howard loved his mother and liked to please her. He could not explain that he had come up against a matter of principle for the first time in his life, because he had no way of identifying the combination of embarrassment and resentment which a church service induced in him. He was experiencing the same trouble with the daily prayer at school assembly, and with any references to God, heaven and such matters as the Resurrection and eternal life. He had voiced none of this; the objections and the doubts took place inside his own head. And the surprising thing was that while he realized that his position was that of a heretic – though without having any conception of the nature of heresy – he felt a calm confidence in his own misgivings. He saw that his doubts were renegade, and was surprised at his own temerity, but at the same time he knew they were well founded. And the matter of the Christmas carol service brought the whole thing to a head. It was a moment of resonance, like that afternoon on Blue Anchor Beach, when he seemed to be directed by some echo of his own future self, when he recognized his own nature, and saw that it would send him in directions that were already suggested.

    'Do you believe in God?' Lucy asked.
    'Of course not,' he said. 'Do you?'

His mother ducked the issue of belief, at first. She harped on the crib, the carols and the merits of social conformity.

'The Richardsons are going. Tim will be there, and Kevin.'

The Richardsons were the next door neighbours; Tim and Kevin were Howard's most intimate cronies at school.

Howard squirmed, wanting to step aside from the whole wretched business. 'I just don't want to go.'

'But why on earth not, Howard?'

'Because you can't prove it,' he burst out, at last.

'Prove *what*?'

'What they say about God and Jesus and that if you pray for things it comes out all right. All that.'

His mother saw that they were in far deeper water than questions of seasonal rejoicing and sociability. She backed off, wisely, not wanting to provoke discord on the third day of the school holidays and with Christmas bearing down upon them. She said very well, then, they'd give the carol service a miss this year but she did think it was a pity. Howard felt much relieved and slightly guilty. And in the event the issue of church attendance was never raised again, while the wider problem was tacitly ignored, until such time as the adolescent Howard was able to make his position clear, and neither of his parents by then wanted to quarrel with it anyway.

Prove it! The playground challenge which is perhaps rooted deeper than we think in early perceptions about the phenomenon of truth. And Howard was in no sense an abnormal child. He was the archetypal child, indeed – behaving as he did in one sense because it was his childish nature to do so and in another because he was unique, one of many but profoundly individual.

When he contemplated his childhood, he could see this explanation gleaming beneath the humdrum assortment of apparently insignificant episodes which serves most of us for memory. He saw it as he considered the six-year-old trying to make sense of an ammonite, and the ten-year-old struggling to balance the opposing demands of principle and compliancy. In fact, he did not bother with this sort of personal analysis very often. He was not inclined to introspection. He shrank from those confessional displays indulged in by most adolescents and, later, from the bouts of self-criticism and exposure of the psyche required in emotional encounters. This gave him a reputation for reticence which was not entirely fair. He was not so much reticent as unconcerned with navel-gazing. His own navel he found of limited interest, and other people's alarmed him. All of which made him ill equipped to meet the demands of close involvement. The first girl he fell for, when he was eighteen, expected him to spend hours discussing her minutest characteristics, varied with an inspection of his own, and resented his reluctance to comply. They parted, both having learned a lesson of some kind.

Subsequently, Howard found himself trying his best to come up to requirements while at the same time retaining what he felt to be his own integrity. Each time he fell in love – or thought himself to be moving in the direction of love – he schooled himself to be responsive. He listened attentively while various women told him what kind of a person they thought they were, and why they had turned out as they had. When they looked to him expectantly for reciprocal revelations he did what he could, and invariably disappointed. It was worst with Vivien, his most enduring partner.

Vivien was not just given to introspection, she luxuriated in it. She presumably engaged in it in solitude, for the most part, but what she infinitely preferred was what Howard came to think of as spectator introspection, in which she carried out the survey and Howard watched, or listened, with appropriate indications of attention and interest. There were strict rules about these. He must not remain in silence for too long, but his interventions must be in accordance with certain regulations. They must complement any statement or diagnosis of Vivien's, rather than dispute it. They should either invite a development of the present theme, or prompt a move on to a related one, in the general survey of Vivien's past and Vivien's personality. They should corroborate, but not intrude.

From time to time the tables would be turned. Vivien would decide that the moment had come for some close scrutiny of Howard. These moments often arrived when they were in bed, as some kind of post-orgasmic indulgence. Vivien, clearly, saw them as that – indulgence of Howard as much as herself. The interrogation was a combination of reward and righteous inquisition.

'What did you feel like the first time you had sex? And who was it with?'

'I can't remember.'

'Don't be silly, Howard. Everyone remembers who they did it with first.'

'I mean I can't remember what I felt like.'

'I find that extraordinary. I can remember perfectly. I wonder why you don't – there could be some sort of problem there. Who was she?'

'A dental student called Elizabeth.'

'A *dental* student? I thought you were in a biology department at university.'

'I was. I'd strayed at an end-of-term party.'

'The end of your first term?'

In the early days of their liaison Howard complied with these catechisms, in so far as he was able. He did not do well. He was definitely short on recollection, it emerged, and a dud at self-analysis, though here Vivien was only too prepared to step in and do the job for him.

'This is interesting, Howard – I'm beginning to see definite signs of a touch of Oedipus complex. Haven't you thought about that yourself?'

'No.'

'Hmmn ... That's interesting too. When *exactly* do you remember first resenting your father?'

'I didn't say I resented my father. I said I once had an argument with him about genetic influence. He didn't know much about genes.'

'How old were you?'

14

'I've no idea . . . About fifteen, I should think.'

'And worrying about genetic influence. You see!'

'I wasn't *worrying*. I was trying to explain to my father about dominant genes.'

'Ah, but *why*?'

'Oh, for God's sake, Vivien!'

He learned how to elude or curtail these sessions. If he couldn't manage that, then he supplied the bare minimum of information that would keep Vivien relatively satisfied and avoid one of those onsets of simmering resentment, in which he was punished by days of pained silence spiced with angry glances, until driven to apologize for a situation that was not his fault, in his opinion. Vivien would have seen it otherwise. And all the time he knew that, just as he had been doomed to Vivien, so, equally, their days together were finite. Sooner or later, he would make the inevitable move and set in train the process of separation.

But it is not yet time for Vivien, in the scheme of things. There is a narrative, whatever the ambiguities of position between what has happened and what is yet to happen and what is happening at this moment. Vivien's time will come, or rather, her time in conjunction with Howard's time. At the moment, she is a circumstance, a tendency, an aspect of the overview of the life of Howard Beamish.

At which moment? A narrative is a sequence of present moments, but the present does not exist, or exists only as a ripple that runs right through the story, a procession of contingent events leading tidily from birth to death. A lifetime is so conveniently structured: it begins and ends. It can be seen as a whole, dismantled and analysed, and can be diagnosed as an uneasy balance between the operation of contingency and decision, with the subject tottering precariously between the two from the cradle to the grave. Which is the stuff of history itself, a conjunction so capricious that it hardly bears contemplation by those unfortunate enough to get mixed up in the process.

2

A Brief History of Callimbia

These events are chronological: they take place in sequence and
are in some senses contingent upon one another. Remove one –
extract a decade, or a century – and the whole historical edifice
will shift on its foundations. But that edifice is itself a chimera,
a construct of the human intellect. It has no bricks or stones – it
is words, words, words. The events are myths and fables,
distortions and elaborations of something that may or may not
have happened; they are the rainbow survivors of some vanished
grey moment of reality. But Callimbia itself – Callimbia today,
as I write and as you read, the continuous fluid Callimbia – is
not thus at all.

Callimbia is brick, stone, sand, sea, petrol fumes and donkey
dung, bougainvillaea, palms and prickly pears. It is advertisement hoardings and discarded bottles of 7-Up and Turkish
fortifications and Roman pavements and the Disneyland
architecture of Samara Palace. It is the trams and tower-blocks
and Edwardian villas of its capital, Marsopolis. It is a Greek
temple and a shanty town of petrol cans crouching among the
sand dunes. It is the boulevards and the statue of Cleopatra's
sister and the Army College and Masrun Prison and the
Excelsior Hotel. It is the beaches and the harbour and the

Military Training Zone (access prohibited to unauthorized persons) and the area far out in the desert where there are curious concrete installations embedded in the sand, razor wire perimeter fencing of a quite astonishing height and depth, and very many armed sentries who are not scrupulous about when or at what they carry out their target practice.

Callimbia itself takes no account of chronology. It is all time and every time; it is impervious and ambiguous. Its stones and bones may bear out the myths and fables, or they may not. Perhaps they are evidence; perhaps they are a subtle deception. But they are there, with everything that that implies. You can look at them, walk over them, stub your toe on them. They cannot be denied, and therefore they prompt history. Or fantasy.

Callimbia lies today between Egypt and Libya, with the desert to its back and the Mediterranean before it. This was not always so.

Once upon a time there was Gondwanaland. A suspiciously fictitious-sounding name, but no more so than Callimbia, though one wonders how the geologists arrived at it. But it was real enough, 150 million years ago, a great slab of land-mass embracing what we now know as South America, Africa, Arabia, India, the Antarctic, Australia and various other bits and pieces. Of course, it wasn't thought of as Gondwanaland at the time: there was nobody, or nothing, to think. Just the ceaseless roll of the globe, the ebb and flow of tides, the blaze of the sun, the cold stare of the moon. Growth and decay; birth and death. Creeping and crawling, slithering and splashing, the gnash of teeth and slash of claws, howling and grunting and trumpeting. Eating and being eaten; plenty of fear, pain and lust. Perhaps even a measure of happiness: a satisfactory meal,

18

the sun on your back on a chilly morning. But no thought. Just time, time, time.

And up at the top edge of Gondwanaland there is an area that will eventually become Callimbia – in a mere trice, indeed, *sub specie aeternitatis*, in the flicker of a few dozen million years. Mountains will rise and fall, seas will change their shape, continents will drift, and lo and behold! Africa will emerge, clean-cut and identifiable, and with it Callimbia, perched up there above the desert and kitted out with a fertile plain convenient for human settlement, a low mountain range in which rise several obligingly prolific rivers, and a fine natural harbour formed by the curve of a most apt promontory jutting out into the Mediterranean. Not to mention the excellent alluvial soil of the coastal plain, ideally suited to the cultivation of many crops, and – more pertinently still – the great slumbering ancient deposits with oil tucked away deep in the desert where what will be Callimbia shades into what will be Libya, amid wastes of sand.

The Earth has heaved, folded and drifted to excellent effect. If it had not behaved as it did – risen at this spot, sunk at that – well then, the circumstances would never have arisen, Callimbia would not have existed and the events here related would not have taken place.

But it did, and they did. And we should spare a thought for that momentous process, for that eternity of infinitesimal change, for the grandeur of the furnishings – the storms, the sunsets, the roaring dawns. The ultimate manifestation of impervious nature. And all for its own sake – no one to take note, to record. No painter frantic to catch the effect before the light changes, no poet wittering on about majesty, sublimity and the celestial scene.

But that innocence and anarchy is to end. The painters and the poets will arrive, and along with them, far more dangerously, the historians. Callimbia comes into existence, and the first echoes are set off. The voices are heard which will reach out into the future. People go there, and talk about what they saw.

Herodotus. Stopping off after his Egyptian sojourn, observing with a clinical eye that combines the precision of a surveyor with the garrulity of a gossip columnist:

The extent of the coastline is fifty *schoeni* and the mountains which lie beyond the flat country are some ten *schoeni* from the coast. The soil is black and extremely fertile. The Callimbians grow vines, olives, millet, sesame, dates and a curious sort of bean such as I have not seen elsewhere. Their women are exceedingly beautiful, and decorate their skin with a green dye. Their religious practices are peculiar to themselves: at the full moon they gather beside the sea and pour libations of wine upon the sand, after which they plunge naked into the ocean. It is said that Rhodia, their queen in ancient times, had intercourse with a gazelle. I have heard that Menelaus visited Marsopolis, the principal port of Callimbia, after he had fetched Helen from Memphis, where she had been taken by Paris and then rescued from her abductor by Proteus. The Greek spent some days feasting and taking his pleasure in that agreeable city, while waiting for a favourable wind. Such, at least, is the story.

3

Lucy

Lucy Faulkner was born in Luton because her father met a man in a pub who had a good wheeze going with cheap leather jackets from Spain. Brian Faulkner decided to team up with him, phoned Maureen who was eight months pregnant and sitting placidly in Broadstairs with her mum, and told her to get herself on up there while he looked around for a flat. In the event, the flat did not materialize and Brian discovered that the wheeze wasn't quite such a good one as he'd thought, and the other bloke was in trouble with the law anyway. So Maureen spent an uncomfortable few months in a bed and breakfast, first on her own and then with an incessantly wailing Lucy, while Brian made forays to Spain and then said they'd better move down to London because he'd heard of something interesting there in carpet sales.

This arbitrary association with a place she was never to know often struck Lucy as odd, when she wrote the word on a form, or glanced in her passport. It induced always a slight *frisson* when she saw it on a railway timetable or road sign: the intimate signal of personal connection. When she was a child she saw it as some kind of paradise from which they had been expelled. She would question her mother on the subject, closely.

'I can't remember it,' said Maureen, with honesty. 'I was too busy feeding you and trying to get the rent money off your father.'

Lucy's acquaintance with her father was to last for a few years only and, in retrospect, seemed as arbitrary as the connection with Luton. She would remain for ever welded to him, just as she remained welded to Luton, but in the same formal and meaningless way. She entered his name on documents. She bore it herself. She had his freckles and his chin. She remembered him – vaguely and without emotion of any kind – as an amiable breezy figure smelling of cigarettes who once took her to a funfair and bought her a stick of candyfloss. The memory seemed appropriately tawdry. And her father – who presumably still existed somewhere out there, older, greyer and stouter – was frozen for ever in her head as that jaunty figure whose manner uneasily combined propitiation with bravado.

Her mother, on the other hand, was constant, unfurling in slow motion from the harassed, loving and cheerily fatalistic figure of Lucy's childhood to the Maureen of today – unfailingly good-humoured, quirkily opinionated, and for ever a great deal younger than her daughter, or so it now seemed to Lucy.

In some ways, it had always been so. Lucy was not like her mother. She was not compliant and trusting. She stared, probed and queried.

'Where does the sun go when it's night-time?' she demanded, aged about four.

'It goes to bed,' replied Maureen comfortably. 'It goes bye-byes, just like you do. All tucked up. And then it wakes up in the morning and shines in at your window, doesn't it?'

Lucy heard her in silence, her mouth knotted in disapproval. And then she burst out, 'No, it doesn't. It can't because it's not a girl.'

22

What Lucy meant was: your claim is impossible because the sun, patently, is not a sentient being. Whatever it may be – up there, wherever it may be – it is clearly not a conscious articulate creature like you and me, capable of putting on a nightdress and getting into bed and going to sleep. Since she was only four, the best she could do to express her insight was to resort to a crude approximation and an outburst of temper.

Maureen, at the time, had two children under five, a third on the way, and a husband who had embarked on the process of gently easing himself out of their lives. So perhaps she can be forgiven for ducking an important issue. She was overburdened and undersupported, but it had always been like that. So far as Brian was concerned, she was not yet aware of what was going on. The easing process was carried out with many a conciliatory gesture, many temporary outbursts of uxoriousness. It was simply that he was away a great deal. It was his work, of course; travelling in pharmaceuticals or something by now – Maureen was never very clear what it was he was involved with at any particular moment, he'd always said she wasn't to bother herself with that side of things, that was his problem. He would be away for a week – ten days – and then turn up with presents for the children and nights of love for Maureen. Then he'd be gone again, with a hug and a wave, diminishing to a series of phone calls, always from call boxes with his small change running out. 'Reverse the charges, Brian . . .' she'd cry into the bleeping receiver, but there'd be a click and he was gone. Rushed off his feet, poor dear. And forgotten to send the housekeeping cheque yet again, drat it.

By the time Lucy was six, the weeks of absence had extended to fortnights and to months. Her father failed to show up for birthdays, and then for Christmas. The phone calls became more infrequent, and then tailed off into postcards, arriving at erratic intervals from places like Scunthorpe or Rhyl, glossy squares of landscape backed with scribbled jollities. Maureen set them up on the mantelpiece and contemplated them without comment. When Keith, the middle child, now four and a half, asked for the umpteenth time, 'When's Daddy coming?', it was Lucy who said crisply, 'Daddy doesn't come any more, silly.' Not looking up from the book she could almost read and which was by now far more important than a man she hardly knew.

And thus did Maureen find herself launched upon an interminable series of sessions with social security people and with solicitors, an activity that soon became a way of life. There she would sit (or stand), always clutching at least one child and a bag of shopping, explaining and trying to follow what was being said by this official or that, and worrying away at questionnaires and at figures which never seemed to come out how they should. She bore no rancour to anyone, a stance which was to exasperate Lucy, in the fullness of time, as she grew up and perceived that there was every reason for rancour to be borne in every direction.

'That's life, isn't it?' said Maureen. Complacently, or so it seemed to an indignant seventeen-year-old Lucy, who did not see why life should be thus at all and considered that those who make it so — feckless husbands, intransigent bureaucrats — should be made to answer for their behaviour. But Brian Faulkner had by now so effectively faded away that he had become simply a series of addresses from which official letters were returned marked *Not Known*. He had converted himself into an absence, a hole into which there vanished the whole sequence of inquiries, threats and admonitions. 'Do you think he could be dead?' wondered Maureen. 'No, dear,' said the social security lady. 'They're never dead.'

The daughters of inadequate fathers all respond differently, no doubt. Lucy, having lost interest in hers by the age of six, became competent, combative and enterprising. Or perhaps she would have been like that anyway. Certainly it is difficult in her case to point to either nature or nurture, let alone to make a triumphant case for either. She would not seem to have derived a vibrant sense of curiosity, a capacity for hard work and a robust refusal ever to admit defeat from either parent or from the hand-to-mouth and airily makeshift circumstances of her upbringing. A mother unwilling or unable to confront a serious question about the nature of the universe was hardly likely to turn out stimulating and inspirational. And yet, and yet . . . Fatalistic and compliant Maureen may have been, intellectually unadventurous and burdened by children and poverty, but she was also resilient, resourceful within her capacities and a doggedly protective mother. She was doing the two things that any creature of whatever species is required to do: struggling to survive and ensuring the survival of her offspring.

Maureen's survival tactic was to keep her head down and weather the storms as they came. She treated the whole process as some inevitable scourge of nature – the defection of her husband, lack of money, the obstacle course presented by the welfare state. There was nothing to be done but grin and bear it, put your best foot forward, and so on and so on. She was the sort of person who makes oppressive regimes possible – to set her within a grander historical context. On a more domestic scale, she was the kind of woman towards whom a man like Brian Faulkner will always gravitate, and she was the preferred fodder of bureaucratic systems. She was the perfect subject for patronage and paternalism: unassertive, unquestioning and equably grateful for anything that came her way. She was also, of course, the politician's nightmare.

Maureen did not relate her situation in any way to history or to a political climate. That was not for the likes of her and anyway she was too busy, down there at ground level. When polling days came round she never voted, having forgotten or being caught up in the crisis of the moment. The truth of it, of course, was that Maureen was on the front line, along with Lucy and Keith and little Susie, historical cannon fodder. Lucy's childhood was dominated by mysterious and portentous incantatory words and phrases: the Family Allowance, the Supplementary Benefit, the Maternity, the Welfare, the Town Hall, the Rent Man, the Insurance ... And eventually she saw, as Maureen never had and never would, that it was they and the likes of them who were the very stuff of which politics are made – the raw material, the bricks and straw.

And Lucy, by the same token, was the very converse of her mother – she was the kind governments dread. She was a natural dissident – a sceptic, a nonconformist. By the time she was ten her voice was raised in query.

'Why can't there be enough houses for people?'

'If we haven't got enough money for the rent, then why does the Rent Man have to have such a lot of money?'

'If you couldn't understand what the Benefit Lady was saying, then why didn't she say it so you could?'

She became more numerate than Maureen, and tackled the accounts, scowling over an exercise book filled with columns of figures, over the Post Office Book and the contents of Maureen's purse, ranged upon the kitchen table in neat and inadequate piles. Instead of accepting the recurrent shortfall as an unavoidable ill, she cast a cold eye beyond the walls of the flat, or the rented rooms, or wherever they were living at the time, and perceived things that Maureen did not. She saw inequality rather than an ordained hierarchy, and a capricious system rather than benevolent paternalism. She saw nosy officials and unsympathetic entrepreneurs and perverse regulations. Whoever was presently interrogating or instructing Maureen would become aware of a source of tension: the small figure of Lucy one step behind her, stiff with righteous hostility. The catechism would falter; the interrogator would avoid Lucy's glare and suggest that maybe the children could be sent out to play.

This makes Lucy's childhood sound like some Dickensian purgatory. In fact it was not so at all. She was short of material benefits, but she had a loving mother, admiring siblings, concerned grandparents who did their best to help, and inestimable natural advantages. She was healthy, intelligent and inquiring. She kept up a barrage of questions.

'Why will the fire burn me? Why shouldn't I lean out of the window?' – or, shifting the level of discussion – 'Are there witches?'

Maureen, for once, was able to answer – this was an easy one. 'No, lovey. Only in story books.'

'But if there are stories about witches,' insisted Lucy, 'then there must be witches, else how could the people who wrote the stories know about them?'

A good point. And years later Lucy would retain an image of that moment of perplexity and of insight. Her mother at the kitchen sink, in a cloud of steam; herself poring over a picture book, confronted with this imprecise and unreliable frontier between the possible and the impossible. And she seemed to retain also a vision of her own sudden childish view into the accumulating wisdoms of a lifetime – that a point would come when she would know about things like this, that the asking of this question implied something about her own direction and capacities. She could recognize other such moments, elsewhere, when a fusion of emotion and opinion sent a shaft of light towards another time and another place, and she glimpsed herself, a Lucy who was entirely different, and yet eerily the same.

'*I thought you were a pacifist,*' *said Howard.*
'*If we're being made to play this stupid game, then we're damn well going to win.*'

The continuity of personality is a remarkable business. Is it fostered by events, or impeded? Maureen was to say, fondly, that Lucy was recognizably Lucy from the cradle.

'She'd lie there watching what you were doing and you could see she was asking questions, except she couldn't, if you see what I mean.'

'Curiosity killed the cat' – a favourite expression of Maureen's. Especially where Lucy was concerned. It may well have done – some cats, under particular circumstances. It does not so often kill human beings; Maureen was quite wrong there. An expedient spirit of inquiry is more likely to be a salvation, to lead to survival and prosperity, let alone a more interesting life. It is the prime indication of mental health, which is why it should never be discouraged, even in cats. And Lucy's habit of query was to make her life as profoundly different from her mother's as could be. And yet, at one and the same time, it was undoubtedly the thought-provoking circumstances of her childhood which sharpened Lucy's wits. If Maureen hadn't had such a rough time, her daughter might have turned out differently.

Lucy adored her mother. And was maddened by her. By the time she was adolescent she found her mother's interpretation of the human condition exasperating, inconsistent and plain wrong. Maureen believed that people got their just desserts but also that life was unfair. She was deeply fatalistic but believed that the Lord helps those who help themselves (the Lord in this instance was a purely abstract concept since – rather surprisingly for one so imprecise in her beliefs – Maureen declared herself to be an atheist). She was an avid reader of astrology columns in newspapers and infuriated Lucy, on one occasion, when she put down £5 for a consultation with a fortune-telling lady.

'Why?' wailed Lucy. 'You *need* that £5!'

'Because if she tells me there's something nice just round the corner I'll feel a lot better,' said Maureen.

And the fortune-telling lady duly forecast some vaguely defined benefaction and Maureen was indeed cheered up, so perhaps she was right.

When Lucy's first boyfriend hove on the scene, Maureen wanted to be told his astrological sign.

'Oh, for goodness' sake, Mum!'

'But it's important, lovey. We need to know if you're right for each other.'

Lucy sighed theatrically. She was fifteen and didn't care that much about the boy anyway, but everyone else in her set had a boyfriend and in any case she needed to know more about sex. The boy served his purpose for a while and was discarded when he showed signs of taking the situation for granted. The daughters of inadequate fathers may respond differently but they share a certain advantage when it comes to shrewd and detached assessment of men.

Lucy thought men were fine, but had no intention of getting mixed up with them except on her own terms and when it suited her. She even fell in love, once or twice, mildly and for a few days at a time. By then she had read enough and seen enough to recognize the symptoms of infatuation, but also to know that what she was experiencing was very far from the consuming passion of literature or poetry. She rather hoped that this would come her way eventually, since she had every intention of living a thoroughly robust and ample life, but she was in no hurry. Clearly, that particular eclipse of reason was a hazardous process and you needed to be in the peak of condition to cope with it. Love could wait. And in the event it did, for longer than she had anticipated.

At around the time of the first boyfriend Maureen took it upon herself to warn her daughter about men. 'What you've got to remember is, there's men and men. I mean, some of them are pretty well straightforward, but there's lots that aren't.'

'How do you tell the difference?' asked Lucy. A slanted question, this, given Maureen's own history.

Maureen considered. 'Well, it's tricky. They can be ever so charming. I mean, take your father . . .' She saw Lucy's expression and changed tack hastily. 'Actually I'm not saying I'm all that much of an expert myself, but the point is, you've got to keep on your toes with them. There's some that's all right, but the trouble is the ones that catch your eye, as it were, the ones that get you feeling interested, well more than likely they'll turn out to be the ones that take advantage. That's what they do, you see, they take advantage.'

'Mmmn . . .' said Lucy, who considered that in her case this was unlikely to happen.

'What you've got to do,' said Maureen dreamily, 'is you've got to keep yourself till the right man comes along. I mean, enjoy yourself, yes, have a bit of fun, but in the last resort you're keeping yourself, see?' She was by now speaking the language of the magazines she read, and it should be noted that such language and attitudes were already distinctly out of date, for this was the seventies, and chastity had been at a low premium for some while. But Maureen — who was herself thirty-three at the time of this conversation, having made her own mistake about men at an early age — was in many ways an old-fashioned girl.

Lucy, who read a different kind of magazine, listened to this with a mixture of incredulity and kindly tolerance. She had long since realized that her mother's advice on most matters was erratic and amateur, to say the least of it, but she usually pretended to take it so as not to hurt her feelings. In this instance she did feel that Maureen was so far out of touch with the current climate as to seem dangerously eccentric.

'You haven't been doing it with that Michael, have you?' demanded Maureen, switching to sudden practicality.

'No,' said Lucy promptly. What she did not mention was that she fully intended to within the next few weeks and was in consultation with her friends about how you got yourself taken on at the Family Planning Clinic.

If Maureen had been as astute and well informed as her daughter about sexual matters, then Lucy would never have been born, in all probability. An observation that leads nowhere but one that, baldly put, can cause distress. Maureen herself, in a fraught moment, had once announced, 'If your dad hadn't happened to come back for a weekend that time because he had the flu and wanted a bit of home comforts I wouldn't ever have had Susie.' Susie, hearing this and taking in the implications of her own retrospective annihilation, had burst into a storm of tears. This so filled Maureen with compunction that she started crying too, which in a funny way cheered her up, as it usually did, and the fraught moment passed, as such moments were wont to do.

Keith and Susie much admired their older sister. They saw that she was possessed of the qualities that their mother lacked, along with a whole lot more of her own, and deferred to her as head of the family in practice, if not in title. They came to Maureen for comfort and for sustenance, but it was to Lucy that they turned for enlightenment and advice. Lucy helped them with their homework, tore into Keith when he went through a bad patch and started truanting, sorted out the bullies who were giving Susie a bad time. She made them street-wise – taught them how to negotiate and survive the daily maelstrom of life in teeming inner-city schools, instructed them in the mysterious codes of adult behaviour and requirements. She was pack leader, dictator, confessor and nurse, according to the requirements of the moment. Neither of them was like her by temperament; Keith was bright but nervous and easily led astray, Susie was phlegmatic and lazy. Lucy hustled her sister and exhorted her brother. And if this makes her appear an intolerable sibling, it must be pointed out that all she was doing was acting as a quasi-parent, in response to some deep-seated instinctive drive of her own. In return Keith and Susie supplied her with support, respect and pliant material – a pack leader needs a pack, a nurse needs a patient.

Lucy grew up knowing that people are best served by their own efforts. She saw that it is wisest to expect little or nothing and to concentrate your attention on first understanding the system and then using it, while at the same time remaining sternly critical and objective. Maureen, in her way, knew this too and as usual had the phrase for it – 'You don't get anything handed to you on a plate in this life' – but she lacked the capacity to fight back. Lucy, by the time she had progressed from the swarming playground of the primary school to the jungle of the comprehensive, had learned to identify her objectives and to avoid distraction and obstruction. She liked to learn and was prepared to work; in a climate where both these tendencies were derided, she had to establish her own credentials also – as a person who was maverick but also to be respected, who had wits, guts and a temper to be reckoned with. She even had a small effect on that climate: if Lucy Faulkner thought it worth bothering with class-work and O levels and that stuff, then maybe there was something to it after all.

She was pre-eminently a child of her time, acting and responding in accordance with its customs. She sprang from it, and was shaped by it. She was what she was because she had grown up fatherless under restricted circumstances in a deprived borough of London at a particular point in the twentieth century. But she was also timeless – the product of a certain conjunction of qualities, capacities and inclinations which happen again and again, in any place and at any period, similar in themselves but adding up on each occasion to a unique human being. Lucy Faulkner, this time.

4

A Brief History of Callimbia

So Menelaus may have visited Callimbia. Or, again, he may not
– you can never be sure how far to trust Herodotus. But the
place is on the map now, and about to become even more so.

Skip a few centuries. In which the Callimbians got on with
the business of procreation, and the cultivation of vines, olives,
millet, and of enduring the wayward political climate which is a
feature of antiquity. *Antiquity.* The word conjures up a scene
which is both remote and precise, like scenery viewed through
binoculars, bathed in golden light and peopled with heroic
figures. Well, it wasn't quite like that, however it may have
been.

57 BC. And we must turn our attention to Egypt, where
Ptolemy Auletes was king, a man blessed (if that is the right
word) with six children: Cleopatra Tryphaena, Cleopatra,
Berenice, Arsinoe and two sons both called Ptolemy. It should
be remembered that the Ptolemaic dynasty was itself the product
of a long tradition of incest, which accounts perhaps for a
somewhat intensified view of the sibling relationship in every
sense. One should bear in mind also that at the time a normal
and acceptable route to success, in ruling circles, was over the
dead bodies of your relations, and thus not be too surprised at

34

the behaviour of this family over the next few years. Ptolemy (father) was obliged to make a business trip to Rome, Cleopatra Tryphaena promptly seized power, only to be assassinated by persons unknown, whereupon Berenice, not to be outdone, stepped into her shoes. Ptolemy, with the two youngest children in tow, hurried home and set about deposing his daughter, after which he had her executed. Six years later he died, leaving the throne jointly to Cleopatra and Ptolemy XIII, aged eighteen and ten respectively. And the rest is what we call history. It is worth noting that Cleopatra, assiduously maintaining the family tradition, engineered the murders of both her brothers and her sister Arsinoe before she was through.

This is the generally accepted version of events. In fact, this is not quite what happened. There is an alternative account, which explains the legendary charisma of Cleopatra's sister and puts Callimbia firmly in the mainstream of Mediterranean affairs in the classical age. Berenice was not executed. She was a girl of compelling physical attraction and commanding personality, irresistible to most who came into her orbit and certainly to Rhamades, a captain of the guard appointed by Ptolemy to supervise her captivity and carry out the execution. Rhamades fell in love with Berenice and ensured her survival by substituting a female slave who was duly dispatched in her place and whose body was whipped away and buried by others party to the conspiracy before the deception could be found out. It is interesting to note that Ptolemy must have ignored one of the basic rules of judicial murder – always check out the corpses of your victims – and we can perhaps suppose that the execution of a daughter was a touch unsettling even in the Ptolemaic context.

Rhamades and Berenice headed hotfoot for the Callimbian

border and thence for Marsopolis, where Rhamades had friends and where he planned to marry Berenice and set up in style as the consort of royalty and a man of substance. But Berenice had other ideas. Callimbia was ruled at the time by Hippostrates, a connection of the Ptolemies, a man pushing sixty and childless. Berenice set about ingratiating herself with the king, whose young wife died soon after from eating poisoned sweetmeats of mysterious provenance. Berenice made the consolation of Hippostrates her especial concern, and in due course they were married. Rhamades disappeared from the story, Hippostrates expired at the ripe old age (by the standards of the day) of sixty-two, and Berenice became Queen of Callimbia.

For the next few years she and her sister Cleopatra glared at each other across the desert. Caesar came, and went. Berenice undoubtedly heard every detail of her sister's gaudy and eventful career, and would have been duly affected. Cleopatra was not only younger, but (according to Berenice's acolytes) less beautiful, less intelligent and less entertaining. But she had all the luck. Such Romans as dropped in at Marsopolis were not of the Caesar class. Berenice observed, took note, and bided her time. And it was not such a bad time, either: a capital city which rivalled Alexandria in civilized appeal, a subservient and industrious population, a compliant entourage, wealth, health and lovers.

And then Antony hove upon the scene. By now Berenice's watchful interest must indeed have been intense. Quite apart from the question of sibling rivalry, there was the matter of international peace and security, with warring Roman contingents rampaging around the Mediterranean, rattling swords at one another and appropriating territory whenever it seemed expedient. Berenice must have feared for the sovereignty of Callimbia. Hitherto, evidently, she had steered a diplomatic course of non-involvement, but now things were getting hot. Antony was busy giving Cleopatra chunks of Asia Minor for birthday presents, while Octavius Caesar and his friends were not known for their sensitive recognition of national boundaries. Berenice looked on, wondering how best to keep her head above water.

Antony and Cleopatra confronted Octavius's fleet at the battle of Actium, and lost disastrously. Cleopatra retreated up-country to rally the troops and consider the next move, but Antony, emotional and impulsive, and plunged into a fit of depression and shame, rushed off along the coast with a couple of friends, Aristocrates and Lucilius. Their ship was caught in a storm, blown hither and thither, and eventually forced into the harbour of Marsopolis, where news of the arrival of these unexpected visitors was brought immediately to Berenice.

What an opportunity! Play her cards right and she could filch Antony from right under her sister's nose. He was disillusioned, depressed and notoriously unstable. Berenice got to work.

It is at this point that Plutarch's sparse comments endorse the alternative account of events, and furnish the first official historical reference to Berenice's existence. It is probable that Plutarch travelled to Callimbia, and indeed the sudden onset of descriptive enthusiasm in his otherwise mundane narrative suggests precisely that.

Mark Antony, with his companions, was forced to take shelter from the storms in the harbour at Marsopolis, the principal city of Callimbia, where he was received by the queen of that country: Berenice, the sister of Cleopatra. Berenice entertained Antony lavishly, and urged him to stay at her court until he was fully recovered from the stresses and disappointments of the recent campaign. And indeed Antony was of a mind to do so, for the city was very agreeable, with many gracious buildings, avenues of flowering trees, an abundance of food and wine, and a climate made pleasant by the prevailing cool breezes from the sea. However, Aristocrates was opposed to this and persuaded Antony to set sail and to rejoin Cleopatra at Alexandria.

This leaves out a great deal. Either Plutarch didn't know any more, or he preferred to be economical with the truth. What really happened was that Berenice threw the biggest party Marsopolis had ever seen. We can assume that she had heard a thing or two about her sister's various thrashes, over the years – the illuminations, the perfumes wafted from censers, the boys dressed as Cupid, that barge. The flutes, the pipes and lutes; the roasted boars. The nights of dalliance. Berenice flung herself into the process of upstaging and outdoing. The ensuing jamboree lasted for three weeks, it is said. There were torchlit processions, phalanxes of dancing girls, cauldrons of roasted doves, vats of Callimbia's choicest wines, honey-baked gazelle, phoenix steeped in herbs, masques and acrobatic displays and a continuous serenade by hand-picked eunuchs. Berenice herself made her entrance in a chariot of onyx and malachite, drawn by leopards. She gave Antony a trireme crewed by Nubian slaves, plus an ivory chest stuffed with precious stones, a cloak of the finest Callimbian linen embroidered with pearls, and finally a bed made of cedar of Lebanon inlaid with gold. No doubt Antony took the hint. What is certain is that he entered into the celebrations with enthusiasm. He stayed on, and on. His companions became concerned. Antony was well known for susceptibility and lack of judgement. Octavius Caesar was stamping around Macedonia, waiting to pounce; Cleopatra would be getting restive, to say the least of it. The companions urged a return to Egypt; Antony waved them away and helped himself to another roasted dove. And finally they took matters into their own hands, slipped a hefty knock-out potion into Antony's wine, loaded him into the trireme and hurried him back to Alexandria to make his peace with Cleopatra and get on with the business of bickering over control of the Roman Empire.

Nothing more is heard of Berenice. From Plutarch or from anyone else. She vanishes, to be transformed into a myth, a legend, a voluptuous marble statue in the central square of late twentieth-century Marsopolis and a provocative suggestion of alternative history. If Antony's companions had not been so forthright. If he had been alone. If Berenice had not given him that trireme. Ah, if . . .

5

Howard

During his twenties, Howard became aware of the curious divide between the life that he lived and the forms of life that he studied. His working days were spent scrutinizing fossil fragments, staring into a microscope, and pondering the construction and performance of extinct species. He worried about digestive systems, reproductive apparatus and modes of locomotion. These mysterious and elusive creatures were both deeply individual and at the same time parts of an intricate network of interdependence. They ate, and were eaten. There were both prey and predators. He sought to identify points of evolutionary success, or of failure. His own professional success depended upon the painstaking or inspired interpretation of a function or a relationship, thus giving a further artificial but ironic twist to the system of mutual obligation.

But if he looked with equal detachment at his own struggle for survival, he saw something entirely different. Or rather, since the detachment was impossible, experienced something entirely different. What you had here was a battleground of emotion, personality and intellectual ability. Physical attributes hardly came into it at all, except in a minor way, of course — those regarded as good-looking have a superficial asset, while it is clearly not an advantage to be malformed or grossly tall, short, fat or thin. But on the whole success lies elsewhere, for *Homo sapiens*. It is only in more esoteric occupations – prizefighting, javelin-throwing, nightclub bouncing – that sheer physical strength or dexterity wins out. Howard had the opportunity to observe this truth at first hand when he was appointed to his first academic post, as an assistant lecturer at Tavistock College. The institution was in the grip of a peculiarly ferocious outbreak of inter-departmental warfare, centred around a power struggle between rival professors. The power struggle had little to do with the disputed matters of course structures and the allocation of teaching resources and everything to do with the conflicting personalities and irreconcilable ambitions of the two men concerned, a burly choleric geologist from Yorkshire and the head of Howard's own department, a bantam-weight Welshman. Confrontations between the two men were a process of relentless emotional manipulation, with Idris Jones seeking to provoke his opponent into a fatally compromising loss of temper and thus of negotiating status, while the geologist concentrated on a campaign of innuendo and imputations of malpractice. If there were a biological analogy, it would be of a fight between members of different species, each equipped with its own means of attack and defence – teeth versus claws, speed against camouflage. But in this case the strengths and weaknesses were aspects of character and qualities of intellect. One man was almost twice the size of the other. Howard, observing their engagements in the Senior Common Room or around a committee table, saw the whole thing as a triumph of mind over matter.

He was twenty-six at the time, and it was his first experience of the brutalities of human intercourse. He had led a somewhat sheltered life. As an only child he had been spared – or deprived of – sibling warfare. His childhood had been spent in a decorous suburban area north of London. The school to which he had won a scholarship was similarly exempt from the more extreme savageries of street life and playground. There was little bully-ing, and the violent aspects of adolescent exuberance were rigorously quenched by the staff. Intelligence and application were neither despised nor penalized, and it didn't matter that much if you were not good at games. Howard was perfectly happy at school, which he was later to realize was a privilege, but perhaps also a drawback in that he was distinctly untrained for a life of competition and contention. By the time he reached university he was so immersed in his particular interests that he ignored most of the extra-curricular student activities, and led his own contented and preoccupied life on the edge of things, occasionally plunging into some smoky gathering over coffee mugs or bottles of rot-gut wine when he felt in need of conversation or sexual stimulus. He was liked, but seen as somewhat aloof. Girls found him faintly intriguing because of his detachment; from time to time one of them would make a dead set at him, and Howard would respond with polite enthusiasm, which usually fizzled out after a few weeks. He enjoyed sex, and became increasingly disturbed by the fact that his emotions were not much engaged. He would be attracted to a girl, want to go to bed with her, do so – provided she was of the same mind – and then fairly soon he would come to realize that he felt nothing much for her at all. And, since it seemed to him distinctly shabby to go on indulging yourself sexually with someone to whom you were pretty well indifferent, he would back out of the relationship, gingerly and with compunction. The campus psychiatrist was on call round the clock, alert for every manifestation of emotional unease or disturbance. Many of Howard's acquaintances spent some of each term officially excused from classes on account of psychological distress; it seemed positively abnormal to profess constant robust mental health. But Howard felt unable to take his particular trouble along for an airing. You could not sit there and say to the man, 'Please, I don't seem able to fall in love.' It would be less embarrassing to be able to claim impotence, or sexual deviance of some kind.

And in any case he was increasingly absorbed in work. He had known for a long time that he wanted to be a palaeontologist. Towards the end of his period at university he became clear as to what kind of a palaeontologist he wanted to be. He found the focus of his interest reaching further and further back in time, and homing in upon smaller and smaller creatures. The more spectacular areas of the discipline were not for him, he realized, turning his back on the Jurassic, on dinosaurs, on early mammals. He was drawn to the beginnings, to that ultimate antiquity, in which anything is possible, where everything is decided, whence, against all the odds, we derive. The first time he looked through a microscope at one of those bizarre, unlikely and immaculate animals of the Cambrian Burgess Shale, he knew that he was hooked. Enslaved, committed. He had fallen – not in love but into fascination. It was as though he stared not just down a tube but through dimensions of time and space – as though his eye reached through more than 500 million years and became intimate with the exotic universe of those delicate creatures which floated brilliantly into vision, unreachable, inconceivable and precise. He became detached, intense, dispassionate, his entire being subsumed into his own eye as he gazed down into that light-drenched other world, at the sparkling surface of the rock on which there sprang into sudden relief the symmetries of miraculous creatures, delicate scribbles on the grey desert – the ridges of a body like dredged silver sand, or the smear of graphite that was the shining whisper of a vanished creature. Using a camera lucida, he would watch the image of his own pencil, straying over the craggy surface of the rock, across shelves and valleys, a ghostly intrusive presence defining now the outline of the animal, lifting it from its silent floodlit world on to a sheet of paper, and he understood that he would spend his life in the service of *Opabinia, Wiwaxia, Hallucigenia* and the rest of them. Here was an array of creatures most of which were unrelated to any species in existence now, all of which had vanished. Here were animals like hairbrushes, or like lotus flowers, with nozzles, struts and frills, occasionally reminiscent of existing fauna, but always eerily different, as though you looked at the fantastic parade of an alternative world. And that, of course, was exactly what they were: the doomed originators of a host of alternative worlds, the elegant biological suggestions which might have led to a contemporary scene populated by the unthinkable descendants of hairbrushes and lotus flowers, if the contingent events of evolution had proceeded differently. The strange conjunction of likelihood and contingency which is the root of life, in every sense. The accident of reality, and of human existence. Howard, improbable heir of the most insignificant of the Burgess Shale animals, the modest slug-like creature, *Pikaia*, which is ancestral to vertebrates, stared at these quivering images, thought of the implications, and knew what he wanted to do.

He did much of the work for his doctoral thesis on the other side of the Atlantic, working on Burgess specimens in the Smithsonian and scrambling around the sacred fossil beds on the slopes of the Canadian Rockies. It was a period that seemed detached from the onward march of things, as though his life were temporarily in suspension, a combination of idyll and purgatory, when he knew that he was probably at his happiest but knew also that the whole thing had to come to an end, and possibly a bitter one. Would he get a job? Would he get a job in the sort of institution he sought, or would he be driven to accept some compromise position, or exiled to somewhere that took in everyone else's rejects? He was far from being without self-esteem, and knew that his work was good and his potential excellent. He had not yet tried his hand at teaching, but thought he would probably get on all right. But he knew now that those who deserve do not always get, and that while the objectives of science may be pure and uncompromising, the process of appointment to an academic position is not. He finished the thesis while anxiously scanning the appropriate Appointments Vacant pages and writing letters to anyone he thought might be able to offer help or advice. When the Assistant Lectureship at Tavistock College came up, he applied at once, though without high hopes. A London job was highly desirable; everyone would be after it.

On the morning of Howard's interview the Professor of Geology, that short-tempered Yorkshireman, had a row with his wife. As a consequence of this he left home in a state of irritation and inattention, drove his car violently into the back of a lorry and ended up in the local Casualty Department. The interview took place without him, and thus without the support he had intended to give to the candidate who was a former student of his. Professor Idris Jones, the chairman of the Appointment Board, whose main interest in the matter was to oppose the selection of his enemy's protégé, was thus able to engineer without much difficulty that Howard got the job. Howard, surprised at this evident favouritism from a man he did not know and who certainly knew little or nothing of him, was fervently grateful to Idris Jones until, months later, a colleague kindly enlightened him as to the correct interpretation of events. Howard was somewhat chagrined. It would have been nice to think that he was the obvious candidate, or that he had captivated those present with his ability and personality. But by then what really mattered was that he had the job, he was embarked on the course that he had chosen, and he could support himself by doing the sort of work that he wanted to do, which seemed an extraordinary privilege.

He found a garret, encouragingly called a studio penthouse, not far from the college, at an exorbitant rent. After a couple of years he exchanged this for a basement, the monthly mortgage payments on which devoured most of his salary. He would have been quite content to remain in the garret, but was goaded into the purchase by his father, who made it clear that without owner-occupancy and a mortgage he would remain locked into some kind of eternal feckless adolescence. Howard would not have cared particularly about this, but he did not like to distress his father, to whom it mattered, so he allowed himself to be propelled into the basement, and let his mother deck it out with curtains and cushions.

The basement, disguised with the cheerful label of garden flat, was in a seedy street near King's Cross down which Howard walked by accident. He had been looking for a place someone had told him about which sold cut-price typewriters, failed to find it, and landed up wandering past this terrace in the process of conversion from grubby boarding houses to cramped maisonettes, the corner of which sprouted the sign which misleadingly offered a charming 2-bed gdn flat. It was the point at which he was under intense pressure from his parents to do something about his living arrangements. He had promised to house-hunt. He hated house-hunting. He made a note of the agent's phone number, saw the flat that evening, and moved in a couple of months later, thus committing himself to three years of litigation and a love affair.

The basement was precisely that – the bottom level of a nineteenth-century terrace house, reached by an iron staircase down into the concrete area with drain-hole and brick facing wall on to which the front room looked. The rooms at the back peered upwards into the ersatz garden, a further concrete space edged by a flower-bed filled with black cindery earth and brickbats in which grew a sickly but determined lilac. The lilac managed a few faded flowers each spring and was to afford Howard a curious kind of comfort on several occasions over the next few years.

The two floors above the basement comprised a maisonette, while the top of the house had become a penthouse. One had to concede a sort of respect for this expedient recycling of a building constructed with an entirely different sort of occupancy in mind. At least it was doing something to solve the problem of inner-city housing needs by cramming as many people as possible into the available space, though at the cost of considerable discomfort and chronic financial crisis for the inhabitants. The flats changed hands frequently, which for Howard had the advantage that the overhead noises also changed in character. The staccato sound of argument between the couple on the verge of splitting up would give way to the rhythmic thump of someone's stereo which would in turn be superseded by the gentle thunder of a two-year-old at play.

Within a couple of years the building began to disintegrate. The roof sprang a leak, cracks appeared in the exterior walls, dry rot was diagnosed above the front door. A soft tidemark of damp crept up the wall of Howard's sitting-room. The leaseholders of the three flats appealed to the freeholder, to whom they had been paying substantial service charges. The freeholder failed to answer letters and was never available on the telephone. The leaseholders consulted solicitors, whose services they could not afford, who wrote more letters to which the freeholder did not reply, and made more fruitless phone calls.

All this created a certain sense of community within the house. Howard formed a Residents' Association and invited his neighbours to a spaghetti supper to discuss tactics. The maisonette was at this time occupied by a gay couple, a second-hand book dealer and his friend, while the top floor belonged to a flautist called Celia. She was a pale thin girl with long fair hair confined by an Alice band, who gave an impression of extreme fragility. Three days after the spaghetti supper Celia knocked on Howard's door to ask if he could come up and help her fix a curtain rail which was giving trouble. He found himself gazing fondly at the childish flaxen strands that lay across her neck, and a week later he went to a concert in which she was playing. Within a short while he was looking up to see if her lights were on when he came back in the evening, or listening for the slam of the front door. He monitored his feelings with intensity, and when he found himself thinking of her in the middle of giving a lecture, or during the precious periods he was able to devote to his own research, he wondered with excitement if this was love.

Celia had the delicate appeal of a porcelain figurine, with blue eyes and rose-petal skin. She was also, Howard soon learned, deceptively resilient and somewhat withdrawn. She earned a living picking up freelance work where she could, vanishing sometimes for two or three days at a time on assignments about which she was vague when Howard made inquiries. She was the most reticent girl he had ever known, which added considerably to her attraction. She did not subject him to psychological scrutiny, and much of the early part of their association was spent in silence, while Celia gazed dreamily at the floor, or walked passively at his side. Up in her room, they listened to music, or Howard read a book or newspaper, a tranquillity disturbed only by Howard's state of sexual agitation and concern lest this combination of uxoriousness and celibacy was to be permanent. He had decided by now that this most definitely was love. He thought of her constantly, had great difficulty keeping his hands off her, and was in a state of deprivation each time she went away. It was not clear what she felt about him. She evidently liked his company and she did not reject his advances, but it seemed to be taking an awfully long time for them to get to bed together. Each time they were on the verge, as Howard felt, the kiss would come to an end, or Celia would gently imply by some look or movement that this wasn't the moment. Quite often she would be out for hours on end without explanation, returning with a look on her face which combined complacency with a curious and uncharacteristic excitement. He wondered jealously if there could be another man.

And then suddenly one evening, while Howard was fondling her hand on the couch in her attic room, to a background of Monteverdi and the remains of a bottle of Soave, Celia suddenly sat up, looked at him, and took off her sweater. She had nothing on underneath. The sight of her breasts reduced Howard to a state of tremulous frenzy; he thought that he had never seen anything so exquisite – small, creamy, and topped with perfectly shaped warm pink nipples. Celia gazed expectantly at him; he put his glass down and set to.

She was not, as he had also wondered, a virgin. Not so at all. Indeed she was surprisingly adept and responsive. It was a rather different Celia with whom he writhed and panted in the twilight of her room and alongside whom he eventually fell asleep. She was both businesslike and enthusiastic. Howard had a wonderful time, and woke up the next morning with a sense of complacent fulfilment. This was it, at last. This was love – sexual, spiritual, the lot.

They began to spend most nights together, in either her bed or his. Now that the relationship was on this sort of footing, Howard expected to find himself taken rather more into Celia's confidence, and to accompany her beyond the confines of the house. This did not happen. Celia's attitude towards him had indeed undergone a subtle change, but not quite in the direction that Howard anticipated. She became more matter-of-fact, and indeed slightly proprietorial, but she was no more forthcoming, and she continued to vanish for hours, or days, about business of her own on which she did not expand. 'I had to go somewhere,' she would say, or 'I had to see some people.' Howard was consumed with jealous doubts but learned not to press the point; on the one occasion when he did, Celia became petulant and ejected him from her bed.

She, on the other hand, expected his attention whenever she required it. He would find terse little notes dropped through his door: 'Came down but you were out for some reason – please let me know when you're back.' He did not mind this, taking it for evidence of love. She showed only a perfunctory interest in his life, or in his work, which hurt him a little, and when on one occasion he asked her to come with him to an end-of-term departmental party she said she would rather not: 'If you don't mind, Howard, I just don't think they'd be my sort of people.' 'But I'm your sort of person,' Howard protested. 'Or at least I hope I am. They're all scientists and academics too.' Celia smiled enigmatically and shook her head.

Howard perceived that all was not absolutely as it should be, but he was too inexperienced in alliances of this kind to be able to put his finger on what was wrong. He simply knew that he and Celia, as a couple, were not as other couples appeared to be. On the other hand, how much did one really know of the intimate lives of others? There was no question but that sex was going very well indeed, and so far as he was concerned all he knew for certain was that he hungered after Celia, wanted to be with her and fretted when this was impossible. He wasn't exactly happy, he realized, but then love was supposed to be an unsettling condition, was it not? He assumed that they would shake down somehow, and began to think vaguely about marriage.

And then, one Sunday morning, Celia sat up in bed, looked at her watch and said, 'I want you to come to church with me this morning, I've told them I'm bringing you. They're expecting you.'

Howard felt himself go rigid. Then he thought he could not have heard aright.

He said cautiously, 'Church . . .?'

'Yes, church,' said Celia briskly. 'We have a special Sunday service in Finchley.'

Howard was silent. The room seemed to have gone extremely cold. Celia had got out of bed and was brushing her hair, an activity he usually enjoyed watching.

At last he said, 'I didn't know you were religious.'

51

'I thought you would have realized. We don't make a point of going on about it to people who aren't born again, but I've told them about you, and they want you to come.'

'Is that where you go,' said Howard slowly, 'when you . . . go off?'

'Well, of course,' said Celia. 'What did you think?'

'I thought perhaps you were seeing another man,' said Howard bleakly.

Celia laughed. She was not a girl who laughed often, and the sound contributed to Howard's sense of disorientation.

'You'd better get up. We have to be there by ten.'

'I can't come,' said Howard. 'I'm not a Christian.'

Celia turned to look at him with a sort of patronizing tolerance. 'It doesn't matter. Nor was I, once. That'll come.'

'You don't understand, Celia,' said Howard. 'I could never be a Christian. I'm an agnostic. It's something I've thought about for most of my life.'

'You'll feel quite differently when you've heard our pastor,' said Celia comfortably. 'He's the most wonderful person I've ever met.' She had finished her hair now and was putting on her bra, another process Howard found aesthetically satisfying in normal circumstances. He lay there looking at her. His stomach felt as though someone had sunk a lead weight into the middle of it. Celia seemed very remote, and entirely alien, as though she were someone he knew slightly, glimpsed across a crowded street.

She continued to talk with fervour about this pastor, and his acolytes. They were members of a fundamentalist sect, it appeared, though a somewhat idiosyncratic one which renounced overt evangelical activities in favour of an intense and exclusive group life.

'But the thing is,' said Celia, 'if any of us gets involved in a meaningful relationship, then we're welcome to bring the person along to meet the group. The pastor usually has a quiet personal exchange with them after the service. It's a wonderful experience. That's how I joined the group originally. I was going out with this fiddle-player, and he was a member and he took me along.' It was one of the longest and most revealing speeches she had ever made.

'Is he still?' said Howard.

'Is he still what?'

'A member of it. This man.'

'Of course not. He went away. That's not important. The point is that if it hadn't been for that I'd never have been born again, never known the pastor, never anything.' She shuddered delicately. 'Do get up, Howard. They don't like people to be late.'

He tried to analyse this unnerving process of the death of love. It was not so much a death, he decided, as a hideous mutilation, a fatal infection. He still lusted after her; he still wanted to be with her; he still listened for her to come in and go out. He also knew that there was absolutely no point in them spending any more time together.

In the end it was Celia who sold her flat and moved out. Not because she was tormented by Howard's proximity but because she had heard of a place for sale nearer to the sect's centre of operations. She said goodbye gracefully and affectionately, hoped they might come across each other again some time, and left him her pot plants. The gay couple in the maisonette, who had observed Howard's comings and goings on the stairs with interest, closed in with sympathetic invitations to Sunday lunch, an unappealing air hostess moved into Celia's flat, and Howard commenced his slow and painful recuperation. He applied himself to work with an even greater intensity than usual. His students found themselves in receipt of his concentrated attention to a degree that was positively disconcerting. He spent long hours in the lab, but when the image of Celia persistently floated above the specimen at which he stared he realized that something more active was required. He harassed every source available until he had secured funding for a field trip, and as soon as the term was over he left London.

During the ensuing weeks Celia faded. Each day Howard found that he had left her further behind, caught up as he was in a healing and demanding ritual of physical exertion and mental exhilaration. He got wet and sunburnt and tired; he saw nothing but the rocks over which he clambered and their elusive treasure. He felt nothing but the wind and the rain and the sun. On every day that he secured a significant fossil, the excitement and the satisfaction eclipsed everything and Celia would fall so far away that when he made a deliberate effort to recover her he could see her face but could no longer retrieve the sensations it used to induce. He could remember sex – oh, yes, indeed – but he could not remember love, or what he had taken to be love. Occasionally there would be a twinge, he would be grabbed by loss as he sat on a hillside, and then he would deliberately apply himself to what he was doing, and would find himself distracted and soothed by the mute presence of the distant worlds he sought. He became nothing but a probing intellect, identifying gills and guts and eyes, in voracious pursuit of those teasing hints of life. After several weeks of this he returned to London feeling thinner, wiser and briskly determined to get on with life, however diminished it might be. And he had enough material for several years' work.

There was also the outstanding matter of the repairs to the building, which had been somewhat neglected during his obsession with Celia. Howard now flung himself into the management of the leaseholders' case as a form of therapy. He subjected the invisible freeholder to a blitzkrieg of letters and telephone calls. Eventually he ran him to ground and found him to be not a single individual but an extended family, each member disclaiming either ownership or responsibility. Howard became obsessed with the whole business. The family, he discovered, owned ramshackle conversions all over London, in each of which distraught leaseholders were festering amid damp, rot and falling slates. He embarked on legal action. In the meantime the gay couple had moved out and were replaced by newly-wed systems analysts, who had to be convinced of the seriousness of the situation. The air hostess sold her flat to an accountant, a tenacious and combative fellow who was to become an invaluable ally to Howard in the pursuit of litigation. Howard found himself locked into his relationship with these arbitrarily acquired associates and enemies. His time away from Tavistock College was spent writing letters about the case, talking to people about the case, pondering the case. He studied the operations and tortuous relationships of the freeholding family with nearly the same intensity of interest that he directed upon extinct fauna. At the end of it Howard had spent a great deal of money, owned a freehold instead of a leasehold, and had vastly extended his range of acquaintance and his perception of human nature. He had lost his innocence, in various ways, and all because, on a particular morning, he walked down one street rather than another.

When he thought about this, it surprised him that we accept the knowledge with such equanimity. The course of an individual life has to be seen as a dizzying maze through which wanders this thread of actuality, an uncertain purpose picking its way up this path and eschewing that one, directed by nothing except the existence of a set of choices. Of course, there is the matter of absence of choices, too, and the intervention of exterior factors, but even so, it is a prospect which should make it almost impossible to face each day with reasonably steady nerves, which most people manage to do.

'Actually, I very nearly took a flight last week. I was just booking it and then I remembered about Mum's birthday, and needing to be back in time.'

'Thank goodness for your mother, then.'

And there is no end to it, this perilous concatenation of circumstance and precarious intent. Howard knew by now what he wanted in life. He wanted to do useful and possibly innovative work in his chosen field and also to be happy. He was not entirely sure what constituted happiness, except that it presumably married satisfaction in both work and the life of the emotions. Well, he had a reasonable measure of the first already, but his emotional life appeared to be grounded. He had recovered from the Celia episode at least to the extent that he could think of her without regret, and mourned only the loss of something which, he now realized, he had never actually had anyway. He saw that it is a great deal easier to achieve some sort of direction in the life of the mind than in that of the spirit. His thoughts about *Opabinia*, *Wiwaxia* and *Hallucigenia* proceeded without impediment; he knew what he was trying to do and the only wayward factor was the performance of his own intellect. But the rest was another matter. He saw human association as a sequence of frantic and feckless conjunctions, and decided gloom-ily that the wisest course, and the best means of self-preservation, was probably to discipline oneself to solitude and celibacy. He doubted that he was naturally disposed to either.

To cheer himself up, he decided to redecorate the basement. With this in view, he bought paint and brushes, and borrowed a step-ladder from the systems analysts upstairs. The step-ladder had a rotten step, which the couple failed to point out, and which Howard did not notice until he had already trodden upon it.

6

A Brief History of Callimbia

So Cleopatra's sister becomes a myth, a statue, an image for alternative history. And of course for most Callimbians she was neither here nor there anyway. Rulers seldom are, unless they start to violate their subjects – chop their heads off, string them up, bludgeon them into the armed forces or tax them into the ground. No doubt Berenice did a fair amount of this – standard practices of the day, and not likely to raise too many eyebrows. But most of her subjects would never have set eyes on her and were far too busy keeping their heads above water to give her more than a passing thought. No doubt there were some who saw the reception of Antony as a disgraceful squandering of public funds, but there would have been plenty more for whom the distant sound of warbling eunuchs, the whiff of honey-baked gazelle, the glimpse of a leopard or a dancing girl were a welcome diversion at a time when the entertainment industry had not really got going.

The first century cannot have been an easy ride, for most. A statement which is loaded with the judgemental absurdities of history. Those in question knew neither that it was the first century or that popular prospects might improve. If Christians occasionally surfaced in Callimbia, as they undoubtedly would have done, their concerns would have been those of any sectarian eccentric — ceremonial niceties, the maintenance of privacy — rather than the significance of the calendar. And it would have taken a genius or a clairvoyant to predict democracy, antibiotics and sanitation. Now is now, for all of us, and ever has been. Few are interested in the conditions of last month, or last century, let alone the treats we shall never experience.

The first century gave way to the second, the third, the fourth. Time was slowing up, if only because of its ever-expanding freight of information. Those aeons of creeping and crawling, thrashing and grunting, when nothing happens except evolution, went whipping by. It was a different matter now that there was the testimony of language. Papyrus, parchment, tablets of stone. What was recorded and claimed and refuted and invented. And it would get worse. It would get to a point when time could barely creep ahead at all for the weight of its cargo of information, and history would have to become an industry rather than an agreeable hobby for the leisured and the curious.

The shores of the Mediterranean were getting complicated. Greek and Roman. Persian, Armenian, Byzantine, Arab. Copt and Muslim. People had to know what they were, stand up and be counted. Or assume an expedient flexibility. For definition is in the eye of the beholder. I am a Greek; you are a Roman; he is a barbarian. One man's Christian is another man's infidel. And Callimbians would have had to be as quick on their feet as anyone else, anywhere else. The smart citizen kept a shrewd eye on the prevailing ideological climate, quite apart from remaining abreast of current events. Unless you were perversely attached to any particular set of deities, it would have been wise to be pragmatic and flexible where religious belief was concerned. A pity to be seen as intransigent. Equally, it would not have done to become sentimentally fixated upon any particular regime. Much better to be sensibly conscious of the inevitability of change. You could do a lot better and live a lot longer if not too unswervingly committed to your culture or your faith or your ruler.

So long as you had the choice. And the capacity to make choices tends to diminish with social status. The first-class passengers get a chance to take to the boats; if you're travelling steerage you go down with the ship. There stands today, in downtown Marsopolis, an assemblage of ruined walls and columns, and a concourse of worn paving, all that is left of the Greco-Roman complex which is supposed to have been Berenice's palace, and which survived in one form and another for a couple of centuries after her reign. The view from there (a delightful one – a sweep of sea, a golden curve of beach) would have been very different from that seen by an occupant of the slave market, another prominent and valued feature of early Marsopolis.

It all boils down to language, in the end. It depends how you see things, and what you care to call them. Callimbia was now a part of mainstream Mediterranean history and accordingly was set for a thousand years of historical negotiation, and all that goes with that. Its inhabitants would have to grit their teeth and be prepared to accept their share of sacking, ravaging, pillaging and looting, with some rape and enslavement thrown in for good measure. But this of course, is the judgemental language of history and is anyway quite disgracefully biased in favour of the Callimbians. Those who visited them to make these necessary adjustments to the status quo saw what they were doing quite differently. They were simply getting on with the normal day-to-day business of an efficiently conducted campaign and –

depending on the appropriate terminology in Greek, Latin, Arabic, Persian – requisitioning enemy property, carrying out prophylactic clearance operations, billeting refugees and resettling displaced persons.

For, in any case, what was Callimbia? A concept, merely. The Callimbian border today plunges straight as a die from the coast into the desert, marking out a neat geometrical tract on the map. Back then during the centuries of negotiation, Callimbia was a strategically placed harbour, a fertile plain, a conjunction of trade routes, a well-appointed city and a population who might come in handy as employees, mercenaries or allies. To a Callimbian it was, quite simply, home: the heart of things, beyond which lay an unimaginable wilderness, out of which roared, periodically, cohorts of strangers whose speech was incomprehensible and whose arrival invariably meant trouble. Thus is born patriotism. Along with insularity, xenophobia, racism and much else.

But for most Callimbians, much of the time, all this was peripheral. Life was a matter of personal negotiation; history could take care of itself. The average Callimbian sweated about love, work and survival, never mind the political narrative. And the sun shone and the crops grew and time passed, unregarded.

Travellers come, and go. In the tenth century the place was visited by the redoubtable Abū 'l-Qāsim Muhammad al-Nusaybī, known as Ibn Hawqal, whose somewhat laconic account strikes a familiar note. A touch pedestrian in style, he reports like any bread-and-butter travel writer – he gives useful guidance on local conditions, sightseeing and shopping facilities:

From Egypt to the kingdom of the Callimbians is a distance of thirty merhileh. There are pleasant cornfields, orchards, and a

61

prevailing breeze from the ocean. To the south of this place is sand, and these deserts may only be crossed in winter. The city of Marsopolis has a most ample harbour. It is a well-inhabited place, remarkable for its white slaves from the quarter of Andalus, which include damsels of great value such as are sold for 1,000 dinars and more. There are black slaves also, of high quality, and coral and ambergris and peacocks and spotted skins and camels, mules and other merchandise. There is a very great mosque here, which was built in ancient times as a place of worship for the Greeks and passed later to the Jews and to the Christians who made use of it also for religious ceremonies, until at last it came into the hands of the True Believers. It is furnished now with pavements of marble, while the pillars are ornamented with gold and with precious stones.

7

Lucy

By the time Lucy was fifteen she had seen that there was no need for her to spend her life as her mother had done. She did not lust after material prosperity – clothes, cars, posh houses – it was just that she knew with absolute clarity that no way was she going to settle for acquiescence, compliance and making the best of things. And it is a question of knowledge, she perceived. If you know what there is to know; if you know how to learn. And Lucy was burning to learn. She wanted to know things because she saw that the things were interesting in themselves, but she wanted another kind of knowledge also – the knowledge that makes people mobile, that gives them the power to negotiate. She intended to correct the balance. She had not the slightest desire to be the officials and the mandarins who had harassed Maureen over the years, but she wanted to be in a position to point a finger at them. She thought she might be a politician, maybe. And, like any protective child, she would one day buy her mother a little cottage in the country.

Lucy negotiated the obstacle course of university entrance for herself and for her brother. Her own arrangements were not too daunting; it was simply a question of getting good enough A levels, mastering the complexities of the application system, and then performing adequately at an interview. Which last, in her case, was almost a foregone conclusion, though she did not know it, for Lucy was the kind of girl who brings tears of gratitude to the eyes of jaded academics. Keith was more of a problem. He panicked at the thought of exams and interviews, and had to be hauled by Lucy to the right place at the right time. Eventually her determination, and his own efforts, got him into North London Polytechnic.

Susie was another matter. Lucy had to wade in and find a way for her to be transferred to a different school at which she might stand a better chance of overcoming a fatal inclination to lethargy and get herself some O levels.

'She's like me,' said Maureen fondly. 'She's dreamy. It's not that she's stupid, she just has a job putting her mind to things. She's not so on the ball as you and Keith. I think she should be a ballet dancer. She's always had that pretty way of standing, and you wouldn't need any O levels for that, would you?'

Lucy pointed out that Susie's lethargy was physical as well as mental and that ballet dancing is strenuous, exhausting and requires years of application. She scolded her mother for conniving at Susie's apparent absence of ambition, and prodded her sister into a school with a more vigorous climate at which she duly achieved a respectable clutch of exam passes and from which she progressed to a technical college to do a course in catering.

Lucy, by this time, was about to leave York University with a degree in Politics and Economics. She had prospered there, from the moment she discovered with surprise that men and women twice her age were prepared to listen with apparent interest to what she had to say, that what she had to say was evidently quite as promising as what anyone else had to say, and that a ferocious taste for argument was an asset and not a serious defect of character. The three years seemed in retrospect to have passed as a single moment, a period of eternal present that was both interminable and crudely brief. At the time, it had gone on and on. And then suddenly it was over, and she found herself ejected into the same raw and real world from which she had slid when she was eighteen. Of course, that world had always been there, and she had returned to it with each vacation, but feeling as though she were on loan, like a sleeper who wakes briefly, poised to plunge back where she belongs. Now she was twenty-one, no longer in transit, and once more a part of that uncompromising reality.

Except that it was a transformed reality. She returned to the same world, but she returned a different person. What she had learned in those three years had confirmed everything that she had suspected as the beady-eyed onlooker of her mother's travails: there are codes, passwords and first-class tickets. Clearly, she was not equipped with a first-class ticket, nor ever would be, but she now knew the codes and passwords. She had the knowledge, like a London taxi driver, and it was up to her to put it to good use. She knew now how the whole infernal system worked.

She no longer wanted to be a politician. The books that she had read, the arguments that she had had, along with some energetic involvement with student politics and three years' close reading of newspapers, had induced a certain cynicism. It would be another matter if you lived at a time or in a place where a call to the barricades was an inevitable summons, where the oppositions and the issues were so stark that no right-minded and red-blooded person could do otherwise than sign up to fight. But the sober and prosaic climate of a politically stable society enjoying reasonable prosperity is another matter.

Lucy saw plenty that was wrong – yes, indeed – but knew now that her interests and her abilities lay in another direction.

She would be a journalist. And as soon as she said it she saw the ambiguities and the contradictions.

'Write for the newspapers!' cried Maureen in dismay.

'Not that sort of newspaper, Mum. There's other sorts of newspapers.'

She knew exactly what was distressing her mother. Maureen did not read papers, any more than she exercised her vote. For her, a newspaper was someone else's copy of the *Sun* or the *Mirror* in which you wrapped the rubbish and maybe read the more salacious items as you did so, or the *Haringey Gazette* which dropped free through the letterbox and was useful because of the small ads. She was envisaging Lucy concocting headlines about sex maniacs or alternatively gathering information about local play-groups and jumble sales.

'After all the hard work you've done! I thought you'd be getting a nice office job, that sort of thing.'

'You don't understand, Mum. Not newspapers like you're thinking of.'

'Magazines,' said Maureen, brightening. 'Now that would be nice. One of the glossies. Fashion and that.' A doubt struck her. 'But you've never been what you might call dressy. Wouldn't you have to smarten yourself up?'

Lucy sighed. She brought Maureen a copy of the *Guardian* and Maureen sat dutifully reading for an entire morning. She looked at Lucy in perplexity and a kind of wonder, perceiving, dimly, the codes and the passwords. 'Could you really write stuff like that, love?'

'I don't know,' said Lucy. 'But I'm damn well going to have a go.'

It was not that *Guardian* style was the summit of her ambitions
– simply that she wanted to show her mother that journalism is
polarized. It is a debased activity, and is also crucial and central
to civilized society. If people do not receive reliable information
about the world they are imperilled. And she now knew that
what she wanted to be was one of the reliable providers. It was
a logical development of the role she had assumed as a child,
when she had been the beady-eyed critic of the bureaucrats who
harassed her mother. She had grown up sceptical and
iconoclastic. She felt equipped to make practical use of these
valuable natural tendencies. There was plenty out there she
longed to tackle.

And of course it didn't turn out like that. It is all very well to
have learned the language and to be able to read the map; it is
quite another thing to achieve your objective. Lucy spent that
first summer of adult sobriety writing letters of application. By
October she had had a dozen brush-offs, half a dozen more
kindly replies explaining that there was no job right now, but
that the writer would bear Lucy in mind in the unlikely eventu-
ality of there being one, and three interviews, at which it soon
became apparent that she was too inexperienced, too ignorant
and too optimistic. She must set her sights lower, and learn
again. By November she had her first full-time paid employment,
proofreading for a firm which produced seed-catalogues. She
stopped drafting polemic editorials in her head, and concentrated
grimly upon scrutinizing entries about large flowered hybrids
and half-hardy perennial varieties.

There can be no profession more amorphous, more all-
embracing. A journalist is he or she who castigates the rulers and
who exposes the corrupt, but may also be one who investigates
computer software, pig farming, makes of motorcycle, or who

writes the captions to the colour spreads in pornographic magazines. As a professional label it is both maddeningly imprecise and conveniently evasive. 'I am a journalist,' said Lucy – tentatively and defiantly – as she rose from the seed-catalogue publishers to junior copy editor for the house journal of a large pharmaceutical company. She inserted commas and corrected spelling for another year, biding her time and amassing skills which seemed paltry beside those already acquired, but which, she had to concede, were necessary. She might not be doing exactly what she wanted to be doing, but she was earning her daily bread, and slotting herself into the chain of advancement.

She moved out of Maureen's flat and into a bed-sitting room, which seemed a perverse extravagance, but a self-respecting twenty-two-year-old cannot continue to live with her mother. Besides, there were the evenings, and the weekends, and Maureen was inclined to take rather too keen an interest in whatever Lucy was currently up to.

'That boy really fancies you. He's got it badly, I'd say. Mind, I quite took to him – you could do worse.'

'Mum, he's just a *friend*.'

Maureen laughed.

'You have a stereotyped view of the relationship between men and women,' said Lucy loftily. 'And an overblown vision of sex, if I may say so.'

'And you're living in cloud-cuckoo-land,' retorted Maureen. 'I know trouble brewing when I see it. It'll all end in tears.'

As indeed it did. Lucy's suitors, at this time, tended to be leftovers from her student days, when she had been cheerfully eclectic in her liaisons, while avoiding any commitments which might be ultimately laborious or exacting. She had been a touch perturbed from time to time at her own ability to remain emotionally detached, and assumed that her day was yet to come. When the men showed signs of becoming possessive or plaintive, she shed them as gently as possible, feeling sympathetic but faintly impatient. She couldn't quite see why they didn't just turn elsewhere – there were plenty of people around whose one ambition was apparently to become locked into some immutable partnership.

'One day it'll be your turn,' said the man whose condition Maureen had so accurately diagnosed, bitterly. 'And then you'll know what it's like.' And Lucy nodded humbly, and wished that he would go, and get it over with.

She saw herself, at this period, as pursuing an inexorable course. She had certain goals and intentions, and a rudimentary, though flexible, plan of action. By the time she was twenty-five she should be here, when she was thirty she should be there. She was not so dogmatic as to exclude the inevitable intrusions of circumstance, but she felt sternly that one must not allow oneself to be unnecessarily diverted or distracted, and she also believed that purpose will prevail.

All of which conjures up a picture of a dauntingly single-minded and obsessive young woman, which was not the case. Lucy was also as intermittently frivolous, indecisive, susceptible and rash as anyone of that age ought to be. It was simply that behind and beyond these inclinations lay the sense of direction and of possibility derived from what she had learned over the last two decades, most of it in reaction to her beloved mother's experience and beliefs.

Maureen too believed in a central purpose, but of a rather different kind. At some point she had come across the doctrine of predestination, which had made an indelible impression on her. No doubt she had met with it at some particularly dire

69

period in her own fortunes, and the thought that there wasn't a lot you could do about things if they were going to happen anyway was an obscurely consoling one. At any rate, she was in the habit of returning to this theme at moments of crisis for anyone in the family, to Lucy's perennial exasperation.

'There's a fantastic new job waiting for you just round the corner, only you don't know it. It'll happen when it's going to happen, and nothing you can do's going to speed things up.'

This was at a point when Lucy was becoming increasingly disenchanted with the pharmaceutical house journal.

'Or, alternatively it isn't,' snapped Lucy. 'According to your theory.'

'Or maybe it isn't,' Maureen agreed. 'In which case it's even less use getting your knickers in a twist and going squinty-eyed over the job ads and rushing around knocking on doors.'

'I see,' said Lucy. 'So if we take the optimistic view, then at some unspecified moment a total stranger is going to ring me up and say, Lucy Faulkner, we can't do without you a moment longer – can you please come and edit the paper, starting Monday.'

'Not quite like that,' said Maureen comfortably. 'But that sort of thing.'

Lucy thought her mother's view simplistic. Or credulous. Or both. You were granted a degree of control over your own destiny and if you failed to exercise it through apathy or indecision or fear – well, that was your own look-out. For her part, she intended to negotiate to the hilt. Or so she said. But in private she might have admitted that sometimes the whole inexorable narrative seemed as though it had you by the nose, as if it led you relentlessly towards the people and the places waiting for you out there, invisible, unthinkable and inevitable.

*

'I've been trying to remember what I know about this country, and it amounts to not very much. Something to do with Cleopatra's sister and that's about it.'

In the event, Lucy got a new job because one day she leapt too precipitately off a bus, fell and grazed her leg, and was obliged to go into the nearest branch of Boots for a plaster and a fresh pair of tights. There she met up with a friend who suggested a reviving drink, over which she mentioned that a mutual acquaintance was about to leave a sub-editing job on one of the quality weeklies, thus creating a vacancy. Lucy rushed home, drafted a letter of application and a month later was installed in a seedy but pulsating office where the talk was of contemporary issues rather than of veterinary techniques and developments in flu vaccines – richer by £5 a week and heady with achievement.

'There you are!' said Maureen. 'See!'

Lucy sniffed, and was silent. There was not much to be said. It was in fact difficult to claim a grazed leg and a chance encounter as a victory for calculated and purposeful job-seeking. Let alone the interaction of someone else's life – the sudden decision of that significant acquaintance to chuck up what she was doing and go off to New York.

'You should be thanking your lucky stars,' continued Maureen. 'That's what.'

'Up to a point,' said Lucy coldly. Sixteen years of diligent attention at school and university cannot be called luck.

Maureen saw her mistake and made hasty amendment. 'I don't mean you don't deserve it. What I mean was it was going to happen sooner or later *because* you deserve it. You've worked ever so hard and you deserve some luck, don't you? What did you say the magazine's called?'

Lucy groaned. Her mother's assessment of the relation between life as it is lived and life as it ought to be lived sometimes seemed to her as unrealistic as the moral message of fairy tales. Those who toil shall be rewarded; the virtuous shall be blessed; the wicked shall perish. And there was Maureen's entire life, a testimony to the contrary.

'If you're not careful I shall bring you a copy every week and make you read it,' she said.

Nevertheless, that unwary leap from a 73 bus had indeed been a climactic moment. The chaotic offices of the quality weekly were rich with possibilities. Lucy blossomed. She met a great many people – a process known as making contacts, she learned. She graduated to writing the occasional piece for the paper, and, more importantly, began to spend her spare time on endeavours of her own. She had articles accepted, here and there, on subjects as diverse as acupuncture, bee-keeping and the prospect of a Channel Tunnel. Her mother read them with reverence.

'I didn't know you knew about things like that.'

'I went and found out, Mum. That's what you have to do.'

'Mind,' continued Maureen thoughtfully, 'once you realize how things in the papers get written, and who writes them, if you see what I mean, you aren't quite so inclined to think it's gospel truth.'

She was not writing exactly what she wanted. She was writing around the edges of things, and not of the more seminal matters to which she aspired. It is a lot easier for a young unknown to place a piece based on something esoteric and entertaining than to find a market for a polemic on a central issue of the day. But this would have to do to be going on with.

It was the best of times, though it should have been the worst of times. Lucy perceived with satisfaction that she was quite out of tune with the prevailing climate of the decade. For she was a natural dissident, and this was the 1980s – the age of the entrepreneur and the opportunist, when the very young could become very rich and the social icons were restaurateurs and commercial emperors. She found it entirely satisfying to go about in a perpetual state of contemptuous outrage – and failed to see the irony of the truth that she herself, in her own way, was no mean entrepreneur and opportunist. Though she could have argued with justification that her own opportunism was never going to lead to wealth, or was unlikely to – merely to a way of life in which there is a satisfying fusion between what you want to be doing and the way in which you earn your keep.

The journal on which she worked was in much the same plight. Trading in radical comment and investigation of the ills of society, it staggered from crisis to crisis as its readership declined, seduced by the spirit of the age. There would be gloomy forecasts of collapse and unemployment, and then somehow rescue would come from somewhere, and everything would go on much as it had before. This was unsettling, but gave everyone a grimly satisfactory sense of embattled virtue. The country was going to the dogs, but at least there remained a few enclaves of sanity and integrity. It was the nearest you could get to the barricades, in the circumstances available.

For Lucy, her student years had been the age of enlightenment. This now became the time of exuberance, the years when she found herself frequently amazed and uplifted by the world, by life, by the simple fact of being. She would walk down a street and experience a sudden uprush, a thrill of excitement at the variety of it all, the vibrancy, the resonances: the myriad faces of strangers, a glowing pile of oranges on a stall, the buses forging on to Leyton, Highgate, Lambeth. She would wake early and lie in bed watching the shafts of light that fanned across the ceiling, hearing the clack of feet on the pavement outside, and feel quite heady at the thought of the inexorable purpose of the place, at the mystery of the day ahead, at her own presence in the midst of it all, hitched to time and change like a surfer poised on a breaking wave. She relished the unfolding of events, the narrative of news which swept ahead regardless, as though history had a momentum of its own quite independent of human agency. And at the same time she was continually surprised by the physical world, brought up short by the sight of silver spears of rain against the tarmac, the glass column of a building floating amid clouds, the sparkling passage of an aircraft against the London sky. You were not supposed to feel like this. You were supposed to decry the squalor of the inner city – and indeed there was plenty to decry, that she could see, but it seemed to her that the place had always this transcendent other quality, that there was always this dimension of unwitting, anarchic wonder – a lovely and mindless alternative universe. She had seen it as a child, she remembered, but differently – now it was newly remarkable, a source not of curiosity but of amazement.

It was odd to be so happy, she sometimes thought. She was hard up and working for most of her waking hours. The magazine underpaid its employees as a strategy of survival, and her weekly rent left her with little to spare. The occasional freelance earnings were a cherished bonus. Nevertheless, she felt rich. She had everything, and not least the daily abundance of expectation. Anything might happen, at any moment.

When Will Lewkowska hove into her life she was not surprised. She had been expecting him, or someone like him.

74

She looked up from her desk one morning to see this lank man with hair dripping over one eye, staring thoughtfully at her and holding out a packet of cigarettes.

'I don't smoke, thanks.'

He lit one for himself. 'No, people don't, do they? I hoped you might be unconventional.'

Will's real name was something entirely different. 'It's some ludicrous Polish name – all c's and z's. No one can ever pronounce it.' It seemed probable that he could not himself, since he had been born in Battersea, the child of immigrants. He earned a precarious living as a freelance arts journalist, and treated the offices of the magazine as a kind of club, dropping by in search of a book to review, a commission to write a piece on some abstruse film director, or simply a cup of coffee and a chat. His courtship of Lucy began with the offer of free theatre and concert tickets, progressed to Indian take-aways in his grimy Kentish Town flat, and moved swiftly to the stance of proprietorial and frequently abrasive lover as soon as Lucy, intrigued and somewhat attracted, had consented to go to bed with him.

Will was two people. Sometimes he was a louche south Londoner and at others he was intense, gloomy and profoundly central European. He juggled these two personae roughly to suit the circumstances. He was at his most European when making love, discussing art or having rows with people. He was a son of Battersea when he went into a pub, watched football on the telly, and argued with his parents, now in their seventies and still running a small upholstery business south of the river. He claimed that they spoke only broken English and needed to be discouraged from talking their own language. Lucy wondered for months if Will could actually speak Polish until one day she heard him do so, volubly, to a visiting painter at the ICA galleries. She was taken aback; you never did know quite where you were with Will.

Will's former wife, Sandra, lived in Camberwell with their ten-year-old son. Their relationship was intense and acrimonious. Lucy would lie in Will's bed while he and Sandra shouted at each other on the telephone for half an hour on end, exchanges which left Will quivering with rage and muttering invective under his breath. Lucy had a great deal of sympathy with Sandra and would have liked to indicate this to her but there was never any opportunity. Will took good care that they never met, and spent much time telling Lucy how unreasonable and vindictive Sandra was, which Lucy did not believe. It was clear to her that Will must have been wildly unsatisfactory both as husband and father.

She suspected that she did not really love him, but she enjoyed sex with him and he added to the interest of life. She refused to move into his flat, but found herself restless when he vanished for any length of time, which he quite often did, usually because of an onset of *angst* that sent him on fatal pilgrimages in search of solace and companionship, from which he returned with a stupendous hangover.

Will wanted to consolidate his position. He would prop himself up on one elbow in the bed and stare down at her. 'Do you love me?'

'Well . . . yes.'

'What do you mean – well?'

'Do you love *me*?' Lucy would say, with a touch of irritation, since she didn't see why she should be the only one to lay her cards on the table.

Will would fling himself on to his back and groan. 'My capacity for love has been warped . . . stunted . . . maimed.'

At other times he would gaze intently at her and say, 'I wonder if we should get married?'

Lucy would change the subject, since she did not feel that this constituted a proposal. Or, if feeling combative, she would reply challengingly, 'I wonder . . . What do you think, Will?' Which would send Will off into a sombre discourse upon the destructive effects of marriage on the creative spirit and the appalling constrictions of domestic life.

Will was writing a novel, and had been for many years. It lay in shaggy piles of yellowing typescript on the deal table in his kitchen, ringed with cup-stains and dredged in cigarette ash. From time to time Lucy was invited to read a chunk of it, a task she undertook with some trepidation. She really couldn't tell if it was any good or not. There was a large and confusing cast of characters, all of whom were given to bouts of introspection which could run on for pages. Will would watch gloomily as she read: 'Well, Lucy – is this the great central European novel, at last?' She learned to dread these occasions and to take deft avoiding action when she saw one looming.

Long after Will had receded into her past, and had shrunk to a sequence of such scenes and to the nostalgic flavour of a particular winter, spring and summer, she saw that – by a whisker – she had escaped a long sentence. She saw how she could well have become a sequel to Sandra, locked into an inescapable condition of indignant recrimination and dependence. Will was essentially intolerable, but he was also solicitous, generous, interesting and attractive. The longer you were with him, the more difficult it became to be without him. She was careful never to let Maureen meet him, knowing instinctively that Maureen would be beguiled by him without spotting the eerie affinity with Lucy's father that Lucy herself perceived.

The initial winter with Will gave way to spring, and then to summer. They had reached a plateau, a point of accustomed partnership from which retreat would be difficult. In any case Lucy was not entirely sure that she wanted to retreat, while retaining a certain unease about the situation, and Will was perfectly happy, in so far as he was capable of happiness. It could have gone on thus for a long time, had Lucy not one day accidentally left a crucial notebook in Will's flat.

She returned for it the next evening, letting herself in with the key that Will had insisted she should have. The flat should have been empty; Will had said he was going to a film première. Instead of which she opened the door upon a familiar sight of table littered with dirty plates and glasses, and the tumbled bed from which stared Will and, alongside, the appalled countenance of one of Lucy's best friends. A classic scene, she thought grimly, as she closed the door and hurried down the stairs.

Later, she was to see the carelessness and mismanagement as typical of Will. He was genuinely distraught; he beseeched forgiveness. Lucy was icily distant, to preserve herself from a change of heart; any concession now, and she could be condemned to Will.

As it was, she did not see him again for a year, when he came sloping across a crowded room to greet her as though she were some favourite niece he had not set eyes on for a while. And in the meantime the quality weekly had folded, leaving a carnage of debts and redundant employees. Lucy's thoughts were not on love or remembrance, but on her bread and butter. She greeted him perfunctorily and edged away.

8

A Brief History of Callimbia

The inner harbour at Marsopolis, today, is still embraced by the massive wall and fortification constructed in the early Middle Ages, at the end of which there stands a small but solid fort, complete with ramparts and a single rusting cannon. The fort is largely derelict and occupied only by a nasty little café – Callimbia has never learned how to make the most of its tourist attractions. The café sells Coke, peanuts and crisps, and is called Dragut's Den, the name being a reference to the famous Turkish pirate (or admiral, depending upon the opinion of the commentator) who marauded and sacked and ravaged in the sixteenth century and indeed annexed Callimbia finally to the Ottoman Empire. Those who swig their Coke on the ramparts today, watching the fishing boats, the coastguard cutter, and maybe the grey silhouette of a US naval vessel perched on the horizon, can reflect that back then those seas meant menace, death and destruction.

The Middle East has changed colour yet again. The Middle East? East of what? And the Middle Ages? Middle of when? That frozen, egocentric vision of history once more. Everything depends on the point of view. And points of view, right now, have never been more fanatical or more ferocious. People have been dying by the thousand in the interests of points of view for several centuries. The Crusaders have been, and gone. The Callimbians, like everyone else in the area, have learned that individuals are defined by their doctrinal allegiances, and that it is not only permissable but entirely admirable to set about killing, maiming and tormenting those who do not subscribe to your own superior code of worship. God is reaping a splendid harvest. More will die in his name, in these parts, than ever before or since. By the time the fort at Marsopolis is erected the finest flush is over. The enthusiasm has faded a little, though isolated pockets of devotees, like the Knights of St John, and Dragut himself, are doing their best to keep up a fine tradition. But the spirit of commercialism has muddied the waters, and indeed has always done so, to some extent. It is all very well exhausting national and cultural energies in the exercise of religious fervour, but trade is trade. Christian and Muslim eye one another with suspicion and contempt while tacitly agreeing that a measure of restraint is in everybody's interests, and that a certain level of tolerance will vastly benefit the import and export business. It would be interesting to know how God feels about this.

Callimbia by now is Turkish. That is to say, those who govern Callimbia are Turkish, while everyone else remains much what they were before except that they must be careful to make expedient acknowledgement of the superiority of Ottoman culture and mores and to conform to the requirements of the regime. Again, it is a question of choice, but in this instance there is not much choice. Callimbia is a small country – indeed it is barely a country. Such places do not argue with empires. And in any case, there are certain advantages. An occupier is also a protector. The dictation of Turkish beys may be onerous, but preferable in many ways to the threats from various other directions, from those who cast a rapacious eye on Callimbia's fertile coastline and upon the charms of Marsopolis.

Callimbia looks towards the Mediterranean, from whence comes almost everything that matters, and turns its back upon the continent of which it is a part. Neither Callimbians nor indeed anyone else knows much about that continent except that it is the source of various interesting trade products ranging from human beings to the spare parts of large unknown animals. The desert, for most Callimbians, is a tedious no-go area out of which arrive oddly spoken nomadic folk with whom you can sometimes do good business. Whence they come, and where they go, is not a matter of any great concern. The coastal Callimbian, busy with the cultivation of vines, olives, oranges and the rest of it, keenly aware of the advantages of metropolitan life, locked into a complex commercial network, is not much exercised about the wider world. A map is a question of how long it takes to get from A to B given a fair wind or decent travelling conditions. A Callimbian has an excellent sense of direction and distance, and an acute eye for topographical detail. Callimbians do not easily get lost, but they have no idea where they are. There is here and there is an elsewhere of unguessable nature and proportions, out of which strangers arrive, talking peculiar languages, queerly dressed, and inspiring panic or cautious interest according to their apparent intentions. It might be necessary to kill them before they kill you, or it might be wiser to act in a propitiatory way from the start, or it might simply be a question of settling down to some productive commercial negotiation. Whichever is the case, there is neither the time nor the inclination for exhaustive inquiry into their home lifestyle or how they got to Callimbia. Those Callimbians who travel do indeed bring back colourful accounts of foreign parts, but these tend to concentrate on climates of belief, political circumstances and the inevitable and abiding question of economic opportunity. They do not contribute to an understanding of global affairs. Globe? What globe?

The globe is a reality. But it is also a concept – one which has not yet arrived in Callimbia. Beyond the coastal fringe Africa reaches away, biding its time. Across the Mediterranean, Europe is already boiling up nicely. The Callimbians, landed with their Turkish masters, settle down to colonial status. And what, after all, is a Callimbian? A Callimbian is a racial pot-pourri, a walking genetic soup whose ancestry is a spiderweb of intricate connections the result of which may be skin the colour of honey, or purple-black like a plum, eyes from a Byzantine icon, or blue as the ocean, hair that is crinkled or that flows straight as water. A Callimbian is the living manifestation of everything that has happened here, a testimony to history, the proof of the past – every bit as much as the fort and the harbour ramparts and the ruins of Berenice's palace. A Callimbian is a wonder, in short. But nobody sees it thus, least of all, probably, the living testimonies themselves, who must get on with fishing, harvesting, labouring, buying and selling, and performing, for the moment, as compliant citizens of the Ottoman Empire.

9

Howard

Howard met Vivien because he fell from a borrowed step-ladder and broke his kneecap. When he was sufficiently mobile, he was referred by his doctor to the Physiotherapy Department of the local hospital, where he found himself doing skipping and running exercises next in line to Vivien, who had incurred a similar injury after pitching down a flight of stairs. It seemed a natural progression to have a cup of coffee together afterwards in the hospital canteen, and to do so again the following week, and the one after that. Howard was flattered by Vivien's matter-of-fact annexation of him, which he took for sexual attraction or intellectual affinity or even, he hoped, both. She was a dark wiry woman a few years older than he was, with large mild brown eyes which she would turn on him with initially disturbing effect. In fact both the mildness and the attention were deceptive, as he was later to realize, but during those first weeks he found her both comforting and enhancing. Someone was interested in him; someone was seeking him out. She worked as a librarian for an institution with academic connections, an occupation of which she made much at the start of their acquaintance ('We're in the same trade, in a sense, then . . .'), though he was soon to discover that her attitude to the place and its concerns was one of contemptuous indifference. But in the beginning it was a bridge; she took him to a reception for a visiting African novelist, he took her to a lecture and drinks party in the college. Before Howard had time to analyse and assess what was going on, they were seeing each other several times a week and making love (if that was what it was). Within months Vivien had moved into his flat and within further months he had sold it and they had bought a larger one on a joint mortgage. He never did know quite how it had happened. He could recall no discussions or decisions; the whole process had been an imperceptible slide into an apparently irrevocable situation.

It was not like the Celia episode. For one thing, it was never an episode, but of course at the beginning there was no knowing that the relationship had this protracted destiny. For all Howard knew, it was a casual and experimental friendship. He was quite attracted to Vivien, but he never really felt in love with her. Vivien herself avoided definition and discussion – as he was later to realize. She simply moved ahead in a series of unspoken assumptions, the effect of which was to compress the normal sequences of a relationship. They seemed to progress in one leap from the opening rounds of courtship to the stale conjunction of a marriage which had long ago run out of steam. Vivien referred to him as her partner, an expression Howard detested. He never found any satisfactory term for her: girlfriend seemed derogatory for a woman in her late thirties. He was reduced to the circumlocution of 'the person I share a flat with', which contained an ambiguity about sexual orientation, but woman, in this context, sounded faintly patronizing. It is a loaded word, he realized – volatile, and to be used with caution. He found this interesting and tried to discuss it with Vivien, who said impatiently that she didn't know what he was talking about. She often said that.

Vivien liked to talk, but only about certain things. She was at her most expansive in introspective analysis of her own antecedents and personality, and in similar inspection and criticism of Howard's behaviour and motivation. She intensely disliked abstract discussion and was quite incurious. There was nothing in which she was particularly interested. She was mildly fanatical about health and fitness, and spent her spare time attending health clubs and swimming baths. To begin with, she wanted Howard to join her and was put out when he declined with increasing firmness; suddenly she gave up, and contented herself with occasional sniping comments about how flabby he was getting. It was his only victory, he later saw, the one area of his life that he kept intact. This was important and possibly his salvation, for it meant increasingly that while Vivien jogged, worked out and swam, Howard worked.

He worked compulsively, during the years with Vivien. He would have done so anyway, in all probability, such were the demands of his teaching load. If he was to pursue his studies, he had to do so at weekends and throughout the vacations. But he was also seeking an immersion in his own preoccupations as an escape from the stagnant alliance to which he was apparently condemned. He knew that he must eventually do something about it, but shirked the necessary confrontation. In the meantime he retreated into the impartial climate of the Burgess Shale, and dissipated his energies in brooding communion with his private alternative universe of faunas. He cherished this solace – the absolute detachment of dissection, when he became simply an eye and a hand, conscious of nothing except the problems posed by the organisms that he exposed, layer by layer, his mind concentrated entirely upon the teasing structure of an animal frozen into a confused mass of component parts. He welcomed also the process of description – the search for language of the right precision and concision to establish on the page the creature that he had reconstructed. At these moments, he became simply the mechanism whereby the animal was rescued from oblivion, the engine of intelligence and curiosity which made this possible. The whole exercise satisfactorily eclipsed the travails of his private life.

Vivien treated his absorption with irritated amusement. He had described some of the Burgess fossils to her, and had shown her drawings, which did arouse a positive reaction, but not one which pleased him. She found them funny: 'I never saw such ludicrous things in my life!' The implications of this diversity were apparently lost on her, however much he tried to explain. 'Howard spends his time digging weird cartoon insects out of bits of rock,' she told people. He saw that along with her incuriosity went a lack of wonder, an incapacity to be astonished. Also, she could not conceive of work which was a compelling pleasure. For her, as for most people, there was an absolute demarcation between the time necessarily spent earning a living and leisure time. It was thus impossible to work voluntarily; if you did a thing voluntarily, then it could not be work. Hence she had a basic conceptual problem with Howard's tendency to work outside what she saw as official working hours. Was this work or some eccentric form of play? Eventually he fed her the notion that these endeavours were essential to gain promotion (in which there was an element of truth). She accepted this, and left him alone with a kind of patronizing tolerance.

From time to time he made attempts to tackle the situation. He did not love her; nor could he suppose, from her behaviour, that she loved him. She treated him with irritable brusqueness, most of the time. Their conversation had deteriorated to a sequence of hurried exchanges about bills, shopping and other necessary arrangements. They rarely made excursions together, or entertained friends. When they did, Vivien became visibly impatient: if out, she would glance ever more frequently at her watch and if at home would start to rattle crockery in the kitchen. She disliked social dialogue that was not inconsequential. When on one occasion a sprightly discussion developed over dinner with friends about historical inevitability, she sat in angry silence and eventually burst out, 'What a ridiculous conversation!'

'Why, Vivien?' someone asked, after the initial startled silence.

'Because it's pointless. I mean, either things happen or they don't. If they do, then there's nothing to be done about it and if they don't, then so what?'

'But you need to know why they did or they didn't,' said Howard. 'And you need to think about what may be determined and what may depend on contingency. It's intriguing, if nothing else.'

'Well, you may need to, but I don't,' snapped Vivien. 'Honestly, I can't tell you how silly you all sound.' She got up and began to slam plates into a pile. The guests shifted uneasily, fell into desultory chatter and soon the evening broke up. Later, Vivien was contrite.

'I'm sorry – it's just that those people were getting on my nerves. Yammering on about *history*, if you please, as though we were back at school.'

'A not uninteresting subject,' said Howard coldly.

'And that fair girl thought she was being so clever and original. I dare say you thought she was too.'

'You started out saying you were sorry,' said Howard. 'Aren't you rather spoiling the effect?'

That particular tiff was patched up, as were most others, more through inertia than anything. Both parties avoided real contention, Howard because he had never had a taste for rows, and Vivien probably because of an instinctive knowledge that this could be fatal. It was clear that so far as she was concerned there was no reason why they should not go on as they were indefinitely. In his glummer moments, Howard used to wonder if she honestly thought that theirs was a normal and fruitful union, or if she simply did not care.

Vivien did not want children. Babies, she explained, made her literally physically ill. And indeed Howard could see her flinch on the occasions when they came into contact with the small offspring of friends, averting her eyes from the gobbets of milk sick, the bubbles of snot, the shiny dribbles on chins. He didn't much fancy such sights himself, but they didn't disturb him as they did Vivien and he supposed himself to be insensitive. It didn't occur to him to wonder how parents come to stomach this. He didn't really know if he wanted children himself or not. It was something he never much considered. He thought perhaps he might be low on genetic drive, which was interesting but did not worry him unduly.

He knew that he must eventually end it. Talk things out with her. Make her see that the longer they went on the more difficult it would be to break up. Suggest that it wasn't working, that neither of them was happy, that both might reasonably hope for some more satisfactory arrangement. He knew this, and continued to do nothing.

A good deal of his time, and much of his emotional energy, was spent in the quest for funding for field trips and the creation of opportunities for these. He often thought that without them he would have sunk into a condition of apathetic desperation, during those years. He pitied colleagues in disciplines which chained them for ever to the lecture room, the library and the desk. His own life was spiced with those heady periods when he could return to the source of his preoccupation, to the rocks themselves. It was one thing to see the detail and complexity of an organism shine up at him from the floodlit landscape of the microscope, but quite another to sit on a windy mountainside and expose the creature in the very strata in which it had perished, the perfect union of time and space. The thrill and triumph of discovery never diminished, and nor did the *frisson* of reluctance with which he interrupted this harmony. A fossil has no scientific value until examined and annotated under laboratory conditions, but it has lost then that freight of implication and association. It is no longer locked into its amazing, emotive and exquisite unity of rock, wind and water – life that has vanished but remains eternally present, the ultimate proof of the past, the revelation of which unites the moment of discovery and that dimly perceived, unimaginably distant world sealed into the rock. At such times, holding in his hand the slab in which hung the *Marrella* or the *Aysheaia*, Howard felt both exultant and tranquil. He would pore over the specimen, feeling the wind, the sun, the formation of the ground under his feet, and his own problems and concerns would be wonderfully diminished. Nothing else, for the moment, mattered – and the moment itself was of such perfection and such clarity that it became imperishable, like the specimen he held. In his head there would remain a shining succession of such moments, polished by the act of recollection, precarious but indestructible.

*

She said, 'Something most odd is happening. I don't feel as though we were where we are any more. I feel as though we had escaped it all somehow. As though we were on another level.'

Back in London, enmeshed once more with colleagues, students and Vivien, those moments would begin to seem as unreal as another ecosystem, and as unreachable. Only the animals he studied were the link – the hard evidence that both he and they had once been elsewhere. The association invested them with a further meaning – they were private totems as well as objects of scientific importance.

Vivien treated his field trips as exercises in personal indulgence. 'Well, have a terrific time . . .' she would say, seeing him off, as though he were bound for a fortnight cavorting in the Caribbean. 'Think of me, festering in the Institute.' He could have suggested that she go with him, but was wise enough not to do so, and mercifully she never seemed to realize that it was feasible. Or perhaps she too knew that such an invasion of his ultimate privacy would have been catastrophic. At any rate, she neither interfered with nor objected to his departures but managed subtly to denigrate what he was doing, so that he would climb on to the aircraft feeling faintly shabby, as though he were a sales manager passing off a spree as some spurious business trip.

Curiously, it was not after one of his own absences that he knew he could no longer live with Vivien, but after she herself had been away for a few days, and he had been alone in the flat. He luxuriated. It was as though the rooms swelled, grew lighter, floated above the city. He felt as though he had broken out of some dark hole and swum free into a translucent ocean. Never had he thus savoured solitude; it was as though he had never before known it for what it was – a freedom and a peace. He spent four days in this state of buoyancy, and at the end of the fourth, as Vivien's return began to loom, he knew that he must not, could not, stay with her any longer.

He said he thought it would be a good idea if they had a talk.

'About what?' demanded Vivien, whisking about the flat, putting her things away, checking the fridge, rearranging a chair that he had moved.

About the future, he said. About where they stood.

'I don't understand,' said Vivien. Her back to him, poised over a handful of mail.

He said he'd been thinking. About them. About the commitment. He'd been wondering.

'Wondering what?' said Vivien. Turning round. Setting down the letters.

He'd been wondering, he said, if they were entirely happy together.

And then she flared up. 'You want to split up, don't you? Is that what you want? Well . . . Is it?' And immediately they were pitched into confrontation – none of the reasonable, measured and merciful discussion that he had intended but a precipitate assumption of positions from which there could be no retreat. He saw that it was going to be worse than his worst expectations.

He said, 'Vivien, you don't love me.' She glowered at him. 'Well, do you? You don't. And I'm afraid I don't love you. I think I may have done once, but I don't now. We haven't got any children. You don't want any children. There really isn't any sensible reason to go on living together and making each other miserable, is there?'

She stared at him. It was impossible to tell if she was shocked and angry, grief-stricken and angry, or just angry. Then she snapped, 'You're one of the stupidest people I've ever known, Howard.' And slammed into the bedroom.

He moved out of the flat and into a rented room from which he weathered the ensuing weeks and months of Vivien's relentless sniping. First she telephoned almost daily with recriminations and insults. Then the phone calls gave way to a bombardment of curt missives: 'The rate bill has come. Your share is £112.60.' The room in which he now lived was expensive and disagreeable. It frequently occurred to him that from the point of view of accommodation he was back exactly where he had been nearly ten years before, when he got his first job at Tavistock College, though he was now a senior lecturer and could claim a modest international reputation in his field. His parents, who tended to measure achievement in material terms, were much chagrined. But they had met Vivien on a couple of occasions and saw his point. His mother said guardedly that she had sometimes wondered if it was working out quite as it should.

Vivien announced that she would sell the flat and give him as much of the proceeds as he had invested in it, with various minutely calculated deductions for failure to contribute adequately to redecoration and for a management charge which turned out to be a recompense for her labours over the sale and attendant paperwork. Howard raised no objections. He now knew that so far as property was concerned he was cursed in some way and dreaded the thought of the recovery of his paltry slice of capital which now seemed for ever associated with misadventure.

But he was alone again. Even Vivien's campaign of attrition, and the combination of guilt and annoyance which this provoked, could not entirely spoil the deep peace of his solitary life. He began to have serious doubts about the pair-bonding system. Maybe it was entirely a social convention, and not instinctive. He now perceived, reflecting upon Vivien and her conduct, that the display of cohabitation, of partnership, was what had mattered to her. He could have been anyone, in a sense. She needed to be one of a couple, because that was the arrangement approved by society. Their association had been centred not on love, or procreation, but on such badges of respectability as a joint mortgage, a shared address and frequent trundling out of that dread word *partner*. He now wished Vivien well (except when in immediate receipt of some especially blistering communication), felt sorry for her, and hoped that in the fullness of time she would find someone better suited to her requirements. As for himself, he envisaged a future in which he remained sternly single, with perhaps the occasional sexual fling if and when he came across someone who shared his state of disenchantment and understood that this was a matter of mutual convenience and nothing else. The prospect did not seem that inviting, but he could see no alternative.

He was thirty-six. Each time he thought of this he was slightly incredulous. Surely there was some mistake? How could this have come about? And for a few minutes he would feel panic-stricken at this acceleration of time, this leakage of years – everything going, youth, powers, prospects, and to what end? And then he would pull himself together, take stock, and cast a coldly rational eye upon a productive and useful career and a record of behaviour in which he could see no major blemishes. He had never killed or injured anyone, was not given to malice, dishonesty or mendacity. He worked hard, paid his income tax, treated others with consideration. He had from time to time sparred with a colleague, castigated erring students and lost his temper with total strangers, but this seemed to him normal if not downright healthy. He was nearer forty than thirty and the fact appalled him, not so much because of the loss of time, but on account of a deficiency which he preferred not to contemplate.

He found himself contrasting the orderly nature of professional life and the anarchy of private concerns. There was plenty of anarchy of a kind at Tavistock College, of course: departmental infighting, recalcitrant students. But where the pursuit of scientific truth was concerned, it was possible to plan a course of action and then carry it out, to set yourself certain goals and then achieve them, making allowances for such imponderables as whether or not you would be able to claw sufficient time for it, and whether or not you would be at a high pitch of achievement. You had a certain control. But life with others was another matter, an unnerving pursuit of harmony. If you were intimately connected with the person you were for ever struggling to balance your words and emotions against theirs. Where friends, colleagues and casual encounters were concerned, you were dependent upon random conjunctions, arbitrarily flung up against those you found congenial and those you loathed. Your daily happiness or distress depended to a considerable degree upon this wayward process. The world teems with people; a minute number of these, fished from a hat as it were, would determine the quality of your existence.

And on occasion some total stranger is licensed to reach in and crucially to manipulate the entire narrative, as Howard was to find on the occasion that his briefcase was stolen at Russell Square Underground Station. He set it down beside him while he felt in his pockets for change to put in the ticket machine.

Someone barged into his back, forcing him into collision with a woman in front of him, who dropped a shopping-bag. Howard restored it to her, apologizing, and, when he turned to stoop for the briefcase, it was gone, along with several books from the college library, various letters including Vivien's latest tirade, an apple, a new umbrella, and the notes for the lecture he was about to give at Imperial College along with the accompanying slides. For a few minutes he strode angrily around the booking hall, rode down the escalator and scoured the platforms. No sign. The briefcase, patently, was gone for ever, and along with it the stranger whose path had so unfortunately crossed with his, and who was probably at this very moment inspecting Howard's possessions with contempt and disappointment.

Fuming, he returned to the college. He made an explanatory phone call and postponed the lecture. He reported the theft to the appropriate authorities, and then fled to the college bar for a restorative drink, where he joined a colleague who was entertaining a visiting curator from the Natural History Museum in Nairobi.

And thus it was that Howard learned that in that museum there resided a recently acquired collection of fossils, as yet uncatalogued and unidentified, which were almost certainly Burgess Shale fauna. The visitor was on the last day of his trip to London, he had a flight home booked that night, would shortly be on his way to Heathrow. But for the theft, but for that now benevolent stranger . . . Howard rushed to his office, fetched drawings and photographs. *Marrella, Opabinia, Wiwaxia*. The visitor studied them and nodded. Yes, there could be little doubt. Within half an hour Howard had dismantled and reassembled his plans for the immediate future. He would not go to a conference in Stockholm. He would not spend a fortnight taking students on a field trip to Scotland. He would pull out every stop and somehow scramble together funds for a quick visit to the Museum of Natural History in Nairobi.

10

A Brief History of Callimbia

Callimbia is poised now to enter the nineteenth century, with all that that implies. Global politics. The European thirst for foreign parts: colonial expansion, discriminating tourism. Callimbia will find itself in the thick of things – blown by winds from Europe, visited by every self-important traveller who had a few days to spare after dealing with Egypt and the Upper Nile.

Starting with Napoleon. It was drawn to General Bonaparte's attention, after the initial months of the occupation of Egypt, that there existed this adjacent territory, also under the sway of the Mamelukes, and that an expedition to sample its attractions and test its recognition of French superiority might be a wise move. In Cairo, the Mamelukes were on the run, but a certain amount of recalcitrance persisted ('Every day I have to have five or six heads cut off in the street,' the general wrote, irritably). It would be as well to make the Napoleonic presence felt in Callimbia.

In the event, the Callimbian expedition lasted for several months. It got off to a bad start when one of the zoologists attached to the Scientific and Artistic Commission became separated from his companions while bird-watching in the countryside behind Marsopolis. Some villagers, mistaking his scrutiny of a flock of lesser egrets for a prurient interest in their womenfolk working in the fields, fell about the man with sticks and inflicted serious injuries. This want of hospitality was summarily dealt with: the village in question was burned, the cattle and corn impounded for the benefit of the Republic, and the sheikh given fifty strokes of the lash.

As an introduction to the advantages of European paternalism this was unfortunate. It may have served to deter the peasantry from jumping to conclusions but it can have done little to persuade the average Callimbian that Bonaparte and his army were there, as he insisted, to rescue them from the oppressive rule of the Mamelukes and acquaint them with the benefits of enlightened government. Things went just as badly in Marsopolis, as the laconic prose of an Order indicated:

> The Commander-in-Chief, being dissatisfied with the conduct of the inhabitants of Marsopolis, decrees that all inhabitants, of whatever nation, must take their arms to the military commander. Those who have not done so after forty-eight hours will be beheaded. Fifty hostages from among those most ill-disposed will be taken into custody and held until the inhabitants of Marsopolis learn to behave better. All horses in the city will be handed over to the military commander within twenty-four hours of publication of this order. Those failing to obey will receive 100 strokes of the cane and will be fined 50 talaris . . .

And so forth, in the same vein, for several pages. It begins to look as though the Callimbian expedition had assumed a rather more serious bent than a mere excursion to get an idea of local topography and greet the populace.

Bonaparte eventually departed. Callimbians, one supposes, sighed, shrugged and readjusted themselves to the systems of repression they already knew. But a pattern had now been established. Callimbia was a must, for the inquiring traveller. If you were doing the Middle East, whether as conqueror or simply as a connoisseur of antiquities and the picturesque way of life, it was essential to drop in at Marsopolis.

And Callimbians, shrewdly, learned how to respond to market forces and exploit their natural resources. Some did so with rather too much fervour, which is why the magnificent sculpture of Aphrodite dug up at the Greek temple now graces the British Museum instead of the Marsopolis Museum of Antiquities. The Turks, not previously distinguished for their antiquarian interests, began scrabbling in the sand with enthusiasm, and had sold off a good tonnage of the spoil before archaeology as a responsible endeavour got off the ground later in the century. At a different level, ordinary citizens discovered that European visitors were naïvely fascinated by the mundane processes of Callimbian daily life, were inordinately acquisitive and spectacularly devoid of the normal skills of economic negotiation. You could sell them anything, for pretty well what sum you chose.

By the time Gustave Flaubert arrived there in midcentury, Marsopolis was accustomed to catering for the discriminating tourist. Flaubert and his companion Maxime du Camp did the rounds – the Greek temple, the Roman baths. They inspected the Grand Mosque and climbed the minaret at sunset:

Effect of the light on the sea, like a sheet of copper, fading within minutes to uniform purple of an inexpressible depth. Glitter of waves breaking upon the beach. In the forecourt of the mosque, the carcass of a dog, picked at by crows, the eyes reduced to bloody caverns. We make our way back through a malodorous soukh, pestered by beggars. A string of slaves brought in by traders from the south: negroes with flesh like a ripe plum, splendid ripple of their muscles as they move, naked except for leather fringes and strings of beads.

He also availed himself of the more personal facilities, patronizing the well-known brothel in the main square:

Two women cross-legged on a divan, one pale-skinned with dark glistening eyes, the other bronze, glowing, diaphanous dress hung with gold piastres. Danced for us. Then a coup with each. The smell of their skin – olive oil and jasmine. A servant brought Turkish coffee and a hookah. The younger woman played the flute. Great heat in the room, and sound of chickens beyond the window. View of statue of the sister of Cleopatra in the square, erected some twenty years ago, a monstrosity in marble.

Poor Berenice, thus glimpsed and dismissed. How are the mighty fallen. But it is a long time now since the first century; Callimbia is racing headlong for the twentieth, and for the achievement of modern statehood, with all its attendant perils. Berenice has become a legend and figure on a plinth, while Callimbia has hard reality to face.

11

Lucy

When Lucy was twenty-nine her mother got married. Technically, she was remarrying, having completed some years before the laborious process of divorcing an absent husband, but it felt to Lucy like a first marriage. When Maureen told her about Bruce – her manner a shifty combination of exultation and embarrassment – Lucy was amazed. As soon as she met him she saw at once that the long years of coping with Maureen's affairs were over. Bruce was manager of the branch of Tesco's at which Maureen herself had risen – rather surprisingly – to supervisor. He had been betrayed in some unspecified way by a wife who had left him with an eight-year-old son and an immaculately equipped house in Cheam. Lucy perceived that he was entirely reliable and luxuriously in love with her mother. He and Maureen sat in the Cheam sitting-room amid stout upholstery, ticking carriage clocks and carpets as thick as summer grass, glancing at each other every few seconds with enlarged and glistening eyes. The little boy leaned against Maureen's knee, besotted. There was a new car in the garage, and a time-share apartment in the Algarve. Maureen was entirely out of place but, Lucy realized, exquisitely happy, and about to adapt to circumstance, just as she had always done. She herself felt like a middle-aged parent whose offspring has flown the coop – liberated and bereft.

It was a precarious period where her own fortunes were concerned. She was out of work for six months after the quality weekly folded. That salary cheque had always seemed derisively small, but now it was like lost riches. Doggedly, she wrote letters and telephoned and peppered editors with unsolicited articles and suggestions. Sometimes she struck lucky and got a commission. She wrote a profile of a woman politician who appreciated her fair-minded approach and tipped her off about a local government row in a complacent cathedral town. Lucy went there, investigated, talked to people, and wrote a piece exposing a rich cauldron of corruption which was snapped up by a national daily. This in turn led to a commission to investigate the controversial siting of a theme park in the Midlands. Her article was noticed by a features editor in search of something sharp and bracing on the heritage industry in general. She was getting a name for abrasive comment, for spotting an issue and homing in upon it. Anxiously, she scoured the press for hints of impending issues. In this trade, she saw, you needed not so much to be abreast of events as ahead of them, lying in wait for circumstance, ready to pounce.

But an article sold every week or two did not pay the bills. She began to contemplate, bleakly, a return to the treadmill of proofreading and copyediting. And then one day she walked into the offices of the national daily which had taken her cauldron of corruption piece and whose features editor had since looked kindly upon her. Having handed over her speculative piece on *in vitro* fertilization, she fell into conversation with an acquaintance and learned that one of the paper's regular columnists had fallen foul of the editor and departed in a cloud of dust. The column, traditionally addressed to matters of the moment and written so as to provoke attention and controversy, was untethered, so to speak. Lucy headed into the street to search for a phone box before her nerve went.

She was given a trial run. Great, they said. We'll let you know, they said. Soon, they assured her, really very soon. She chewed her nails for a fortnight, and read the contribution of the seasoned hack who succeeded her, which she saw with absolute clarity was succinct, incisive and original. Or just possibly anodyne, banal and plodding.

And then, amazingly, the phone call came. A weekly column; her own by-line. Her photograph, postage-stamp size. A salary cheque.

Success. Celebrity. Immortality.

'A start,' she said to Maureen and Bruce. 'It's a start, anyway.'

'I think you're better with your hair a bit shorter,' said Maureen. 'Or maybe that's just not a very flattering picture.' Bruce, a *Daily Express* man, was dismayed at the prospect of the newspaper he was now going to have to read, but put a brave face on things and volunteered to keep her supplied with inside information on developments in retail trading.

She had security. And opportunity.

'They could fire me at any moment.'

'Just let them try!' said Maureen belligerently. Bruce offered to put her in touch with a friend in insurance, who had all the latest on pension schemes.

'I'll have to find something sizzling to write about every week, or get the chop.'

'She did some lovely essays, at school,' said Maureen, to Bruce. 'I wonder if I've still got any of them put away somewhere.'

Lucy knew that this was a piece of good fortune. She refused to allow the word luck. She was young yet, and this was something of a plum. She had got the job on her merits, she told herself, along with whatever assistance there may have been from the inadequacies of others considered for the appointment, or the failure of yet further competitors to apply. What she was never to know was that in fact the editor had been on the verge of offering the column to the seasoned hack – had been about to pick up the phone – when the colleague he most disliked had walked into his office and spoken with satisfaction of the prospect of closer association with this old crony of his. The editor listened with mounting indignation, first at the assumption that this would be his decision, and then at the notion of these two ganging up under his nose. As soon as the colleague was out of the room he reached for the phone. And rang Lucy.

And so it began, that time during which she was so feverishly hitched to events that in retrospect it was to seem as though she hurtled from day to day with the onward rush of the news, denied any of the lethargy of individual existence. Public life never stops. And most issues whisked out of sight as soon as she turned aside, dipping as she did from one concern to another. As soon as she had got up a head of steam about injustice in immigration procedures, that issue would have evaporated and the indiscretion of a cabinet minister would send her off in pursuit of an angle on the abuse of power. Every day, something happened to twist the direction of public interest. Wait, she felt like saying, we're not through with this one yet, we've barely begun. But there was no holding it – the inexorable plunge ahead, the scandals, the revelations, the new names, the new voices, the shifty fusion of private and public drama, to which she must supply a breathless commentary. It was both exhilarating and alarming. There you were in the thick of things, helpless. And not just in them but of them. Part of the flotsam. Sometimes she glimpsed a shadowy *alter ego*, propelled by inconceivable happenings.

'There's this feeling of unreality. Half of me doesn't really think this is happening, but the other half knows it damn well is.'

She lived in a welter of newsprint, a babble of information. She would seize upon a subject when it was in mint condition, untarnished by discussion, before people knew that they were concerned about methods of sewage disposal, that they did indeed feel strongly about the absurd sums earned by a twenty-year-old footballer, that they shared Lucy's indignation at revelations of financial irregularity in the affairs of a leading charity. But by the time the letters of support or of condemnation reached her, those matters had already been eclipsed, swept aside by something newer, more compelling, more urgent. And most of it unpredictable, a continuous unfurling of surprise – the developments you could not have allowed for, the smashes and crashes, the reckless moves, the triumphs and the humiliations. And behind it all some invisible unstoppable force, charging ahead.

She was invigorated by what she had to do, and occasionally unnerved. She would glance at the mounting pile of her pieces and see nothing but obsolete opinion. Nothing ever finished; a sequence of interrupted testimony.

'Well, I think you're very clever,' said Maureen. 'Finding three new things to get cross about every week.'

'Hmmn . . . Maybe. But it's as though you were a character in a novel, living it out without any idea how it was going to end.'

'I'll be in a Catherine Cookson,' said Maureen. 'One of the historicals. No – her in *Gone with the Wind*, what's her name?'

Bruce remarked that there is only one way it can end, for any of us. Lucy looked at him with surprise – he was a superficially bland man, capable of occasional pungent accuracies.

'Don't be morbid,' said Maureen. 'Speaking personally, I'm going backwards from now on – getting younger and younger.'

This did indeed appear to be the case. She had bloomed in this undreamed-of climate of love and prosperity, though clearly it was the love that mattered a great deal more than the prosperity. Maureen moved gingerly amid the lavish furnishings, the sound-system, the microwave and the marble-effect bathroom suite, but Bruce she treated with the uncomplicated ease of pure affection. She had lost a good deal of weight and looked extremely pretty.

'Do you know,' she confided to Lucy, 'I had no idea there could be men like that. And another thing, I know now why I used to eat chocolate all the time. It was instead of you know what, if you see what I mean.'

And Lucy, now, was thirty. When she looked at herself in the mirror she saw the faint imprint of another face imposed upon the familiar contours of her own. She observed this without the squeamishness of vanity, but with a certain perplexity; it was as though you cohabited with a mysterious stranger, and conducted a subdued and secret struggle for house-room. She was not so much perturbed by the prospect of ageing as by this involuntary metamorphosis. What would one turn into? She remembered the same bewilderment tinged with alarm when she was a child, trapped in that bizarre and inescapable process of lengthening limbs and an inconstant external world, in which trees and buildings appeared to shrink as you yourself so confusingly expanded.

Her sister Susie, stalwartly upholding the family tradition, had become a mother at twenty-one. She was living with her two offspring and their father (a cheerful fellow her own age who worked on a building site and played the saxophone with a jazz group at the weekends) in conditions which Lucy grimly saw as a nostalgic re-creation of her own childhood. Maureen either ignored this resonance or was not aware of it. From time to time she made oblique references to Lucy's own status.

Lucy would retort, crisply, 'Mum, children are not on the agenda.'

She thought that she probably meant this. She found Susie's infants engaging, but did not detect any powerful maternal yearning in herself.

Besides, she had not the leisure in which to sit around examining her state of mind. A busy life is the enemy of introspection, and Lucy, whipping about the place, thought less about herself than about the world on which she commented. She would pass within a day from exhilaration to shock, from amusement to dismay. She saw the extraordinary conjunction of distress and prosperity, of vice and valour, of rationality and mayhem, and wondered how it could be that people come to terms with this. She could talk, within hours, to people whose assumptions, expectations and wisdoms were as far apart as if they inhabited different centuries. And all this within a small country in which the large majority enjoys a fair standard of living and reasonable educational standards. What of the rest of the globe? Thinking this, she would become restive. Work came flowing in, now. She took on more assignments, found that she could even pick and choose – spend several days on something that attracted her, say no if she pleased. Sometimes she would get so involved in some piece of freelance writing that the deadline for the column would loom and she would find herself guiltily scrabbling for material. She took stock one day and saw that she had been writing it now for nearly two years. How could this be? How had so many weeks peeled off and slid away? Riffling through old copy, she was astonished by that vehement language and those extinguished issues. How could she have thought this, or been so demonstrably wrong about that? Above all, she detected here and there a note of frenetic insincerity. And no wonder. Nowadays, she applied herself grimly to the papers, the radio and the television screen in pursuit of this week's quarry. What had once been uplifting was becoming mechanical. She was indeed writing frequently of seminal matters – she was no longer tethered to fringe concerns, but she did so in such a spasmodic way that any real commitment became impossible. She was in danger of losing her capacity for indignation, for incredulity and even for surprise. She made cold-blooded calculations, and came to a decision. She could survive now, probably, as a freelance. It was time to stop.

'Why?' said the editor.

'I'm getting stale.'

'That's for me to say, not you.'

'I think I'm slightly shell-shocked,' said Lucy.

To which the editor pointed out coolly that this was London, not Belfast or Beirut. What Lucy had meant to say, but could not, was that she feared she might cease to believe in reality, or to take it seriously. A somewhat histrionic response perhaps for a woman required to supply a weekly column of topical comment, but Lucy's feelings were genuine enough. It was not that she doubted her choice of profession, but that she no longer wanted to play the part of a sibyl or a soothsayer.

'Well,' said the editor, 'it's up to you. We shall miss you. The best of luck. Keep in touch.'

Maureen was dismayed. 'But what about that nice regular income? And you won't have your picture in the paper any more.'

Bruce, who was inwardly rejoicing that he could now revert to the *Daily Express*, asked what she had in mind.

'I want to travel,' said Lucy, who had not until that moment realized that this was her intention. 'I am a bad case of insularity and cultural complacency.'

All my life, she thought, I have lived in a small country perched near the top of the northern hemisphere. I speak only one language with any efficiency, and properly understand only my own society – if that. But we live in global times, or so we are told. Out there, down there, are other worlds and other actions, as alien to me as another century.

'You're a bad case of itchy feet if you ask me,' said Maureen. 'But I suppose there's no harm in it at your age and seeing you've no one but yourself to think of.' Bruce commented that the buzz these days was about going into Europe. Maybe Lucy should be thinking along those lines. They were doing French and Italian recipe dishes in Tesco's now, and a special Greek wine promotion.

And so she embarked upon the next stage, a free spirit, accountable to no one but herself. Absolutely independent, and also entirely dependent – upon her own energies, upon a supply of work. She set about a systematic round of visits and phone calls. She drew up a list of potential subjects in which she hoped to interest her various contacts. But she was prepared to go anywhere and write on anything. And she could trade now upon a modest reputation. She was known for eclecticism and astringency, as someone who could turn out a brisk, informative and thoughtful piece, who combined reliability with a certain maverick approach. She felt reasonably confident, and occasionally terrified.

She got off to a slow start. A magazine commission to do a piece on vineyards in Alsace. A profile of an Italian novelist. Gradually, things picked up. Sometimes she was alarmed by the state of her bank balance. At other times a rush of work had her feeling heady with achievement. And after eighteen months or so she was able to make a sober assessment and to decide that it was working out, that her stock was pretty high and getting higher, that she could carry on.

She wrote about Chinese refugees in Hong Kong and Mormons in Salt Lake City and aborigines in Alice Springs. She climbed in and out of aeroplanes, skipped from continent to continent, and began to wonder if her sense of time and space had been corrupted. She passed from today into tomorrow while sitting in the sky eating a meal, and back into yesterday while watching a movie. She leaped across oceans and over mountains, careless and accepting, indignant at minor delays. Her unconsidered bounds from one hemisphere to another made a mockery of those other laborious and anguished voyages, of the long slow conquest of the globe. She would step down the aircraft's gangway, five thousand miles from home, into steam-heat and exotic scenery, with the complaisance of a fictional time-traveller. When she found herself grumbling with a fellow-passenger that it should take so long as twenty-four hours to reach Australia, she knew that her disorientation was complete.

We do indeed live in global times, she thought. That is the problem. The globe has lost its mystery and its terrors. It no longer has oceans, deserts and forests, it is reduced to time-zones, flight numbers and the logo of an airline. We are all travellers now. In airport departure lounges she contemplated the boredom and the composure of those who circumnavigate the world today, in tracksuits and anoraks, slung about with electronic goods and cheap liquor, surprised by nothing, lords of the universe. It has come to this. Once upon a time a stranger was to be wondered at, questioned, attacked maybe, but never, for heaven's sake, accepted with indifference and a yawn. In the linguistic babel of arrivals and departures the itinerant hordes are barely aware of one another, moving between destinations as impervious as the baggage trundling round the carousels. Only language survives, and the cast of an eye, the colour of skin.

In Los Angeles, she fell in love with a Swede. He was a documentary film-maker who roved the world, living out of suitcases in hotels, and while the passion raged Lucy shared with him a private capsule floating free of time and place, waking with a thrill to the sound of her phone in the small hours, and Lennart's voice in Bangkok, or Sydney, or Rio. They talked to each other for weeks and months with the private intensity of obsession, fuelled by this majestic overriding of natural laws. Love conquers everything. It became more exciting to live in expectation of Lennart's calls, and to hear that voice, loaded with erotic significance, than to be with him fleetingly when he touched down in London, or when they could contrive a meeting somewhere else. And eventually she realized that the pleasures of expectation had long outstripped the reality, and that she quite liked Lennart, but that all passion was spent and she didn't like him enough to keep readjusting her life in order to snatch a night in Paris, or to gaze into his eyes across a restaurant table in Milan. They drifted asunder, but Lucy would long mourn those heightened conversations, those magical transmissions of desire around the globe.

She had met Lennart because they fetched up checking in at the same hotel reception desk, had exchanged glances, met up later for a drink ... An arrival in the same place at the same moment so capricious and so improbable that it seemed appropriate to Lucy, with the wisdom of reflection, that in the end the whole appeal of the affair should lie in the triumph over distance and the dictation of the clock. She began to forget Lennart's face, but the sound of the telephone ringing in the night would for ever cause her heart to leap.

Things were going well. She felt sufficiently secure to put down her savings on the deposit for a flat, and take out a mortgage. The sums of money involved appalled her. What possible connection could she have with £64,000? She who had grown up in rented rooms and council flats, who had carefully stacked the loose change from her mother's purse on the kitchen table? She who had learned to add and subtract by labouring to balance the Family Allowance and the Social Security and the Supplementary Benefit against the rent money and what Maureen owed the Indian family who kept the corner shop. She had run a tight ship, back then, aged nine. Now, so far as she could see, she owed astronomical sums to faceless men in charge of financial empires. And this was called the security of home ownership. Every month you relinquished a large proportion of what you had earned. If a shortfall threatened, you were in trouble.

Thus it was that a £60 increase in her monthly mortgage repayment was to direct Lucy on board CAP 500. She read the building society's letter, bemoaned the economic climate and did some rapid calculations. Not good. Not good at all. A thin couple of months on account of a commission falling through, and a whacking great plumbing repair bill and now this.

And so Lucy was all ears when, later that day, the features editor of a Sunday magazine telephoned. Well, yes, she might indeed be interested in doing a travel piece. Love to, she said. I could fit it in pretty soon, as it happens. Sunday magazines pay well. With the mortgage demand smouldering in front of her, Lucy scrapped every arrangement for the immediate future, picked up the phone and rang the travel agent to make inquiries about flights to Nairobi.

12

A Brief History of Callimbia

The extent to which an individual can manipulate the course of history is a matter of intense debate. The Cleopatra's nose theory of history refers to the operation of contingency, but it also implies that personality is everything. Well, maybe. It is impossible to deny that the mad ruler – and indeed the occasional sane ruler – is a real determinant, and moreover one which has achieved new heights in the twentieth century. Callimbia now becomes a case history, and it is necessary to home in upon the life of Doreen Winterton, born in Bexhill in 1918.

Shortly before the Second World War, Doreen, then twenty-one, went out to Egypt as nurserymaid to a British diplomatic family. While the Libyan campaign raged, Doreen knitted and gossiped with the other nannies on the emerald turf of Gezira Sporting Club. She had a good war, and during the course of it she left the diplomatic family and went to work for a wealthy Lebanese couple whose lifestyle was more exotic and who offered better wages. Moreover the mother never interfered; Doreen ruled supreme in the nursery and was waited on by a posse of attendants. She was an adaptable and congenial young woman, and more cosmopolitan by inclination than most of her kind. She learned to speak some Arabic, along with a smattering of French and Italian. England began to seem very remote and unappealing. When in 1945 the Lebanese family moved from Cairo to Marsopolis, where they had extensive trading interests, Doreen went along, willingly.

Marsopolis was picking itself up and putting itself together again after the depredations of the desert campaign, when it had been in the hands of the Italians, the Germans and the British alternately, shelled by three navies and under siege twice. It had not had a good war, and most of the inhabitants had conceived a hearty and entirely understandable dislike for Europeans. On the other hand, many of them had made a good living catering for the requirements of the armed forces of three nations. There was plenty of money around, and every prospect of prosperity in the post-war period. The harbour was repaired and enlarged; the debris was cleared away and concrete apartment blocks began to replace the nineteenth-century façades and the Edwardian villas.

Doreen loved Marsopolis. Within a year she had met and married Yussuf, a Callimbian army officer. She parted from the Lebanese family with expressions of mutual affection and settled down to a life of contented domesticity and maternity. She bore Yussuf three daughters and at last the essential son, Omar, at which point her parents-in-law, who had been getting restive, forgave her the daughters and lavished her with presents and attention. Her own parents had disowned her at the time of the marriage – a breach which, as the years passed, disturbed Doreen less and less. She lived in a great deal more style than she ever would have done in Bexhill. She had a comfortable villa, plenty of servants, and nothing much to do except keep everybody in order, a task for which she had been perfectly equipped by her Norland Nanny training. Her Arabic was now fluent. She spoke English to the children when they were small, but as they grew older she became irritated by their inadequate grasp of the language and ceased to do so. The reticence and decorum required of Muslim women appealed to a certain prudishness in her own disposition. She wore the *chador* with enthusiasm and took happily to a shuttered life of gossip and intrigue with the female members of Yussuf's extended family. This was not so very different in kind from the life she had been accustomed to among her cronies at Gezira, but with the added advantage that there were minions to take the children from under your feet and you only had to clap your hands if you wanted a cup of coffee or a tray of sweetmeats.

Marsopolis was flourishing again by now. The corniche had been reconstructed, the hotels and restaurants had reopened. In the centre of town the tower blocks soared, dwarfing the statue of Cleopatra's sister in Tahriya Square (formerly Piazza Benito Mussolini, previously Place Napoléon). In the suburbs and along the coast the villas rose again, in pink stucco and gleaming white, draped in bougainvillaea and morning glory. Yachts and power boats appeared among the fishing vessels beyond the harbour. The beaches glistened with the oiled flesh of Callimbia's *jeunesse dorée*.

When little Omar was six Doreen became pregnant again. Tragedy struck. The child (a boy, to compound the disaster) was stillborn; Doreen died of post-natal complications. Yussuf was shattered. The marriage had been a genuinely happy one and he was a devoted husband. For six months he was inconsolable, and then he succumbed to family pressure. He had previously refrained from taking the second wife to whom he was entitled under Muslim law, partly in deference to Doreen's cultural susceptibilities and partly because he didn't want one anyway. He now acquired in quick succession two new wives – an older lady to manage the children and the household and a younger one for other purposes. The three girls and little Omar adapted themselves as best they could to the new regime. After a few years the voice of Bexhill and the Gezira Sporting Club was almost extinguished, surviving only in the family folk memory and a few catch-phrases on the lips of the children, who were after all half English. By the time the girls were in adolescence and Omar was ten their mother was no more than some photographs in an album, a residual memory of nursery pastimes and a few battered props – toys, board games – and an occasional pinched expression upon the faces of Amina and Nadia, her successors, both of whom knew quite well that they fell short and for ever would. Yussuf retreated into a premature middle age, spending most of his time with his cronies at the army barracks. The household suppressed the memory of Doreen by becoming as Callimbian as possible.

Callimbia itself was for the first time independent of foreign domination – assistance, protection, guidance, call it what you will. Callimbians were free to rule Callimbians – or to exploit, oppress and deceive, as the case may be – and set about doing so with gusto. An initially optimistic period under a relatively stable government with an enlightened policy of educational reform and economic expansion gave way to a decade of slithering uncertainty, as one precarious regime succeeded another and the country slid from the post-war boom into debt and insolvency. Corruption became the norm. Here and there fortunes were made and quickly salted away in Swiss banks. The average citizen grew poorer and watched in bewilderment and disillusion as rival parties slanged each other, as yet another heralded saviour fell from power, or disappeared in mysterious circumstances.

The Americans muscled in, their eye on the strategic possibilities. The Russians and the Chinese slipped into crannies. All three competed in the provision of advisers and technological experts and the supply of various commodities from dried milk to unspecified bulk deliveries of hardware for the heavily guarded research and development sites out in the desert. The oil prospectors, who had been quietly foraging for many a year, suddenly struck lucky. The oil began to gush – albeit in a small way by Middle Eastern standards but liquid gold none the less – and the attentions of those dispassionately concerned about Callimbia's future were redoubled, along with the furious struggles for power between those Callimbians convinced that they alone were equipped for leadership. By 1990 there had been eight changes of government within the last ten years, four political coups, with and without bloodshed, seven ministerial assassinations and a small revolution. Those Callimbians with long historical memories must have had doubts about the nature of progress.

Young Omar had followed his father into the armed forces. There, though, the resemblance ended. Yussuf was a punctilious and conscientious officer, a touch unimaginative perhaps, and inclined to emphasize the bureaucratic and disciplinary side of army life, but then he had never been required to go into action and had signed up in the first place in search of a respectable and relatively undemanding occupation. Omar's military career took a rather different form. He became known for insubordination, deviousness, and a capacity for violence which disturbed even his superiors, who were in the business of producing fighting men. He also appeared to have some charismatic quality. Many feared him; others gravitated towards him. His commanding officers were wary of him and tended to look the other way, in the hope no doubt that a tiresome and vaguely worrying phenomenon will disappear if ignored. A grave mistake. As time went on the intractable and hot-headed cadet became a more disturbing figure, the subversive leader of a claque, the focal point for manic and destructive elements in an already unstable society. It was impossible to identify what he offered, or stood for, to clarify his vision or his political intent. His power and his allure lay simply in furious purpose, a megalomaniac concentration of ambition which mesmerized and ignited his ever-growing cohort of supporters. Those observers who appreciated the situation were chilled.

Why the union of a meticulously reared English woman and a decent and law-abiding Callimbian should produce a moral renegade must remain a mystery. Suffice it to say that at the age of forty-one Omar, fighting fit, utterly unscrupulous, raving of the national destiny and his own potential, came roaring from the shadows, with perfect timing. The government of the day, a creaky affair ripe for demolition, never really knew what had hit it. Within twenty-four hours Masrun Prison was full, various people were no longer available, Samara Palace, the state broadcasting centre, the airport, the barracks and indeed anywhere of any interest were occupied by friends of Omar, and Omar had declared himself President, Chief of Police and Supreme Commander of the Armed Forces.

Part Two

1

'And when would you like to travel?'

'Well, some time in the second week of September. Coming back a fortnight later,' said Howard.

Which would get him home nicely in time for the beginning of term. Now that the slog of raising funds was over, the grant in his pocket and the trip within his sights, he felt an almost childish thrill of excitement.

The woman behind the Lunn Poly counter was scrutinizing her screen. 'Tuesday the ninth? There's a 10.30 flight. And a Nairobi–London flight on the twenty-third at midday.'

'That sounds fine.'

'I'll check availability.'

There were glossy posters lined up behind her head. Sunset in the Seychelles, Miami Beach. Autumn in Vermont. How little of the world I've seen, thought Howard. An assortment of strata, and that's about it. 'I've never been to Africa before,' he confided.

'Really?' said the woman. 'They have availability. Do you want me to confirm the bookings?'

'Yes, please.'

'We shall get the tickets early next week. How do you want to pay?'

'Visa,' said Howard. 'I'll call in for them. Thanks very much.'

'Enjoy your trip.'

'Off again?' said Lucy's friend at the travel agency. 'Nairobi? I thought you said you'd never go near Africa again after that trip to Ibadan.'

'Beggars can't be choosers. I'm skint, and it's a good commission.'

'And you want something around the middle of the month. Hang on a minute . . . The fifteenth – how's that?'

'That'll do nicely.'

'And they have availability. Right. How are you for jabs? You need the lot for there, you know. Typhoid, tetanus . . . You name it, they've got it.'

'I'm probably up to date, but I'll check.'

'My mum had a typhoid for Singapore,' said the friend, 'and actually she needn't have anyway, and she was ill for three days. What you should do is ask . . .'

'Oh, God . . . you've reminded me. *My* mum. It's her birthday on the eighteenth. Look . . . is there a flight a few days earlier? Then I could be back in time.'

'Let's see . . . Tuesday the ninth, what about that? 10.30 Heathrow.'

'I'll take that,' said Lucy.

Howard did his packing at the weekend, rearranging everything several times in an unsuccessful attempt to manage with one bag only. The special purchase of short-sleeved cotton shirts and cotton underpants from Marks and Spencer, essential apparently for the heat, of which he had been frequently and fervently warned by his new acquaintance at the Nairobi Natural History

Museum, John Olumbo. Some rough gear and his climbing boots, in case there should be a chance for a field trip. Various off-prints and books for which Olumbo had asked. The boots he wrapped in a couple of sheets of the *Independent* which caught his eye for a moment because of a photograph of the statue of Cleopatra's sister in Marsopolis. He hadn't realized Cleopatra had a sister. The accompanying article was about political instability in Callimbia, but he did not read it. He was wondering what he could take Olumbo as a personal gift and eventually settled rather lamely for a bottle of something from the Duty Free.

Various notebooks and other essential documents went into a small haversack which he would use as a flight bag. He pushed in also a change of shirt, a sweater, and his washing and shaving things, plus a book by a colleague. He would have to pick up some lighter reading matter at Heathrow. Sun-tan lotion and a stick of insect repellent might be a good idea, too. He checked his passport and tickets again. He was looking forward tremendously to this excursion. Whatever awaited him in the Nairobi museum – and undoubtedly these were Burgess Shale animals, though it was difficult to tell at this stage of what significance – it was a chance to go somewhere completely new, to meet new people, Olumbo himself was extremely pleasant. It was the ideal break before the *longueurs* of the new academic year and the London winter.

He went over the contents of his case once more, and added a compass and binoculars, with the idea of a field trip still in mind.

Lucy was working on an article all through the Monday. She finished at about six, faxed it in, and then went to meet some friends for supper. It was after ten when she got home, but the packing took only twenty minutes. She never travelled with more than one bag, of the dimensions acceptable as hand luggage by any airline, and this remained permanently stocked with the essentials of toilet equipment, nightdress, hairdryer. After that it was just a question of adding a small basic wardrobe, adjusted to climatic requirements. Which in this case was wonderfully simple – a cotton skirt and a few tops, a dress lest some more sartorially demanding occasion should turn up, and a couple of pairs of sandals. She would travel, as always, in trousers, T-shirt, sweater and a jacket.

At 10.30 she rang her mother.

'It's all right for some,' said Maureen. 'Swanning off to tropical islands.'

'This is *work*, Mum. As usual. And it isn't a tropical island.'

After which they discussed other matters until Bruce, who liked to keep early hours, could be heard becoming restive in the background. 'See you on the eighteenth,' said Lucy. 'I'll bring you a coconut for your birthday.'

She rang off, and set about a final check of the bag. She added a bathing costume and a copy of *Anna Karenina*. Always advisable to have a long and absorbing book on hand: you never know what will arise by way of delays.

Howard arrived at Heathrow's Terminal Three ten minutes ahead of the recommended check-in time, somewhat fazed. The tube had been crowded and he had had to stand for much of the way, astride his two grips and with the haversack slung over his shoulder. But he was in plenty of time, and his flight was on the departure board without indications of delay or disruption. He joined the shortest British Capricorn check-in line.

126

'Smoking or non-smoking?'

'Non-smoking, please. Window seat if possible.'

She handed him the boarding pass. '39K. Window. Your flight leaves from Gate 19. You'll be called at around 9.45.'

He headed for the Duty Free and spent ten minutes trying to decide if Olumbo would prefer whisky or brandy. He then bought a newspaper, and a couple of paperbacks. He also picked up a tube of sun-tan cream and some insect repellent. It was now twenty-five to ten, which should just about give him time for a quick cup of coffee. He dumped his possessions at the only empty table in the cafeteria and lined up at the counter, casting a wary eye from time to time on the haversack, a garish blue nylon job which he had acquired on one of his Canadian trips, the colour deliberately selected with the notion that if he fell down a rock face his corpse would at least be clearly visible to his rescuers.

Having achieved his coffee, he took off his anorak and settled to his paper, with frequent glances at the departure board. He was an edgy traveller, a legacy perhaps of family journeys in his childhood, when normal practice was to arrive so early for trains that they caught the one before. He therefore saw that CAP 500 had rippled up to the top and signalled boarding before the call came. He rose at once and headed for the departure gates.

'Smoking or non-smoking?'

'Non-smoking. Window, please.'

'Hmmn . . . Window I can't do, I'm afraid.'

'Never mind,' said Lucy. 'Is the plane on time?'

'It is. No bags to check in?'

'None. Just hand luggage.'

'My . . .' said the girl. 'You've got travelling light down to a fine art, haven't you! Here you go – 39J. Gate 19.'

'Oh . . . is that an aisle seat?'

'No, it's centre. Did you want aisle?'

'I'd rather, if you don't mind. Sorry . . . I should have said.'

'No problem, I'll do you another boarding pass. 36H. Have a good trip.'

Just time for a coffee. She snatched up an armful of papers at the shop and made for the cafeteria. She queued up, and then, coffee in hand, looked round for somewhere to sit. The nearest table was occupied by a solitary man reading an *Independent* propped on a haversack. Lucy made to sit down on the chair opposite him and then she saw that a table further away was being vacated by an Indian family, so headed for that instead.

She ignored the first flight call, still busy going through the papers. She was adept at gutting a page of newsprint, isolating what should be read and passing an eye over items that need only be noted. Into this last category came a few lines of an *In brief* column reporting unrest in the Callimbian capital of Marsopolis. She discarded the papers except for a couple, which she stuffed into her hand grip. They were putting out the final flight call now and she hurried for the gate, having to rush back when she realized that she had left her cherished black leather jacket in the cafeteria. Mercifully it was still there.

Two hours into the flight they served lunch, and Howard abandoned his efforts to concentrate on his book. He had drawn the short straw so far as seating was concerned, and was landed with a couple of computer salesmen as neighbours. They were now into their third Bloody Mary and a sequence of long anecdotes with inadequate punchlines, to which he was obliged to listen. The only hope for the future seemed to be that the combination of drink and food might render them unconscious for the rest of the flight. He ate his seafood salad and beef stroganoff rather glumly, aware of a headache coming on. His mood of cheerful anticipation was somewhat dampened, but would no doubt recover upon arrival at Nairobi. As soon as the trays had been cleared he got up to stretch his legs and have a wash.

There was a line for the toilets. He stood looking down through the window on to the carpet of quilted cloud below. Ahead of him was a young woman with short dark curly hair leaning up against a bulkhead reading, he observed, a copy of *Anna Karenina*. She looked up and caught his eye; Howard concentrated quickly upon the window again, embarrassed to be caught prying.

The plane seemed pretty full. A cosmopolitan lot, too. There was a clutch of Japanese faces, an Indian enclave with many children whose small heads bobbed up and down among the seats, a lot of Africans. One whole block of seats was occupied by a party of male Americans with old-fashioned crewcuts, whom Howard identified by means of some shrewd eaves-dropping as the staff of a mission school, returning from vacation. He amused himself identifying languages: he listed English, Arabic, Japanese, German, hesitated over something Scandinavian that might be either Swedish or Norwegian, or possibly Danish, guessed at Swahili and then gave up. They were setting things up for the movie now, which with any luck would silence his companions. The Japanese were taking photographs of each other. He headed back to his seat.

'Shit!' said the girl next to Lucy. 'It's that stupid thing about

129

three guys who get landed looking after a baby. I've seen it already. If I'd known they'd be showing that I'd have taken the Thursday flight.'

Lucy smiled noncommittally. She knew by now all about her neighbour's job at the United States Embassy in Nairobi, about her vacation trip to the Everglades and her boyfriend in the construction business. *Anna Karenina* had proved an inadequate defence.

'You seen it?'

'No,' said Lucy firmly. 'But I think I'll get some sleep.' The girl turned disconsolately to the flight magazine in the pouch in front of her. The blinds came down. When Lucy slid a glance sideways, she saw that her neighbour had put on her headphones and was staring at the movie screen. She wondered if she dared switch her light on and return to *Anna Karenina*.

Howard dozed. His neighbours were pole-axed by alcohol and snoring, as he had hoped. The plane roared and hummed around him; voices came rooting into his sleep; he still had a headache. An outbreak of turbulence brought him swimming up into consciousness; he opened his eyes and saw the flickering movie screen, figures mouthing and gesticulating. He closed them again and dropped back into that noisy throbbing state of semi-oblivion. He dreamed that he was holding in his hands a plastic model of a *Hallucigenia*, constructed evidently as a toy. He thought that distant hordes were shouting some refrain, like football mobs.

And then a voice was saying loudly, 'Hey! Where's the rest of the movie?' He whipped wide awake. The cabin lights were on and the screen was blank. All over the plane people were stirring and turning. The FASTEN SEAT BELTS sign was lit up.

One of the cabin crew hurried down the aisle. The computer salesmen had come to and were staring round dopily. One of them said, 'Christ! Are we there already? I could have done with a bit more kip.'

Howard lifted the blind and looked out of the window. It was still daylight, and the white mantle of cloud stretched as far as he could see, delicately tinted with grey and, in the distance, suffused with apricot reflections from an invisible sun. He looked at his watch. They had been flying for some four and a half hours.

The cabin was becoming restless. One or two people left their seats to make for the toilets, and were shooed back by the cabin crew. Others craned uneasily over the seats. An Indian stood up and was shouting excitedly at a passing steward, who ignored him and vanished into the business section. The aircraft seemed to be losing height. The unrest and agitation increased.

The intercom crackled. 'This is Captain Soames speaking. We are experiencing some engine trouble and will have to interrupt this flight at Marsopolis. We have been given permission to land and will be starting our descent within a few minutes. We apologize for the inconvenience and hope to let you know what length of delay to expect as soon as possible.'

Howard's immediate neighbour groaned. 'Bugger that – a night in the Holiday Inn at Marsowhatsit, that's what we can expect, I imagine.'

'Where the hell is it, anyway?'

'North African coast somewhere, isn't it?' The man turned to Howard. 'You know this place, by any chance?'

'It's the capital of Callimbia,' said Howard. 'That's all I know about it.'

The air crew were patrolling the aisles, with reassuring

131

smiles. The blinds rattled up on both sides and light flooded in. Turbulence began as the plane descended more steeply. A baby began to cry.

'Jesus!' said the girl from the United States Embassy in Nairobi. 'Wouldn't you know it! Larry's got a table booked at the best restaurant in town – welcome-back party. I guess I can kiss that goodbye.' She peered across and out of the window; her expression changed. 'Or is this what they say when you're going to crash and they prefer not to mention it?'

'I don't know,' said Lucy. 'I don't think so. I was in a plane that got engine trouble once before and it just came down and we got into another one. Eventually.'

'Eventually,' said the girl. 'That's what I'm afraid of. Oh, well. It's on the coast, this place, isn't it? Maybe we can go to the beach while they fix us up.'

It is also in some kind of political difficulty, thought Lucy. Something about reports of disturbances at the army headquarters. I should know more about Callimbia. Oil. Those boxes of dates you buy at Christmas. Different governments every six months.

They were in cloud now, white mist streaming past the windows, the plane shuddering. The baby was screaming and someone was being sick.

Howard could see a group of airport buildings in the distance. The plane had started to taxi towards them and then came to a halt, in the middle of a waste of concrete. There were a lot of people about down there, a good many of them soldiers with rifles slung over their shoulders. He wondered about this. Most of the vehicles buzzing to and fro were army vehicles, too. The only other grounded aircraft to be seen carried the logo of the local airline: there were several unmarked helicopters.

The cabin crew now hurried up the aisles in the direction of the flight deck. Five minutes passed. Ten. People were fidgeting. Children broke loose and ran up and down. The FASTEN SEAT BELTS sign remained on, but a number of passengers got up to take things from the overhead lockers.

'Oh, come on,' said the computer salesman. 'I need to put through a call to the office.'

Several vehicles had now converged upon the forward end of the plane. A gangway was being wheeled into position up there. There was a lot of activity on the ground; people hurried to and fro. A minibus had arrived. The crew appeared suddenly on the tarmac and stood in a group; there seemed to be an argument going on; Howard could see the Captain talking vigorously to a man in a dark suit. And then a couple of soldiers began to shepherd them towards the minibus. A stewardess who seemed reluctant to get in was shoved unceremoniously through the door.

Howard's neighbour was also peering out. 'What the hell's going on down there?'

'I don't know. They seem to be letting the crew off first.'

There was disturbance now further up the plane. Howard lifted himself to look over the top of the seats and saw figures advancing down the aisles.

'It's something to do with immigration,' said the computer salesman. 'Passports. Why the devil don't they take us into the airport and do it there?'

When the official drew level with their row they saw that he was amassing passports into a large canvas bag. There were a couple of soldiers behind him.

'What's this about?' said the computer salesman. 'No, thank you. Here's my passport. You can check it over and I'll have it back, if you don't mind.'

'All passports!'

'No. You look at it here, OK?'

One of the soldiers now stepped forward, thrust his face down and shouted incomprehensibly.

The computer salesman flinched. 'For Christ's sake! All right, then, here you are.'

Howard fished his passport from his pocket and handed it over. The cavalcade moved on to the next row.

'God Almighty! What is this place? They could take a few lessons in customer relations.'

'Maybe they don't have a tourist industry,' said the other computer man.

The whole cabin was chattering now. Heads craned over seats, following the progress of the passport collectors and the soldiers. One of the Americans from the mission school got up and sauntered down the aisle after them. 'Excuse me . . .' Howard heard him say. 'Hey . . . excuse me . . .'

A soldier turned and hurried back towards him, snapping an instruction.

'Look,' said the American. 'Some of us are wondering . . .'

The soldier poked the butt of his rifle into his stomach and the man fell back into his seat.

The computer salesman swung round to Howard. 'Did you see that! This is crazy. I can tell you one thing. I'm going to be putting in a complaint when I get back to the UK.'

'Do you know, we've been sitting here for precisely twenty-five minutes?' said the girl from the embassy. 'I mean, this is

134

ridiculous. And why did they take the passports *away*? I don't get it.'

'Neither do I,' said Lucy. From where she was sitting she could see little out of the window except the occasional truck or lorry bumping over the tarmac, and people standing around. Most of them seemed to be staring up at the plane.

The passport collectors and the soldiers now came back up the aisles. The passport collectors disappeared but a soldier remained standing in each aisle, at the curtain into the business-class section.

'And what are these guys for?'

Lucy tried to see beyond the soldier into the further cabin. Through there, an altercation was going on, someone shouting that they'd been waiting quite long enough now . . . absurd delay . . . demand to see the airport controller. And then another voice cut in, lower, inaudible. And the first voice shouted again and the soldier turned round and disappeared and the voice ceased, abruptly.

The soldier returned and stood in the centre of the aisle again. The intercom came on, with someone saying something inaudible, and then another speaker took over, talking clear precise English with a tinge of an accent: 'All passengers should now disembark at the forward end of the plane and proceed to the airport building as instructed. Please take your hand luggage with you.' He spoke again in French, and then in Arabic.

'And about time too,' said the American girl. 'A hot bath and a martini, that's what I need.'

Lucy thought, but whose was that voice? And where are the cabin crew?

The plane came to life, people reaching up into the lockers, stretching, commenting. The aisles filled up; the lines shuffled forward. As they passed through the business-class section Lucy saw a man wiping blood from his mouth with a tissue. The woman with him had her hand on his arm and looked tearful.

'Did you see that guy? What d'you think happened?'

'I don't know,' said Lucy.

'Maybe something fell out of one of the lockers.'

'I expect so.'

From the top of the gangway they could see the passengers ahead of them moving across the tarmac in a long straggling line. At each side of the line, every ten yards or so, there was a soldier. Soldiers stood at the top and bottom of the gangway. Lucy looked across at the airport building. There were projections of some kind on the flat roof. As she stared it came to her that they might be machine guns. A helicopter circled overhead.

'This is the craziest airport I ever saw!' said the embassy girl. 'What do they think they're doing, for goodness' sake? You don't need half the army to help a few people get off a plane.'

I don't like this, Lucy thought. I don't like this at all.

2

Howard eyed the soldiers as he walked towards the airport building. Their uniforms were motley and ill-fitting, but the rifles with which they were slung looked authentic enough. Not that he was any expert. They were an interesting range of physical types, he noticed – some quite negroid in appearance, others pale-skinned and Greek-looking, Semitic faces and lean brown Arab features. But why were they all over the place like this?

The passengers were marshalled into what appeared to be the main arrivals hall of the airport, where the more restive began at once to investigate the facilities. Howard joined the American mission-school party whose apparent leader – he who had accosted the soldier on the plane – returned from a tour of inspection.

'You're not gonna believe this, but there's not one airline desk active in this place. PanAm, BA, TWA ... closed down, the lot of them.'

'Maybe it's their Sunday,' someone suggested.

'Oh, come on ... Airlines run on the sabbath, the world over. You know what, I think we should call our embassy. I don't like the way these people are handling this.' He was a big gangling man with penetrating blue eyes and a loud voice; you could imagine him running up and down a games pitch, blowing a whistle at small boys.

Howard pointed out that the flight crew were still nowhere to be seen.

'That's right.' The American teacher pondered. 'You'd think they'd be telling us something about our onward journey. This is the last time I'll use British Capricorn, I can tell you that. I'm Chuck Newland, by the way – Naivasha Boys School.'

'Howard Beamish.'

'Ah . . . Here we go . . . They're making an announcement.'

The voice that came over the public address system was the one which had issued instructions on the plane. 'Will passengers from CAP 500 please divide up into national groups. United States citizens to Exit A, British citizens to Exit B, Japanese to Exit C, EC countries to Exit D, African and Asian nationalities to Exit E, others remain here. This procedure is necessary for administrative purposes.' The instruction was repeated in French and Arabic.

There was an instant babble of comment. People began to mill about, and to move towards the various exits.

'For heavens' sake!' said Chuck Newland. One of his group suggested that the intention must be to return the passports.

'I guess so. But it seems a pretty screwy way to go about it.' He heaved his flight bag over his shoulder and turned to Howard. 'Well, see you later. On our way to Nairobi, let's hope.'

The British group made its way out into a corridor, closely supervised by a posse of soldiers, who ushered them for some distance and eventually into a large room furnished with rows of moulded plastic seats, and screened off from the corridor by a glass partition. The opposite wall was entirely window, but blinds had been drawn down so that it was not possible to see out. The passengers – there were around forty of them – drifted towards the seats and began to settle down.

'Here we go for another two-hour wait,' said the computer salesman. 'This is the worst travel cock-up I've been in for quite a time.' Howard nodded polite agreement and headed for a different part of the room.

He saw that the young woman who had been reading *Anna Karenina* on the plane was alone at the end of one of the rows of seats. He sat down alongside her, dumping the haversack at his feet. She was not reading now, but looking round intently, apparently taking stock. Howard observed covertly. He saw a small, trim person dressed in brown trousers and a sea-green sweater, with a black leather jacket. She was pretty without being arresting: a cloud of dark hair, a face with neat, crisp features, a particularly agreeable set to the nose, an appealing line to the lips. No make-up. A drift of freckles.

She too was glancing now, aware of his scrutiny. He said hastily, 'We seem to be being shoved around rather, I must say.'

'We certainly are,' said Lucy.

She recognized now that lurid haversack, and remembered that she had also seen this man on the plane, waiting in the toilet queue. He was of medium height and rather thin. Thick brown hair, long face and a light beard. Alert expression; pleasant smile. Greenish-brown eyes and curiously luxuriant eyelashes. Somewhat shabby appearance – crumpled cotton chinos, a veteran anorak.

'This is a most peculiar airport,' she went on.

'All the airline desks are closed down.'

'Yes. But not just that. There aren't any planes. Listen. Nothing coming in or going out. Just these helicopters.'

139

They sat in silence for a few moments.

'I don't know what to make of it,' said Howard. 'It begins to get a bit worrying, frankly.'

'I think there's been some sort of coup. I saw something earlier in the paper about disturbances here. I think there's been a political coup and they've closed the airport down and we've fetched up in the middle of it.'

Howard considered. 'That would make sense. In which case presumably they're just sussing us out and then we'll be on our way.'

'I suppose so,' said Lucy. 'I hope so.'

'Well, what point would there be in making us hang around here?'

'I can't think of one,' replied Lucy after a moment. And indeed she couldn't.

'Why did they let us land, though?' Howard continued.

'Quite. And why didn't our captain pick a different airport?'

'One must assume,' said Howard, 'that he didn't know there was a problem here, or else that the engine trouble was such that he had to get down as quickly as possible, no matter where. Either way, it's about time we were offered some sort of explanation.'

Others felt the same, clearly. People peered through the glass screen into the corridor, and the more daring accosted the soldiers posted at the entrance, who stared impassively back.

'They will have to get us another plane,' said Lucy. 'Unless this one can be fixed, and in any case what does engine trouble mean? Is it like your car hiccuping on the motorway? And the A A man does something deft with a screwdriver and hey presto! Or is it one of those cases when they shake their heads gloomily and you end up being carted off on a breakdown truck? Whatever, I imagine we're here for the night. And I'd be a lot happier if we were told something. Politely, by someone in authority, if anyone is, and with less of the Callimbian army standing around. My name's Lucy Faulkner, by the way. Who are you?'

Howard introduced himself. The odd thing was that he did not now feel unhappy. The headache he suffered on the plane had vanished, and he was in no great hurry to reach Nairobi after all, he found. This delay was indeed perturbing, he supposed, but it would undoubtedly be sorted out in due course and in the meanwhile ... Well, in the meanwhile he had achieved a rather congenial companion. He really must try not to look at her so intently, though.

There was a burst of activity now at the entrance to the room and a trolley appeared loaded with cans of soft drink and packaged snacks. People began to get up and converge upon it.

'Would you like something to eat?' said Howard. 'There doesn't look to be much choice but I can forage.'

'Thanks. Just a cold drink.'

He returned with a couple of cans and some packets of crisps and chocolate biscuits. 'I've brought rather more than you asked for, on the grounds that we seem to be living from moment to moment and it may be wise to make contingency plans. If you don't want this now you can always stash it away against hard times.'

Lucy laughed. She looked directly at him and then away again, quickly. The queasy feeling she had developed earlier was ebbing; instead, she was slightly exhilarated. But I still don't like what's going on, she thought. Why don't they *tell* us something?

'Handing out food is definitely a bad sign. We're being softened up.'

'Do you think so?' said Howard. He bit into a sandwich and then put it down. 'If that's the case, they're not going about it very cleverly. This is inedible. I've been trying to remember what I know about this country, and it amounts to not very much. Something to do with Cleopatra's sister and that's about it.'

'It's had a series of unstable governments. It was under Italian administration before the war. Before that I think it was Turkish. It exports dates and in the sixties the tourist industry got going a bit. There were package holidays for a while, and then all that folded up because of the unstable governments, and the economy going haywire. It has oil, though, on a relatively small scale.'

'You're better informed than I am,' said Howard.

'I'm a journalist. It's a tendency of the trade – to have a smattering of information about a great range of things. Seldom enough to be really useful.'

'Well, you impress me, anyway. But I'm relieved it's professional. I don't feel quite so ignorant.'

'What do you do?' Lucy asked after a moment.

'I'm a palaeontologist.'

'I've never met a palaeontologist. Could you tell me exactly what that involves?'

And so he did. And she listened, he noticed, with absolute attention. When she asked a question it was pertinent and succinct. She made him repeat the names of Burgess Shale animals.

'And the reason that they're so interesting is this huge disparity? And that lots of them don't relate to anything that's around today?'

'Exactly,' said Howard. 'Most of them are evolutionary

142

dead-ends. They include animals which are ancestral to the four major kinds of modern arthropods, but there are a whole lot more which are completely weird and wonderful and which have to be classified as entirely separate phyla, all of which have vanished. I'm sorry, I'm probably boring you . . .'

'Do I look bored?'

'Well, no – but I tend to get a bit carried away if given encouragement. I forget that others may not see the point of it. Especially when they've never set eyes on these creatures.'

'The point being,' said Lucy, 'the implications for the way the world is today. The fact that there is the existing fauna, including us, instead of something entirely different.'

He gazed at her with gratification. 'Just so. The whole process becomes both remarkable and precarious. An accident of contingency. That's not to say that there wouldn't always have been certain tendencies – the emergence of creatures that fly, or run on four legs, or reproduce in a particular way. And there are those who insist that the appearance of intelligent life is an inevitability. Nevertheless, it gives pause for thought.'

'I am feeling distinctly envious. I've always had quite a lot of job satisfaction myself, but your line sounds amazing. Picking up bits of rock in scenic places and then unravelling the secrets of the universe.'

'I've left out most of it,' said Howard sternly. 'I spend the bulk of my time teaching students, many of whom aren't much interested in what I'm trying to tell them. I also spend many hours squabbling with my colleagues about time-tables and the allocation of space.'

'All the same . . . Do you have a particular favourite, out of these creatures?'

'I'm pretty fixated generally. You tend to have a special

respect for the ones which have not yet been definitively studied and described. And the ones of which there are only a very few known specimens. I'm rather fond of a thing called *Hallucigenia*, which really is like some sort of Salvador Dali dream object, with a bulbous excrescence at one end and a tube at the other, and spiky struts on top and a row of tentacles beneath. And indeed it has thrown everyone recently because it turns out the original description had it upside down. It's as though these mysterious little animals get the last laugh.'

'And you think there are some of them waiting for you in Nairobi?'

'I'm sure of it. One of the exciting things is the way in which they are now turning up in all sorts of places.'

'It must be driving you mad, being held up like this.'

'I suppose so,' said Howard, without conviction. In fact, the delay was becoming more acceptable by the minute. 'As it happens, I've not met so very many journalists. Was it something journalistic that was taking you to Nairobi?'

'Yes. Extremely mundane, though, I'm afraid. I was going there to write a bread-and-butter travel piece about game reserves and suchlike for a Sunday paper. Bread-and-butter in every sense. I'm feeling a bit skint and they pay well. Someone rang up out of the blue, so I jumped at it.'

'That sounds exotic enough to me. What rates as non-mundane, then, in your trade?'

'Things you really want to do as opposed to things you have to do to earn your keep, I suppose.'

'Such as?'

'Well,' said Lucy. 'Finding out about something important of which you reckon people don't know enough – or don't know the truth about – and then telling them. That, basically.'

'Which is roughly what I buy a newspaper for, now you mention it. Information and informed opinion. I take it you're the informed opinion side?'

'I suppose I am. Though put like that, I worry about the opinion bit. It seems to stick out. Opinion but not opinionated, is what you hope.'

'Presumably if it were the latter, people would cease to hire you.'

'Oh, no,' said Lucy. 'They'd jump at you, in some circles.'

'What papers do you write for, by the way?'

She told him.

'Then I must have read you. Lucy Faulkner . . .'

'People never notice by-lines.'

'Ah, is that what you say. By-line.'

'I thought I was entitled to my own touch of professional jargon. You had arthropods and phyla and heaven knows what.'

'I *was* boring you,' said Howard.

'On the contrary, I'd like to hear more.'

'I fear there may be all too much opportunity, if things go on like this.'

They both glanced towards the corridor, where the soldier still lounged at the entrance and fellow passengers banged in frustration on the glass partition wall.

'This opinion business . . .' said Howard. 'Do you ever find yourself without one?'

'No. Or at least hardly ever. That can be a problem. I'm a person who tends to leap into a position. You have to avoid that. Stay detached, at least while you're finding things out.'

'It's beginning to sound a bit like science. And what sends you off after something?'

'Curiosity. Wanting to get there before someone else does.'

'Definitely like science.'

'Up to a point,' said Lucy. 'Remember plenty of journalists manipulate the truth and do fearful things with evidence.'

'*You* don't.'

'So I claim.'

At this point the tranquillity of their conversation was threatened by a somewhat raucous family party encamped near by, so they moved away to a solitary table with a couple of chairs close to the shrouded windows, and talked there, becoming more and more impervious to the gathering restlessness of others in the group. An hour passed, and more, during which Lucy and Howard were too absorbed to notice an incident in which a soldier threatened one of the computer salesmen with the butt of his rifle and another in which a battle was fought and won over the right to visit the toilets in small, escorted parties. When eventually they were distracted by a couple of squabbling children and the by now fairly explosive atmosphere in the room, it was late afternoon.

'Heavens! We've been here going on two hours,' said Lucy.

'So we have. It hasn't seemed like that.'

'Perhaps we should be making more of an effort to find out what's happening.'

'I think other people are doing precisely that.'

Indeed, there was one group haranguing the soldier on the door, clearly to no effect, while individuals were knocking angrily on the glass partition every time anyone with any appearance of authority walked by in the corridor beyond.

'It really is getting past a joke,' said Howard.

'I'm beginning to feel a bit knackered, I must say.'

He looked at her solicitously. 'Are you? Shall I see if they've got any drinks on that trolley?'

'I'll survive,' said Lucy. 'Don't worry. Anyway, something seems to be going on. Look.'

The door had opened and the soldiers were apparently being issued instructions by a more highly ranking colleague. The door remained open, with the officer standing there. The soldiers toured the room, indicating that the group should gather up possessions and depart.

'Where are we going?' said Howard.

The man shrugged. 'Go in buses.'

'Yes, but go where in buses?'

At the door, others were pressing the point with the officer.

'Transport is waiting. Hurry, please.'

'Are we being taken to a hotel? How long before there is another plane for us?'

'There will be statement of information very soon.'

The party straggled along the corridors again and out on to the tarmac at the back of the airport building. There were several coaches parked and in the distance people were getting into one of them.

'That's the Japanese group,' said Lucy.

Howard suggested that perhaps they were being allocated a superior grade of hotel.

'Maybe . . . It does seem peculiar to keep on segregating us like this, though.'

They got into the coach. The Americans had now come out of the building and were being directed to other vehicles. Howard caught sight of Chuck Newland, who waved.

The driver got in, the engines revved, the coach set off.

They drove along anonymous airport access roads and on to a dual carriageway. The landscape was flat, with a distant grey smudge of hills. There were fields of sugar cane, beans, and the

147

occasional patch of olives or orange trees. Once they passed a village of squat mud-walled houses interspersed with low breeze-block apartment buildings. A string of camels prompted a buzz of comment.

There was very little traffic. 'The only thing I'm learning about this place at the moment is that they have an extraordinarily high accident rate,' said Howard.

At intervals, ever since leaving the airport, they had been passing the carcasses of cars and lorries, pitched on their sides by the road and, in some cases, burnt out.

'I've noticed that too,' said Lucy. 'I suppose this must be the beginning of Marsopolis.'

They were driving through suburban sprawl now. Apartment blocks, small concrete villas with gardens, shops and petrol stations. There were people about, who stared briefly at the coach as they passed. As the city thickened around them the dishevelled appearance of the place became more pronounced. An overturned bus; debris of bricks and stones on the road; buildings with broken windows.

'I'm afraid you're right,' said Howard. 'There has definitely been something going on here.'

Lucy nodded. The army was still much in evidence. Soldiers lounged on street corners, or patrolled entrances and bus stops. People appeared to be going about their business, though perhaps rather hurriedly and in smaller numbers than one might have expected. Many of the shops were shuttered.

They had reached the seafront now. The corniche road ran alongside a long beach, entirely deserted except for the odd gang of children. The coach passengers gazed at it with interest. The atmosphere of anticipation grew stronger as hotels were spotted on the other side of the road; Beau Rivage, Plaza,

Excelsior. 'Whoa, there!' someone shouted. 'This'll do nicely.'

But the coach forged on, and indeed shortly turned off the corniche to a distinctly unprosperous hinterland of shabby shops and housing set among warehouses, depots and small factories. A stir of discontent and apprehension spread through the bus.

Lucy sighed. 'It's not going to be the Beau Rivage or the Bella Vista, I'm afraid.'

'Wherever it is, will you have dinner with me?' said Howard.

She looked directly at him. She smiled.

'I was rather thinking along those lines, as it happens.'

The coach was now turning into a large concrete compound with a high wire perimeter fence. In the centre was a sprawl of buildings, at the entrance to which the coach drew up. The door was opened and the passengers disembarked, looking around with dismay. The attendant military waved them towards the barrack-like structure.

'We want a hotel. Tell the driver to take us to a hotel.'

'Is here hotel,' said one of the soldiers.

'Oh, for God's sake!'

The group milled about, conferring mutinously.

'This is ridiculous. We shouldn't go in there. We should get back in the coach and sit tight till they take us to one of those places on the coast road.'

'We should get hold of the embassy.'

'Where the hell are the airline people?'

More soldiers and a handful of official-looking men in suits had now emerged from the building. The coach started up and made for the exit. The gates were closed behind it and padlocked by a sentry. One of the officials was addressing those of the group who were nearest the door.

'What's he saying?'

'It's something about the passports.'

'They're going to give the passports back.'

'Presumably then they'll take us to a hotel.'

'But why has the coach gone?'

The passengers straggled into the building, still expressing doubts. The official stood at the entrance, holding a sheaf of papers and looking harassed.

'Why have we been brought here?' demanded Howard.

'There are immigration procedures.'

'All that could have been done at the airport.'

'Please go inside.'

'I want to telephone the British Embassy.'

'Very soon. Please go inside.'

He had become detached from Lucy. She was somewhere ahead, among those now filing through a door opening off a bare entrance hall furnished only with an unmanned reception desk and some empty noticeboards. Concern about this separation at once swamped his annoyance with the bureaucratic stonewalling. He abandoned the exchange and hurried into the building.

The room into which they had been herded was stark. There was a long trestle table at one end, with three chairs behind it. The concrete floor was distinctly dirty. The walls were peeling. Howard eased himself through the crowd to Lucy's side, and then felt an uprush of uncertainty. Would she think he was pestering her? Maybe she had been trying to get rid of him?

Lucy had been processed into the room with the rest of the group and then had found that Howard was no longer there. She looked round and could see him nowhere. And she felt a twinge of deprivation, quite distinct from her general condition

150

of increasing weariness, annoyance and vague alarm. This is absurd, she told herself. You only met this man a couple of hours ago.

And suddenly there he was; somehow things weren't so bad after all. They beamed at one another. Howard said, 'I couldn't see you, I . . .' and then pulled himself up short and began to talk of his bout with the official at the entrance and to speculate as to why they were being incarcerated here.

'People seem to think we're going to be given back our passports.'

And, sure enough, a soldier now appeared with a briefcase containing the passports, which were ranged upon the trestle table in a disorderly display. The passengers surged forward to claim them, and were shoved back.

'Wait! Everybody wait there!'

The official from the entrance now appeared, perusing lists.

'Anderson?'

Someone stepped forward.

'Take passport please and go in there. Take luggage also.'

The rest waited, grumbling. There were only a dozen or so chairs in the room. It was clear that this was going to take some time. People leaned up against the walls. Those who had initially appropriated the seating offered it to the elderly and the pregnant.

'We're developing group solidarity,' said Lucy. 'Interesting. I don't think I've seen that happen before.'

Howard's name was now called. He collected his passport from the table and was directed into a room occupied by a single man behind a desk equipped with a pile of forms, one of which he handed to Howard.

'Fill in form, please.'

151

Father's name, mother's maiden name. Religious status. Occupation. Howard sighed and set to work. He handed the completed form to the official, who studied it closely. It seemed that he was unhappy about something. He stabbed at the paper with one finger.

'What is this?'

'Palaeontologist,' said Howard. 'It's what I do. Occupation.'

The man scowled. He rose and went into the next room. Through an open door Howard could see him conferring with colleagues. The form was handed from one to another. Now Howard's original interrogator reached for a telephone and held a lengthy conversation. Howard could only suppose that his profession had never caught on in Callimbia.

The interrogator returned, set down the form and looked at Howard with irritation and suspicion.

'What is the purpose of your visit to Nairobi?'

'I really don't see what business that is of yours. This is not Nairobi.'

'It is necessary information for immigration procedures.'

'Oh, rubbish,' said Howard. 'I was going there to study some fossil specimens in the museum, if you must know.'

The man made notes, laboriously. Howard hoped the term 'fossil' would give pause for thought.

'How long do you intend to stay in Nairobi? Have you previously visited Egypt, Libya, Algeria, Morocco . . .? How much currency are you carrying with you?'

The catechism continued. And as he provided perfunctory answers it suddenly occurred to Howard that the whole thing was a charade. They don't really want to know all this, he thought. It is to wear us down. Or play for time. We are being used in some way. And for the first time he felt deep cold unease.

152

At last it was finished.

'Give me luggage now, please.'

'Why?' said Howard.

'Customs inspection.'

'Oh, for God's sake . . .' He handed over his flight bag. The official rummaged within, examined with care his electric razor and flipped open the books. He closed the bag, returned it to Howard, and nodded to a colleague who stepped forward and carried out a body search, investigating Howard's pockets and running his hands up and down his trouser legs.

'Go back to group now and wait, please.'

'What for? And for how long?'

'Information will be given soon.'

The interrogator had taken Howard's passport from him for inspection. He now dropped it into a wire tray beside him along with a couple of others.

'I'd like my passport back.'

'Is not possible at the moment.'

Howard got up and marched out of the room. When he was once more beside Lucy he was shaking with anger, he discovered.

'What happened?'

He shook his head, trying to calm down, not wanting to dismay her. 'It's just that they're a thoroughly cussed lot, these people. They bombard you with questions. And they're not giving the passports back. And they search both you and your luggage.'

Lucy was silent for a moment. 'There's something odd going on, isn't there?'

'I'm sure it'll be all right. Don't worry.'

She looked at him. 'I'm not going to get in a stew. I tend to be fairly calm.'

'I'm sure you do,' said Howard. Each time he studied her face afresh there was now this incredible sense of familiarity. Not so much that he had always known it, as that he had always needed to, but been unaware. As though a void had been filled. And how on earth was it possible to be simultaneously uplifted and profoundly apprehensive?

The group had disposed itself around the room, slumped against the walls or seated on the floor. Indignation was giving way to weariness. It was by now early evening. A mellow light filtered in through the dirty windows, through which could be seen only the compound and the wire perimeter fence, which was patrolled by a guard. One by one the passengers carried their passports into the adjoining room and returned, empty-handed and resentful. The several children in the group had passed through restlessness to tears and in some merciful cases to sleep. No refreshments were offered. Those demanding the toilet were escorted to a single offensive facility at the back of the building.

At last the entire party had been interrogated. The door into the adjoining room was closed. The officials vanished. Three soldiers remained in attendance at the entrance to the corridor. Those of the group whose exhaustion had not reduced them to a state of total apathy now gathered to take stock of the situation. A putative leadership emerged, principally comprised of a forthright woman called Molly Wright, who was the chairman of a local health authority on a visit to Nairobi to advise on hospital administration, and James Barrow, director of a film company, a more flamboyant and loquacious figure. Howard and Lucy joined the small gathering which was now debating what could or should be done. It was generally recognized and accepted that they had become unwittingly involved in some kind of Callimbian political crisis.

'It seems to me that they're looking for someone,' said Molly Wright. 'Hence the intensive screening. Maybe they think there's someone on the plane they want.'

It was pointed out that this would be a curious coincidence, since the plane had never been destined for Callimbia in the first place.

'True,' said Barrow, 'but they're very interested in nationality. This segregation process. That has to be significant in some way. I can't fathom what the hell it is they're at for the moment, but I think we're being much too bloody compliant.'

Howard observed that there was not really a lot of choice, given the presence and attitude of armed soldiers.

'Yeah, but I doubt they're actually going to take a pot shot at any of us if it comes to the point.'

'They hit someone, on the plane,' said Lucy. 'At least, there was a man with his face bleeding.'

'If you want to try making a run for it, feel free,' said Molly Wright briskly. 'But where to, anyway? What we need is a line to our embassy. Have they any idea we're here, one would like to know?'

It was now quite dark outside. Lights had been switched on and there sounded to be activity in the corridor. Outside, some large vehicle was heard to arrive.

'Aha,' said James Barrow. 'Action of some kind. A nice air-conditioned coach to take us to the local Hilton, maybe.'

There was now a great deal of coming and going without. Shouted instructions. Footsteps to and fro and the thump of objects being dumped on the concrete floor. Those of the group who had been slumped semicomatose around the room stirred and watched the door, which opened to admit a couple of porters staggering under the weight of a pile of mattresses.

'Oh, no!' exclaimed Molly Wright. 'This is unbelievable.'

For the intention, it soon became apparent, was to transform the room into a makeshift dormitory. The mattresses — thin lumpy affairs, a number of which bore disagreeable stains — were disposed about the floor. There were not quite enough to go round. The group now hived off into those who had perceived this and began furtively to appropriate a mattress and those who concentrated on vociferous objection. These converged upon the soldiers at the door.

'No!' said James Barrow, pointing at the mattresses. 'No good. We refuse to sleep here. You get your commanding officer, right?'

'Is not possible.'

'Oh, shit, don't give me that. You go and get someone right away. Now!'

The man stared without apparent emotion. It seemed indeed that he might be about to comply. And then with a single neat action he unslung his rifle and slammed the butt of it downwards into Barrow's stomach. Barrow bent over, clutching himself.

'Are you OK?' said Howard.

'I will be in a minute. Christ!'

A concerned group gathered round. A chair was brought. Barrow subsided into it, retching. People were angrily admonishing the soldier, who shrugged and returned to his post at the door. Molly Wright tried to persuade Barrow to lie down on one of the mattresses. 'I'll be fine in a minute. He's winded me, the bastard, that's all.'

More soldiers now arrived with a heap of insalubrious blankets and a trolley furnished with a pile of bread rolls and a tea urn. The initial horror and disbelief gave way to a kind of exhausted acceptance. Those who had grabbed mattresses began to establish private enclaves in the corners of the room. There was a rush for blankets. The trolley was rapidly stripped bare.

Lucy went along the corridor to the washroom, escorted by a soldier who looked all of sixteen and who stood sternly at attention outside the door while she was inside. There was a single cold tap above a sink, and a foetid lavatory. She washed as best she could and re-emerged. The boy motioned her to go ahead.

'What's your name?' said Lucy.

He shook his head.

'Name?' She pointed at him. 'My name's Lucy. What's yours?'

The boy looked panic-stricken and motioned her ahead of him. 'Go! Go!'

Back in the room she looked at once for Howard. And felt again that surge of pleasure. This is absurd, she thought. Everything is absurd. I don't understand.

'I've got a mattress for you,' he said.

'But what about you?'

'I'll manage. I managed to grab a blanket. And I've got my anorak.'

They found a space under the windows and established themselves.

'You'd better have my jacket as a pillow,' said Lucy. 'This is going to be a fairly horrendous night, I'm afraid.'

'Up to a point,' said Howard.

He did not appear particularly dismayed. Either he's a very phlegmatic fellow, thought Lucy, or . . . or what, exactly?

She delved in her flight bag. 'Would you like to join me for dinner? I seem to have two packets of crisps and one of chocolate biscuits.'

3

At some point in the small hours Howard plunged briefly into a black pit of sleep, and awoke to an instant of wild confusion. He sat up, saw huddled figures around him, shadowed in the light of a single naked bulb slung from the ceiling. He saw the closed door, a standing man who held a gun. The room rustled and murmured. It was both cold and stuffy; there was a disagreeable smell. The whole scene was nightmarish and yet eerily significant. And then he turned his head, saw Lucy, and was instantly slotted back into a sequence. He knew where he was, and why.

She was asleep, facing him, hunched into a foetal shape. Her mouth was slightly open, with a thread of saliva at one corner, and there was a smudge of dirt on her cheek. He gazed at her, and then felt intrusive. Her position suggested that she might be cold; cautiously, he laid his anorak over her. He was stiff and numb from lying on the concrete floor. Taking care not to disturb Lucy, he inched himself to his feet and moved towards the window, where he could see James Barrow leaning against the wall.

They conversed in whispers.

'That fellow must have given you a bit of a bruise.'

'I haven't had a chance to inspect,' said Barrow. 'But I've spent the night working out exactly what I'd do to the bastard given half a chance.'

It was beginning to get light outside. Above the dark line of the perimeter fence the sky was streaked with grey and lemon. The compound within was lit by sodium lamps and bare except for a line of parked lorries and stacks of oil drums and petrol cans.

'What I want to know,' said Barrow, 'is where the hell is our embassy in all this?'

'Maybe they're not aware we're here.'

'They have to be. A plane full of people doesn't just vanish into thin air.'

The door opened. A soldier entered and held a brief muttered exchange with the one already present, who departed.

'The changing of the guard,' said Barrow.

Howard saw that Lucy had woken, and was sitting up. He moved back to his blanket and sat down beside her.

'You managed to sleep a bit?'

'Yes. I seem to have got your anorak on me.'

'I put it there. I thought you looked cold.'

'That was nice of you,' said Lucy. She smiled, and Howard was suffused with pleasure. He sat there on the dirty blanket, in this squalid room, and wondered if he were becoming slightly unhinged by circumstance. Lucy had fished a comb out of her bag and was trying to tug it through her hair. He watched, entranced.

'I don't suppose you've got a mirror on you?'

'No, sorry,' he said.

'I seem to have lost mine. Oh, well – least of our worries. Is my face filthy?'

'There's a smudge on your right cheek.'

She licked a kleenex and rubbed vigorously.

'That's better,' said Howard.

'You know something? I'm really glad I found you – all this would seem much worse otherwise, I'm sure.'

'I'm glad too,' said Howard. 'Quite extraordinarily glad.'

'How bad do you think it is?'

He looked straight at her, startled. 'How bad what is?' he said cautiously.

'This situation. These people locking us up here like this.'

'Oh . . .' He collected himself. 'I can't think it's going to last long. Presumably they'll sort themselves out and get us another plane.'

'Hmmn . . . Well, I hope you're right.'

As dawn broke those who had achieved some sleep awoke. The room, awash with mattresses, blankets and their dishevelled occupants, looked like some refugee rescue centre. The door remained closed, and was opened only to allow escorted visits to the toilet. There was another armed soldier on the outside, and more who patrolled the corridors. Each turned a blank face to questions and demands. At eight o'clock a trolley was brought with an urn of watery coffee and a supply of bread rolls. The sun was beating upon the windows and the chill of the night had given way to an increasingly oppressive heat.

Groupings and alliances had now developed within the party. The several families with young children had set up a corral by the door. The computer salesmen, Jim Rankine and Tony Saunders, had joined up with some other single business travellers; a desultory card session was in progress. Four Irish nuns returning to their convent school in Kenya kept themselves to themselves. Howard and Lucy were drawn into the small cabal

160

trying to assess what was going on and work out a strategy of response. Molly Wright and James Barrow had been joined by a slightly bombastic but evidently acute and forceful man called Hugh Calloway, the managing director of a big engineering company with interests in Kenya.

'As I see it, we're blocked until we can get access to someone in authority. The blokes we're up against here are rank and file. They're under orders to stonewall, and to clobber anyone causing trouble.'

'I doubt if they're under orders to start a bloodbath, though,' said James Barrow. 'What if we rush them? Put them on the spot? Announce we're not staying in this dump any longer and walk out? I can't see them risking a massacre.'

'Try it if you like,' said Calloway drily. 'I'll pass, if you don't mind.'

Molly Wright broke in. 'It would be thoroughly unwise to provoke them. We have to get to someone higher up – I agree. But we mustn't be compliant, either. We must keep up the pressure.'

'If I knew more about what's going on here it would help,' said Lucy. 'What's the political situation? Is someone in control, or is it chaotic? If anyone's got a radio . . .'

'No one's got a radio,' said Barrow. 'Not any more. I've asked around. That search they did was for radios just as much as for weapons. Nobody had so much as a blunt instrument on them but one of the kids had a transistor, and so did a couple of other people. They took those.'

There was silence. It's like when the lights go off, thought Howard. Or your car engine cuts out. That feeling of being set aside – grounded. But this is worse, much worse. The less you know the more helpless you are.

'I don't like it,' said Calloway. 'Up to now what's going on could have been sheer muddle. Conflicting instructions, what have you . . . This is positive and deliberate and I think we have to take it seriously. Ah . . . something's happening!'

The door had opened to admit a couple of soldiers bearing what appeared to be recording apparatus and an amplifier. They were followed by another carrying a table. An area of the room was unceremoniously cleared of mattresses and occupants, and the table set up. One of the men arranged the apparatus on the table and connected it to the power supply. Adjustments were made, and a blast of martial music swamped the room.

'Oh, Christ . . .' said Barrow. 'This we do not need.'

Everyone was now alert; many were protesting. The soldier, apparently satisfied, surveyed the room and switched off the music. He fiddled further with the machine. There was a burst of static, a silence, and then a male voice, speaking precise and only slightly accented English. It was the same voice heard over the tannoy on the plane and in the airport.

'Good morning. The Callimbian government regrets the inconvenience to passengers on CAP 500. This is due to temporary disturbances in Callimbia which make it necessary for passengers to remain a little longer in transit before continuing their flight. This is in the interests of your own safety. The representative of your government has been informed and is satisfied that all steps are being taken by the Callimbian authorities to ensure your comfort and safety. Further information will be given when this is available.'

The tape was switched off and replaced with the martial music, at full pitch.

James Barrow strode across to the soldier and pointed at the machine. 'Turn that thing off, please.'

162

'Is not possible.'

'Then I'll bloody well make it possible myself.' He reached out a hand towards the machine. The soldier lunged at him.

Lucy pushed forward. 'Don't. Let me try.' Barrow hesitated and Lucy confronted the soldier. She beamed. 'Please. Too much noise!' She put her hands to her head and pulled a face. 'Not good. People tired. Children crying.'

The soldier considered. Lucy continued to beam at him. Finally he stepped in front of the machine and turned the volume down by several decibels.

'Well,' said Barrow. 'Bully for you. Softly does it.'

'He'd obviously been instructed that the thing wasn't to be turned off, but not that it couldn't be turned down.'

Everyone was now talking. Speculation and interpretation ran around the room. The prevailing mood was one of exasperation and anger allied with a grudging acceptance. Maybe the airport had been put out of action. Maybe there was fighting going on still. Maybe the communications centres had been knocked out.

'Balls!' said James Barrow. 'If you have a reasonable explanation you give it in person, not like this.'

'And if the representative of our government is satisfied, then he or she isn't doing their job,' added Molly Wright. 'Where are they, I ask? Why aren't they down here kicking up an almighty stink? Because nobody has said one word to them about us, is my guess.'

'And what about the Foreign Office . . .?'

'Surely London must be . . .'

'They have to know the plane came down here . . .'

It doesn't wash. None of it, thought Lucy. The Callimbian government regrets . . . It is just a stalling process. A way of keeping us quiet while . . . While what? While they decide what they want to do with us? While something goes on that they don't intend to tell us about? She looked at Howard and read in his expression similar thoughts and questions. 'I don't care for this at all,' she said.

He put his hand on her arm. 'Nor do I. But I still prefer to think that they're inept rather than dangerous, these people.'

The military band blared on. A baby was yelling. Molly Wright embarked on a tussle with the sentry about opening a window, and won. A hot wind blew into the room and somewhat dissipated the smell.

Howard and Lucy returned to their encampment.

'Share the mattress,' said Lucy. 'We can put it against the wall and make it into a kind of sofa. If this is some sort of endurance test then we may as well endure stylishly. Would it be pretentious to read *Anna Karenina*?'

'Not pretentious, but perhaps a touch antisocial.'

'I'd rather talk too. I thought you might be too exhausted.'

'Not as much as I'd expect.'

'There's the feeling that you need to keep your wits about you,' said Lucy. 'Keep track of time, and that sort of thing. I hope my mum hasn't heard anything about this. She'll be doing her nut.'

'Are you married . . . or anything?'

'No. Neither married nor anything.' She paused. 'And you?'

'Me neither.'

She kept her eyes sternly upon the turbulent room and, imperceptibly, sighed. Molly Wright was busily talking to people, and seemed to be making a list. The nuns had emerged from their isolation and were improvising entertainment for the children. I am in a place I never wanted to come to, Lucy

164

thought, apparently imprisoned and thoroughly uncomfortable, and yet I feel . . . happy.

Howard also sighed, an involuntary release of stress which he turned into a discreet cough. The husbands, lovers, partners and attachments for whom he had already devised physical attributes and lifestyles evaporated in a trice. How amazing, he thought. How incredible.

'It's my mum's birthday at the end of the week,' said Lucy. 'I hope we'll be back by then.'

'I'm sure we will. God knows what these people think they're at, but I imagine the wires are humming out there and sooner or later they'll come to their senses and we'll be on our way.'

'And you'll be able to get down to your fossils in Nairobi at last.'

'I suppose I will,' said Howard.

'As though none of this had happened.'

'On the contrary. It will inform subsequent events. Everything does.'

'You mean you'll always notice what's going on in Callimbia, and you'll make a point of never taking a holiday in Marsopolis?'

'That. And I'll never feel the same about military brass bands. And I shall get a new anorak in case I ever again need to lend one out as a blanket. And . . .'

'Yes?'

'And if this hadn't happened I wouldn't have met you.'

'Nor you would,' said Lucy breezily. 'Actually, I very nearly took a flight last week. I was just booking it and then I remembered about Mum's birthday, and needing to be back in time.'

'Thank goodness for your mother, then.'

They looked, now, at each other, and at once had to look away again.

'My mum got married recently, she . . .'

'I'm sorry, I'm afraid I'm being . . .'

'Medical conditions and dietary requirements?' said Molly Wright, looming suddenly over them. 'Sorry to interrupt, but it seemed a good idea to get together a dossier and a list of demands. We've got a diabetic and a chap with a heart condition plus a pregnant lass and a three-year-old with diarrhoea. The mothers are running out of disposable nappies and if either of you happen to have any antihistamine on you one of the children has a bee-sting. Both of you in good nick yourselves, are you? Jolly good. Would you like to try your charms on our friend at the door, my dear, and see if he'll turn this blasted racket down some more. It's driving people crazy.'

There was a different soldier now on guard duty, a pale, thin man with a face like a Byzantine icon, in utter contrast to the ebony-skinned broad-featured person who had preceded him. You could get interested in this, Lucy thought, this jumble of people, which means something, which is a code, which tells a whole story that you cannot understand. She gestured towards the amplifier, and made damping down motions with her hands. 'Please . . . Music too much. Too loud. Too much noise.'

The icon stared at her, impassive.

She decided to change tack. 'I want to go to the toilet.'

The icon ushered her through the door and shouted for a colleague. The washroom was by now disgusting, the floor soaking wet, and the lavatory pan encrusted with faeces. When Lucy had finished she peered out of the small window, which offered a different view of the compound. Beyond the fence was a field with a crop of scraggy beans. A donkey trotted along a

166

track, followed by a man who flicked idly at its legs with a switch. Somewhere out there ordinary life was going on; there were people for whom this view was quotidian, unexceptional, who were thinking about the day's work or the housekeeping bills.

The soldier waiting outside the door had aquiline features, a copious moustache and mild brown eyes. Lucy said, 'How many people live in Marsopolis?'

He shook his head.

'Never mind.' She pointed into the washroom. 'Very nasty in there. Dirty. Ugh! It should be cleaned.'

'Tomorrow,' said the soldier.

Returning to the room, she saw it suddenly with astonishment – the figures heaped about the floor, the fretting children, the glazed expressions on faces. How could she have been pitched into this place? What was she doing here? What were any of them doing here? In the mind's eye she saw these same people the day before, unwrapping their airline meals, switching on headphones, flicking through magazines. How could a single day be so treacherous? She felt unsteady and stood still for a moment, gathering herself. The music continued to trumpet forth and the noise made her suddenly furious. She eyed the instrument, identified the volume control, stepped up to it and turned the sound down to an endurable low thump.

The sentry instantly leapt towards her, shouting. He shouldered her aside, adjusted the volume to the previous pitch, wagged a finger angrily at Lucy and returned to his post.

'Well tried, dear,' said Molly Wright. 'Orders is orders, clearly. Now I'm going to have a go at him about the disposable nappies. And some cold drinks before we get dehydrated.'

The day inched onward. At noon a meal of sorts appeared –

bread sticks filled with dry and curling slabs of cheese, hard-boiled eggs and bottles of fizzy soft drink. The sun was by now beating on the windows; some of the blankets were made into improvised blinds. From time to time there were outbursts of activity beyond the room; vehicles came and went, boots clattered in the corridor, instructions were shouted. On several occasions there was another sound, much more distant and hard to identify through the crashing from the amplifier.

'That is gunfire, isn't it?' said Lucy.

'I think so,' said Howard.

Successive sentries were subjected to a barrage of requests, mostly to no avail. A supply of nappies appeared, but pleas for permission to exercise in the compound in small escorted parties were repeatedly refused. By late afternoon despondency began to set in as the prospect loomed of a second night in the barrack-like room.

It became dusk. The sodium lights were turned on around the perimeter fence. And then the door opened and an officer snapped out an order to the soldier on duty, who sprang to attention, rushed over to the amplifier and switched it off. The silence was startling.

Everyone watched the door, which had been left open. A man came in. He wore civilian dress – an immaculate and exquisitely fitting grey suit, white shirt with gold cufflinks and silk tie with fleur-de-lis motif. A perfect triangle of white silk handkerchief jutted from his breast pocket. The passengers of CAP 500, dirty, dishevelled and red-eyed with exhaustion, stared at him sullenly.

'Good evening, ladies and gentlemen. I am instructed by the government of Callimbia to welcome you to Marsopolis. It will be necessary to delay your departure a little longer owing to continuing disturbances in the country which have affected communications. However, I can assure you that everything possible is being done to make your stay in Callimbia as pleasant as possible. You will shortly be taken from this hospitality centre to alternative accommodation which I am sure you will find agreeable. Thank you.'

There was a momentary silence, and then a barrage of query and objection. James Barrow pushed to the front and confronted the visitor.

'That isn't good enough. Why haven't we been allowed access to our embassy? We have been locked up in this dump for twenty-four hours with inadequate facilities and no information whatsoever. Why have our passports been removed? Why were we searched?'

Calloway broke in. 'What is your status? Do you represent the Callimbian government?'

'I am an interpreter.'

'Then we demand to speak to a government representative, in the presence of an official from our embassy.'

'That will not be necessary,' said the interpreter. 'The arrangements have been made. Please take your luggage and proceed to the transport which is waiting.' He left the room.

People began to gather up their possessions. There was a babble of speculation, but also an atmosphere of weary relief.

'At least we're getting out of this dump.'

'This bloke does seem as though he knows what's going on, anyway.'

'So long as we get a decent bed tonight . . .'

The group straggled out of the building and on to the tarmac, where they were processed into three minibuses. The interpreter stood at the entrance to the building, supervising the departure. He listened gravely to each query and returned the same reply: 'Unfortunately I am not in a position to give that information.'

Howard and Lucy were among the last to leave. They got into the front seat of the third minibus. The interpreter had gone back into the building. Soldiers stood around; each minibus was equipped with a driver and an armed companion in the passenger seat.

The interpreter re-emerged. He inspected the minibuses and then climbed in alongside Howard and Lucy, placing himself at the far end of their seat and issuing a brisk order to the driver.

They drove out of the compound, followed by the other two buses.

'Where are we going?' said Howard.

'Unfortunately I am not in a position to give that information.'

'Are we going somewhere else in Marsopolis?'

'Marsopolis is a very ancient and beautiful city. There are a number of Greek and Roman remains and the harbour is most interesting. The coastal scenery is extremely pleasant.'

They were now passing through an industrial development – shabby factory buildings and warehouses interspersed with smallholdings.

'Callimbia has today an important industry of light engineering. You see there the state battery component factory. There is also considerable export of dates, oranges and olive oil.'

'What is the average per capita income?' said Lucy. 'What proportion of children are in secondary education? Is there an agricultural co-operative system?'

The interpreter shot her a startled glance. 'These questions are difficult to answer.'

170

The industrial hinterland gave way to a suburban sector with apartment blocks and small villas and then to a densely built-up area with narrow streets, shops and offices. The minibus rounded a corner and came to an abrupt halt. An army truck was slewed across the street. Beyond could be seen a car with soldiers clustered around it, intent in some way upon those within.

The driver of the minibus hesitated, his hand on the gear lever. Howard and Lucy, staring over his shoulder, saw that a pair of trousered legs hung from one of the open doors of the car. And now the soldiers were hauling a man from the passenger seat. His face was momentarily visible between them, bright with blood. And they were bundling him, doubled up, towards the truck.

The minibus driver began simultaneously to reverse and to signal to his colleagues behind to do the same. The convoy backed from the street.

'The driver has taken a bad route,' explained the interpreter. 'We go another way.'

Howard, craning over his shoulder, saw that the soldiers had now pulled a limp body from the car and dumped it in the gutter.

'These disturbances you've been having here — are there many people killed or injured?'

'I do not think so,' said the interpreter. 'I am sure that is not likely.'

They turned into a wide boulevard lined with trees and shady pavements. Most of the shops had shutters pulled down. The cafés had chairs stacked upon the tables; from the only one apparently doing business a solitary man drinking coffee stared with interest at the minibuses. The traffic was sparse; military

171

vehicles were conspicuous. A posse of soldiers was shovelling rubble from the façade of a damaged building.

'What was the cause of the disturbances?' said Lucy.

The interpreter paused. He seemed about to give his routine reply, and then apparently changed his mind. He spoke almost confidentially. 'Unfortunately there were people in this country who were opposed to change. It has been necessary to remove some personnel. And as a result there were those who made difficulties. It is a local problem and has been satisfactorily handled by the authorities. The people making difficulties are not doing so any more. Ah!' His tone became brisker. 'Now we are entering the central square of Marsopolis. You will see that there are many fine buildings. And in the centre you see the statue of Cleopatra's sister, Queen Berenice. It is the work of a very famous French sculptor. Please look. Berenice was the most beautiful woman of her day and had many lovers, among them Alexander the Great.'

'That's impossible,' said Lucy. 'They didn't live at the same time.'

'Excuse me,' said the interpreter. 'I do not know so much about historical things. I studied engineering at Cambridge University. Do you perhaps know Professor Wilcox?'

'No.'

The interpreter was looking intently at Howard now. 'I think you are a university professor, yes? Mr Bealish?'

'My name's Howard Beamish. I work at Tavistock College in London.'

How does he know who is who? thought Howard. Oh . . . the passports, of course. There's been some careful scrutiny going on.

'London also has very distinguished universities. I was for

172

four years in Cambridge and then for two years in London. I know your country very well.'

The bus was now circling the square, in the centre of which Cleopatra's sister was enthroned upon a plinth, a sumptuous figure, one bare breast jutting from marble drapery, one hand languidly trailing a fan of palm leaves.

'I am very familiar with the British way of life,' continued the interpreter. 'I think British people are very nice. Most friendly. I am sending still a card every year to my landlady in Cambridge.'

'If you have such a high opinion of us,' said Howard, 'you could demonstrate it by giving us some more straightforward information and a telephone line to our embassy.'

'Ah . . .' The interpreter shrugged delicately. 'I am obliged to carry out instructions, you understand. I can assure you that the situation is entirely under control. There is no cause for concern. Soon there will be full information, I am sure.' He straightened his tie, brushed a fleck from a sleeve, and stared ahead. 'In a minute we reach our destination. Please look down this street and at the end you see the flag flying upon Samara Palace, the residence of the head of state of the Callimbian nation.' He spoke in tones of deep respect.

The minibuses were now proceeding up a wide boulevard flanked with shops, banks and cafés. Parallel lines of tamarisk trees converged upon some distant edifice. And then they swung suddenly off the street and into the awning-covered forecourt of a substantial building. There was a waiting group of military, who leapt forward to open the doors of the buses. The passengers of CAP 500 clambered out, staring round them with expressions of mounting relief as they recognized the reassuring furnishings of a luxury hotel – the dripping foliage of carefully tended pot plants, the revolving doors with carpeted approach, the brass, the marble, the curtained windows.

'The Excelsior Hotel,' said the interpreter, 'has been temporarily requisitioned to provide accommodation for passengers from CAP 500.'

The group, however, was already advancing eagerly up the steps, and few heard him.

4

They rapidly established that the Excelsior Hotel was equipped with a swimming-pool (empty), a sauna (inoperative), a bar (closed) and a skeleton staff of uncommunicative attendants. But there were rooms, there was food, and there was space. These benefits were seized upon with positive gratitude. As though, Lucy thought, it were generous of the Callimbians to provide them.

All floors of the hotel but one were empty and barred off. They were allocated rooms on the one surviving functional floor and told that a meal would be provided shortly. Lucy bathed and washed her hair. It was quite dark now. She looked out of the window, saw street lights and the occasional passing car, but sensed as on the drive to the hotel a city which breathed softly, in which many people were silent and careful behind closed doors. She felt suddenly leaden with tiredness, and looked with longing at the bed.

When she returned to the ground floor she found everyone else already assembled in the dining-room, where a single long table had been laid and dinner was in the process of being served. Lucy joined Howard, James Barrow, Calloway and Molly Wright at one end of the table and found them taking stock. The interpreter had apparently vanished; none of the staff knew where he was or when he might return. The hotel was guarded by soldiers on every side. Every telephone was out of use. Anyone attempting to leave the building was firmly turned back by the military.

'And where the hell are the other groups?' said Barrow. 'Where are the Yanks? The rest of the plane, for that matter?'

'In different hotels?'

'Why, in that case? This one is empty except for us.'

'Not in Marsopolis any more?' suggested Howard thoughtfully. 'Gone home. Or on to Nairobi.'

'At this precise moment,' said Molly Wright. 'I don't care. All I want is to crash out. That bathroom is pure paradise. And this is the best prawn cocktail I've ever tasted.'

Around the table, the prevailing mood was one of weary acceptance. Most people disappeared to their rooms as soon as the meal was over. James Barrow engaged in a long and ultimately fruitless negotiation with the head waiter in pursuit of a bottle of whisky.

'Not even for $50! Either these people are genuinely incorruptible or they're scared stiff.'

'The latter, I imagine,' said Calloway.

'Well, there's nothing for it but bed, in that case, I suppose. And to think I walked around the bloody Duty Free at Heathrow and thought, no – I don't need to lumber myself . . . God!'

Howard and Lucy travelled up together in the lift. When they got out he turned to her. 'As a matter of fact I've got a bottle of whisky in my haversack. I felt unspeakably mean but . . . well, the last thing I need right now is an all-night drinking session. But if you'd like . . .'

176

He hesitated, looking at her. They stood in the empty corridor. Lucy was so tired that she seemed to be fizzing, as though her limbs were slightly aerated. She and Howard were the only stable objects in a quivering frame of gilt-striped wallpaper, receding ranks of doors and a long river of chevron-patterned carpet. She gazed at him, and then he put out a hand and held her elbow for an instant. 'No,' he said, 'you're exhausted. Go to bed. Sleep. I'll see you in the morning.'

Alone, she pulled off her clothes and dropped into the bed. She put the light out and lay flat on her back in the darkness, her mind emptied of thought. She saw, with the detachment of exhaustion, a succession of images, all of equal clarity and equal emphasis: the orange tongue of dry cheese protruding from a bread roll, the glint of sunlight on the brown hair of Howard Beamish's beard, the clockwork action of a donkey's hoofs, a stumbling man with blood on his face. And then she fell into a profound and dreamless sleep.

Howard dreamed. At least, the climate was that of a dream. He awoke, in a strange bed, to the sound of hurried footsteps in a street beyond a curtained window that he did not recognize. Shouts. A sharp crack, and then another. He got up, went to the window, and looked out to see a man running, in the light of street lamps. The man was pursued by others. Soldiers. And then, as he stood there, it came to him that this was not a dream.

One of the soldiers stopped, raised a rifle, and fired. He heard the shot. The running man was now out of his vision, beyond the window frame. The soldier fired again, and they all paused, observed, and then moved forward once more, but in a leisurely way. A couple of them were laughing.

Howard stood at the window until the street was empty once

more. Opposite was a chemist's shop. In the window, a smiling girl in an advertisement praised in Italian the performance of a Japanese make of camera. Alongside was a gigantic dummy bottle of Chanel perfume and a display of German hairdryers. Film posters on an adjoining wall were captioned in Arabic; the showrooms beyond sold Ford cars. The place was now silent and unpeopled, bathed in neutral light; above the shops rose apartment blocks with shuttered windows. A wafer-thin cat slid from a window ledge and walked down the centre of the street, paired with its own elongated shadow. The commotion of a few moments ago – the running man, the rifles – seemed preposterous, an illusion.

He went back to bed, and looked at his watch. It was 4.30. A glossy brochure on the bedside table described in three languages the videos available on the inoperable television set. The room had all the familiar props, but when you investigated them they were a sham: the minibar was empty, the radio dead, the telephone silent. They were as reassuring, and as useless, as the universal references in the street beyond the window. Behind the perfume and the Japanese cameras were running footsteps; the brochure's wares (Family Viewing, Humour, Adult) were a wry reminder of normality. He had again that sensation of being set aside, flung into some eerie purgatory parallel to the real world, and was afraid. Resolutely, he turned over and tried to sleep, and when at last he did so he was thinking of Lucy, not of the running man.

'Did you hear a racket in the small hours? Soldiers in the street outside, and shots?'

'Not a thing,' said James Barrow. 'I was out cold.'

Coming down late to breakfast, Howard found the dining-room already full. Lucy was at the far end of the table and he had to take a seat where he could. Nobody else had seen or heard anything, except Molly Wright who had had an impression of a car backfiring. Most people were more exercised by the fact that the hotel's hot water had given out and by the absence of fresh milk. With a return to surroundings that approached familiarity, the mood of resignation had given way to a more combative one, centred on the supply of normal facilities. The family groups were keeping up a barrage of requests that the swimming-pool be filled. The head waiter, as the only apparent figure of authority, was subjected to a stream of demands and complaints. Hugh Calloway watched with incredulity.

'I find this amazing. We have now been held incommunicado for nearly forty-eight hours and people are fretting about cold bath water and powdered milk.'

'I suppose it's a way of suppressing anxiety,' said Howard.

Calloway took out a calculator and tapped for a few moments. 'I stand to lose somewhere around £400,000 worth of business. My own time, at a conservative estimate, is worth about 100 quid an hour.'

'Send in your bill to the Callimbian government,' said James, 'I'm sure it'll be given top priority.'

And out there, thought Howard, in this city most of us had barely heard of until yesterday, there are people who are certainly not thinking about bath water or the value of their time.

An argument had now broken out about the comparative expediency of patience or protest as a tactical approach. Howard applied himself to a bowl of cornflakes with powdered milk and waited for the table to disperse so that he could join Lucy.

It was becoming apparent that the hotel was a limbo. The British passengers of CAP 500 were the only guests, and were restricted to the floor containing their rooms and to the ground floor, which provided the dining-room, foyer and lounges. Such staff as remained were there to supply basic services and had clearly been instructed to say as little as possible. The receptionist, sitting idle behind a reception desk which received no one, whose telephone was silent and computer screens blank, had nothing to do but parry queries and requests. The soldiers lounging at the entrances were impassive unless challenged, when they became belligerent.

As the day proceeded the group tended more and more to foregather on the ground floor. Those who retreated periodically to their rooms would soon drift back, afraid of missing some news or development. At noon the doors on to the patio beyond the foyer were suddenly opened, enabling the children to run around outside. A few people took chairs there and sat in the sun. The discovery of a colony of lizards on the wall became a matter of intense interest. There was rather good seafood salad for lunch, and a selection of Italian ice-creams.

'You must tell me,' said Howard sternly, 'if you feel that I am monopolizing you. Or if you simply want to be alone.'

'I don't think anyone else is after my company. And solitude isn't that appealing. One begins to worry.'

'Then I needn't feel guilty. Good.'

'Of course,' said Lucy, 'there's the danger that we may run out of small talk. We could yet end up playing noughts and crosses.'

'I doubt it.'

'Well, we've managed nicely so far. And with barely a disagreement. There was a tricky moment over voting habits. I am clearly several notches further to the left than you. And I think you are quite wrong to be so dismissive of novels. There's a lot to be said for fiction.'

'It's the scientist's disability,' said Howard. 'A terrible addiction to fact.'

'Well, if we're here long enough I can always read *Anna Karenina* to you.'

'I'm sure that would do the trick.'

'Are we being frivolous?' said Lucy after a moment. 'Talking like this. With what's going on. Whatever it is. Whatever it's going to turn out to be.'

'Possibly. But solemnity isn't going to help. And as you say it takes one's mind off it. And . . .' He looked at her. 'And life has to go on.'

'Oh, it does. It does.'

Lucy looked away first. 'You saw something last night? The sort of thing we saw on the way here yesterday?'

'Yes,' he said. 'Something like that.'

'It's hard to believe. Sitting here. In the middle of this . . .' She waved a hand at the gilded hotel foyer, the framed posters for TWA and Lufthansa and Air India, at the other members of the group playing card games, chatting, trading paperbacks.

'I know. But it won't do us any good to harp on it. Why don't we . . . Well, why don't you tell me some of the things I don't know about you.'

'That's a tall order,' she said. 'You can't be serious. All right, then. I was born in Luton for a reason that may seem bizarre . . .'

During the course of the day the three-year-old with diarrhoea took a turn for the worse and a doctor was summoned by the hotel authorities, after relentless pressure from Molly Wright.

181

The doctor supplied medication and declared the child in no danger. The parents were too preoccupied to press the man for information but Molly cornered him on his way out and elicited from him the comment that there was much trouble in Callimbia and for some people it was not good, not good, before he clammed up and scuttled from the hotel. In the middle of the afternoon there was a great din of passing vehicles from without and those who hastened to the front windows of the foyer were able to see a convoy of jeeps crowded with armed militia rattling past before they were hustled away by an irritable sentry and the curtains firmly drawn. At five the hot water came back on again for long enough for those with quick responses to grab a bath. Someone found a cache of glossy magazines behind a sofa, a discovery which raised morale in some quarters and prompted lengthy discussion about fair distribution and exchange. Alliances and antipathies were becoming more pronounced. James Barrow joined the businessmen for a poker game which degenerated into a barely suppressed quarrel. Barrow left the game and went out on to the patio, where he proceeded to expose a startlingly hirsute chest to the sunshine. The nuns had taken under their collective wing a sixteen-year-old girl travelling alone to rejoin her parents. Various unassertive people had emerged from relative anonymity: an English-language teaching expert on his way to an assignment with the British Council, who proved a dab hand at improvising board games for the children, a young woman teacher called Denise Sadler, a very young bank employee, Ted Wilmott, the only member of the group so far to show serious signs of demoralization. He was rallied by Molly Wright, and later joined the poker game. In the early evening there was an unexpected service of soft drinks. This reawoke the lust for alcohol and brought James Barrow in from the patio for a further unproductive set-to with the head waiter.

'I was born in Enfield,' said Howard. 'A fact of no significance whatsoever.'

'What's the first thing you remember?'

'Picking up a fossil on a beach in north Somerset. I have it still.'

'What sort of fossil?'

'An ammonite. *Psiloceras planorbis*. I use it as a doorstop. When we get back to London perhaps I could show it to you.'

'I'll look forward to that,' said Lucy. 'When we get back to London. Goodness, London ... You know, I have this odd feeling of having been flung sideways. Into some other dimension of time. Not unreal, exactly. Surreal, maybe.'

'I know what you mean. So do I, in a way. In another way, very much the opposite.'

'How do you mean?'

'Well,' he said. 'You.'

'Me ...'

'You don't seem unreal or surreal or other-dimensional or anything of the kind.'

'Good,' she said. 'That's a relief.'

'I feel as though I've known you for a long time. Oh, God, what an unbelievably crass remark. Please don't hold it against me.'

'I shan't. Actually I quite like it. I feel a bit the same way.'

'Do you?' said Howard. 'Honestly?'

'Yes.'

'If we weren't where we are ...'

'Mmn?'

183

'I mean, if there weren't all these people all round . . .'

'Yes?' she said, not looking at him.

'Nothing. Just . . . Well, maybe at some point we . . .'

'Look,' said Lucy. 'Perhaps you should go on telling me about being born in Enfield.'

'I've exhausted that topic, I'm afraid.'

'And you feel it doesn't signify. The fossil, on the other hand, does?'

'Oh, resoundingly. Thence springs, I suppose, my entire life. Including, come to think of it, being here now.'

'Definitely I have to see this fossil,' said Lucy.

As dusk fell, the group's mood became more querulous. The girl on the reception desk was subjected to endless questioning and hectoring until eventually she fled and was replaced with fresh blood, a young man evidently well rehearsed in parrying the complaints of disaffected travellers. Yes, he said, interpreter is coming back here very soon. In the morning. Certainly in the morning. Yes, telephones will be working again very soon. Tomorrow, bar will open tomorrow. There are some problems in Marsopolis, but soon everything will be very nice again.

'Look, we don't want to be in bloody Marsopolis,' roared James Barrow. 'What we want is to get out of bloody Marsopolis. You get on to that telephone and tell that interpreter guy to get over here, right?'

'Very soon.'

Dinner was late but lavish. Some members of the party were so mollified by lobster salad and a choice of elaborate desserts that they lapsed into a state of relative quiescence. Others did not, and continued to harangue the hotel staff and debate amongst themselves as to the best course of action. There were

184

by now internal conflicts between those like Molly Wright whose instinct favoured collective discussion and united decision and those who preferred lone moves. Several people – including Barrow and Calloway – tried private bribery of the hotel staff for access to a telephone. None of them got what he wanted. Others appeared to be becoming slightly traumatized by the situation, and to be settling into a sort of glazed compliance. A couple – the bank clerk Ted Wilmott and one of the young mothers – were on the edge of hysteria.

'Are we being antisocial?' said Lucy.

'Possibly.'

'Do you think it matters?'

'Actually,' said Howard. 'I don't really care.'

'I have the feeling that people may be beginning to avoid us.'

'Ah.'

'We are becoming a bit conspicuous, if you see what I mean.'

'I think I can live with that,' said Howard.

'We've been talking for hours . . .'

'Have we?'

'We have indeed,' she said. 'And at lunch and dinner. Some of them think we're travelling together, you know.'

'Do they?'

'In fact that mother with the baby – Ann something – asked me if we were on our honeymoon. Oh, shit – I shouldn't have told you that. It's made me blush. Now I'm embarrassed in every direction.'

'It's intensely becoming,' said Howard. 'A sort of rosy glow, including even the ears.'

'And the more you look at me like that, the worse it gets. Please stop.'

'I'll try,' he said. 'I can't promise.'

Night fell upon Marsopolis. A velvet Mediterranean night that drew the group out on to the hotel patio beyond the foyer. The back of the hotel and those of neighbouring buildings rose around it like the walls of a canyon; far above was a square of indigo sky spiced with stars. Moths glimmered in the shafts of light from the hotel, and amid these the group sat or wandered. The talk was of everyone's pressing need for a change of clothes, of the prospect of hot water, of the moths, the heat, the pervading smell of kerosene. Behind and beyond this chatter there hung the sense of anxiety resolutely held at bay. Periodically tension was manifest in an irritable exchange, a hectic movement, a commotion over a fretting child. The day had been very long, and now the evening and the night seemed static, an immobile lump of time. Some people went glumly to their rooms; others embarked upon defiant diversions – card games, paper games, an absurd ant-racing contest with bets laid and money changing hands.

'It's nearly midnight,' said Lucy.

'So it is. Go on about your sister's boyfriend.'

'My sister's boyfriend,' said Lucy, 'is a bricklayer and saxophonist. A feckless guy in some ways, but a good sort. How can you possibly be interested?'

'Oh, but I can,' said Howard.

'You've heard about my sister's boyfriend, and about my mum, and my brother, and my entire life history, just about, not to speak of my views on just about everything. Either your stamina is amazing, or you have extraordinarily good manners. Or . . .'

'Or what?'

'Or nothing. I think maybe I should go to bed. Soon we'll be the last people left down here.'

'Would that matter?'

'Well, not really. It's just that . . .'

'That what?'

'It's just that here are we, sort of absorbed in each other like this and meanwhile there's this happening. Whatever it is that's happening. To all of us stuck here. To this country.'

'I know,' said Howard. 'I've thought of that too. But we can't help it, can we?'

'No,' she said. 'We can't.'

And so, presently, they rode up once more in the lift and stood again in the empty, padded, floodlit corridor. In silence, looking. The air between them humming, it seemed, with the unstated issue.

'Good night,' said Lucy, at last.

And, 'Good night, then,' replied Howard. He moved towards her, hesitated, and put his hands for an instant on her shoulders. 'It may sound absurd and inappropriate, but this has been a wonderful day.'

And then he turned and walked down the corridor to his own room.

5

_____

'Everyone leave hotel now! Get luggage and leave hotel –
quickly! Bus is waiting!'

They were in the middle of breakfast. Everyone stopped
eating and gazed in bewilderment at the army officer who had
appeared suddenly at the dining-room entrance. Then a babble
broke out. Chairs were pushed back, the meal abandoned.

'They must have got us a plane – about bloody time too!'

'Why couldn't they have told us last night, for heaven's
sake?'

'At least something's happening . . .'

Hugh Calloway accosted the officer: 'Where are we going?'

'Information will be given very soon. Get luggage now,
quickly.'

Twenty minutes later, attentively supervised and counted by
a posse of the military, they were climbing into a coach which
sat with engine running in the hotel forecourt. The windows
were blacked out. As the last passenger sat down the officer
came on board to carry out a final head count.

'Why are the windows covered?' Howard demanded.

'Is better like that.'

'How far are we going?'

But the man had already departed. The doors were slammed to; the bus set off.

'Pity,' said Lucy. 'I wanted another look at the statue of Cleopatra's sister.'

'Did you sleep all right?'

'Not too badly. You?'

'Reasonably,' said Howard.

They had barely had a chance so far to talk, that morning. Lucy had come down late and, looking round for him, had experienced that thrill of emotion pitched somewhere between ecstasy and panic. She had picked at a melon and they had smiled, and she had tried to hear what he was saying to Molly Wright, further down the table. And then the officer had arrived and they were plunged into activity.

'Where *are* we going, do you imagine?'

'It's anyone's guess. The airport, let's hope.'

'But if we are, why not tell us?'

Howard was silent, and she knew that he shared her doubts, but did not want to make her anxious. She could not remember when last someone had been protective towards her. You could get a taste for it, she thought.

The coach rattled through the invisible city, pausing at traffic lights, turning this way and that. Traffic noises could be heard, a siren, and, as the coach slowed down or stopped, the sound of feet on pavements or a snatch of conversation. Out there, a few yards away, eyes must be noting their shrouded progress. Close by, and yet immeasurably far. Lucy thought of these hidden people with whom, for a few moments, she shared the same bubble of time and space.

And then the coach turned off the street, bumped over a ramp of some kind and came to a halt. The engine was switched off and the driver jumped out. There was a racket of orders being shouted, boots ringing on tarmac. The passengers rustled in apprehension.

'This is not the airport,' said James Barrow loudly. 'No way is this the bloody airport.'

The coach door was flung open. The officer put his head inside and said, 'All get out now.'

The group filed out and found themselves being processed into an impressive stone building with wide steps running up to an entrance portico. The green and purple Callimbian flag hung limp above the entrance. There was little time in which to take stock – they were chivvied up the steps and into the building by soldiers.

Once inside, they were hustled through a large marble-flagged entrance hall flanked with balustraded staircases and into a big carpeted room with ornate ceiling and chairs around the perimeter. At one end hung a huge glossy portrait of a man in military uniform encrusted with decorations, the camera angle such that his large bovine eyes gazed into those of the viewer with a Big Brother effect. The same picture had dominated the entrance hall.

The door was closed on them. They stood about, or sat, and discussed the situation.

'This must be a government building of some kind,' said Molly Wright. 'A good sign, surely.'

'My hunch is we're getting to the authorities at last,' announced Calloway. 'They've come to their senses, and not before time. Apologies all round, I hope, and I for one will be slapping in a compensation claim, let me tell you.'

'Against whom?' asked James Barrow.

'Against the Callimbian government. Against the airline for

being so damn cack-handed as to put us down here. My company can start working out the damage just as soon as I get to a phone.'

The door was now opened by a soldier and a further small group was ushered into the room. Its members wore casual dress, but were instantly recognizable as the crew of CAP 500. They looked as dishevelled and uncertain as everyone else.

'Well,' said Barrow. 'You may as well get going with your case right away. I'm sure these guys will be most sympathetic.'

And now the interpreter came into the room. He was preceded by several military, who took up position at either side of a small gilt table beneath the glossy portrait. The interpreter seated himself behind this table, took some papers out of a briefcase and quickly glanced through them. The group watched, mesmerized.

'For Christ's sake!' exploded Calloway. 'We've had enough of this! Look here, my friend . . .'

The interpreter rose to his feet and raised a hand. The attendant militia glared into the room.

'Good morning, ladies and gentlemen. I am instructed by His Excellency Omar Latif, President of the Republic of Callimbia, Supreme Commander of the Armed Forces, to welcome you to the Callimbian Ministry of Foreign Affairs. You will shortly be taken from here to a secret destination, in the interests of your own security. In the meantime . . .'

No one, now, was talking. They stared, in silence. One of the children began to wail, and was desperately subdued. The interpreter frowned, cleared his throat and began again.

'In the meantime I am instructed to give you some information about the reasons for your continued stay in this country.' He paused, as though to make sure he had their attention. As he continued his precise and mechanical tone took on a curious note of confidentiality allied with fussy severity. 'There is a problem about some people who have attempted to question the recent election of His Excellency the President. These people are a potentially dangerous and disruptive element in the affairs of Callimbia. They have now fled to your country and it is of course essential that they should be repatriated immediately. Unfortunately your government is not being so co-operative. This is very foolish and unconstructive. It is therefore necessary that you should remain here until your government understands that these enemies of the Callimbian state must be returned to Marsopolis. This is an unfortunate event but you will appreciate that His Excellency has no alternative but to take this action in the interests of the security of the Callimbian state. We must all hope that the British government will soon abandon its obstinate refusal to repatriate these undesirable elements in the interests of friendship with the Callimbian nation, and of course the safety of its own citizens. Thank you, ladies and gentlemen.'

For several seconds there was an absolute silence. The interpreter gathered up his papers, aligning them neatly as he did so, and stowed the pile away in his briefcase. He nodded to his military escort, and moved towards the door. His words sank in and pandemonium broke out. Everyone was talking. Those nearest were trying to confront the interpreter as he made his way out.

'Why is there no one from our embassy?'

'There are young children . . .'

'There's a man here with a heart condition . . .'

'This is criminal behaviour . . .'

'You can't do this. You just can't do this.'

The interpreter was resolute. He forged through the gathering, past the passengers of CAP 500, stained and tawdry in their tracksuits, jeans and T-shirts, their crumpled skirts, himself spruce in pinstripe suiting, emitting a waft of perfumed after-shave, patently the force of reason in a disorderly universe. 'I am sorry,' he said. 'It is not possible to make exceptions.' 'Information has been passed to British government represent-atives.' 'I am sorry, no further commentary is possible.' He achieved the door and was gone. Two of the soldiers remained, observing the group without apparent interest.

'So that's it,' said James Barrow. 'You know, I've had a nasty feeling it might be something along these lines.'

They milled about, protesting: shocked, indignant, some people verging upon hysteria. The dominant note was one of disbelief and incredulity. A voice rose vehemently above the others: 'It's so bloody unjust. I mean, whatever's going on here is really nothing to do with us, is it? It's not our problem.'

But it is, thought Lucy, it is. And it always has been, only we never knew it. All our lives this place has been waiting for us. This room. That ceiling, with its plaster cherubs and roses and stuff. These spindly French-Empire-looking chairs. The marble tables and the photograph of this man who is presumably His Excellency Omar Latif. Those men standing there with their guns and their shiny belts. All our lives we've been converging upon this – slowly, slowly.

Howard was saying something to her.

Just as I've been moving towards Howard Beamish, she thought, and he to me.

'Sorry,' she said. 'What did you say?'

'Just that I think we should take this calmly. All we know is what this fellow cares to tell us. Presumably there's a great deal going on we don't know about. In London. Everywhere. Yes, it's unpleasant, but . . .'

'Howard,' she said. 'I'm a journalist, you know, I read newspapers rather closely. I've heard about things like this, often enough. Just as you have. Sometimes it works out fine, quite quickly. Other times, it doesn't.'

He looked at her. 'OK. Sorry. You're quite right. I was only trying to forestall alarm and despondency.' He reached down and took her hand. 'May I do this?'

She felt his fingers twined into hers, warm and immediate. 'You may,' she said.

'We must assume that elsewhere all hell is being let loose on our behalf. There's not a lot we can do but wait, and try to keep a clear head.'

Molly Wright approached. Howard relinquished Lucy's hand.

'Well, at least we know what we're up against now. It's almost a relief, after all this hanging around. People seem to be being moderately level-headed about it. There's a bit of panic with some of the mums, and that lad Ted Wilmott's rather on edge, but mostly I think people are going to cope. I suppose we've got to assume that it could be days rather than hours before our government sorts something out with this wretch. Ah, it looks as though we're on the move again.'

The door had opened and the officer reappeared. He was shouting that everyone must come this way now. As they filed out through the door and back through the entrance hall, Lucy looked intently around her. Keep a clear head, she thought, but clear eyes too. Notice things. Learn what you can. Keep notes – eventually I shall need them. She felt reasonably collected, but with a knot of nausea somewhere deep down.

There were many military about, and a scattering of civilian underlings. She observed again that allusive range of physical

194

types. She thought of the mysterious narrative of this place, flowing also towards this moment, towards this morning when it and they, she and Howard, Molly Wright, that soldier lounging there behind a desk, would collide here. And then she was jolted back to mechanical observation: the baroque extravagance of a staircase that looked French, a great dark Italianate oil painting on a wall, a certain dishevelment about the desks and administrative arrangements, as though functionaries had recently moved in here, or out, or both. The only sense of permanence was in the building itself; otherwise the whole atmosphere was one of haste compounded with confusion. Men came and went, carrying papers, shouting at each other.

The coach was still parked outside. They were shepherded back into it. As soon as they had been counted on board by the officer, the engine was started and the vehicle moved off.

'One can put two and two together now,' said Howard. 'The other groups weren't at the hotel because, quite simply, they aren't in Marsopolis any more. They were allowed to go because these people had no interest in them, once it was established where the political refugees had gone.'

'But what about the other British there must be in Marsopolis? Are they being held here?'

'That's a point.' Howard pondered.

'There may not be so many of them. We've not been exactly *persona grata* here for some time. But there must still be a few around.'

'Well, we may shortly find out.' Howard peered at his watch. '10.15. Let's see how long it takes to get to wherever it is we're going.' He slid his fingers between hers and glanced at her. 'Feeling OK?'

'Not bad,' said Lucy. 'By and large and all things considered.'

They were rattling once more through the unseen city. She could see the backs of heads above seats down the length of the coach, recognized Hugh Calloway's balding pate, Molly Wright's unkempt greying thatch. The familiar world, one's reassuring personal frame of reference, was this group of comparative strangers. Beyond it was an inchoate and unreliable alternative universe, whose codes were impenetrable and intentions obscure. It was as though you stepped suddenly from firm ground into a shuddering quagmire. Today was Friday. On Monday she had been sitting in her flat in London writing an article about Turkish immigrant workers in Germany. The man had come to read the electricity meter. Her mother had phoned, and a colleague, and someone from the BBC. In the evening she had gone out to dinner with friends. Now, all that was inaccessible, out of reach, available only in the mind. Unreal. Reality was this darkened coach, and these now-familiar faces. And Howard Beamish. It occurred to her that she would like to share some of this with him.

'Do you believe in God?' she said.

Howard turned to gaze at her. A wary gaze that indicated surprise, unease, and the profound hope that she was not about to say something that would oblige him to fall out of love with her.

'Of course not. Do you?'

'No. But it must make things much simpler if you do.'

'Simpler?' queried Howard, savouring his relief.

'Well . . . Divine purpose, which I suppose is some sort of consolation. And the prospect of better things in the hereafter.'

'Oh, come now,' said Howard. 'I don't think our situation's that bad.'

'That's not what I mean. I was thinking more of fate, or whatever you like to call it. One thing happening rather than another. Us being landed in this.'

'I take your point. Personally I've always been more outraged by the suggestion of mysterious purpose than by random circumstance. Up to now, I admit, it has never been quite so devastatingly random.'

'The nuns,' said Lucy, 'are praying. Quietly, but you can just hear. Back there.'

Howard peeked behind. 'So they are. Well, I wish they wouldn't. It will undermine morale.'

'I suppose it relieves their feelings.'

'Which makes it the more self-indulgent an activity.'

'They presumably don't see it like that, since if God intervenes it will be on behalf of all of us, not just them.'

'And will we then be expected to feel beholden to them, or to a benevolent deity?' said Howard crossly.

The praying nuns had made him genuinely indignant. He fell silent. The indignation passed, and he recognized it as a sign of good health. He was responding to circumstance in what was for him a normal way and according to character. He was under control. So far, so good. His mind now began to whirl, juggling the events of the last half-hour, the implications thereof, possible outcomes, possible parallel developments. Why had the aircrew suddenly reappeared? Held separately hitherto, presumably, for some reason. Was the interpreter's account to be believed? What was being said and done in London? What would be the most expedient attitude to adopt towards their captors? How would they be treated?

Lucy's fingers were still entwined with his. It came to him with a great rush that if anyone attempted to hurt her, if anyone so much as touched her, threatened her, gestured in her direction, he would . . . he would . . . Since he was a man to whom violence did not come naturally, his flailing responses fell short at this point. He sat there in a further spasm of outrage until that too subsided and he was able once again to concentrate on the moment, on what was really happening. Lucy withdrew her hand, with a little sideways smile of apology, and took out a notebook and pen.

The coach appeared to be moving out of the central area of the city. There were fewer pauses at traffic lights or intersections, the traffic sounds diminished. It thundered along some long straight road. The darkened windows were disorienting. You lost any sense of distance or direction. Which was perhaps the intention. Was the contrivance in order that they should not see, or in order that they should not be seen?

Lucy said, 'I feel distinctly queasy, and yet at the same time I'd kill for a cup of coffee. How can that be?'

'I imagine it's the nervous system making demands. Nothing to get worried about.'

'I see. That's why people administer tea to those suffering from shock. Well, nobody's going to administer tea – or coffee – to us.' She began to ferret in her handbag. 'I've got some Polo mints. Would you like one?'

'Thanks.'

'There's this feeling of unreality. Half of me doesn't really think this is happening, but the other half knows it damn well is.'

'What most disturbs me,' said Howard, 'is the guessing element. Not knowing what is hard fact and what is not. What's true and what isn't.'

Lucy was silent for a moment. 'They can't possibly hand over these people. Our government can't, I mean.'

'I don't think we should even be considering the implications yet. Not until we know more.'

The coach now slowed and turned, evidently off the road and into some enclosed area. There were sounds of comings and goings, of orders being issued, doors slamming, boots on a gravelled surface.

'We're there,' said Lucy. 'Wherever there turns out to be.'

They were told to get out of the coach. The building into which they were hustled was a large plain stone construction of two storeys, with shuttered windows and mansard roof. It might have been the residence of a prosperous lawyer or doctor in some French provincial town. It stood back from the road behind high walls screening a driveway and turning circle for vehicles. Both entrances to this were guarded by soldiers. More stood at the front door, through which the group was now ushered.

Within was a long stone-flagged corridor with doors opening off it on both sides. The place smelled of carbolic and floor polish – a vaguely reassuring institutional smell that could not be immediately identified. The group was directed along the corridor and into a large bare room at the end. On the way Howard observed in bewilderment several framed religious texts in French, a fly-blown nineteenth-century engraving of the Virgin and Child, and a garish Crucifixion in painted wood.

The room in which they gathered was bare and whitewashed, with a long refectory table pushed up against the wall, and chairs stacked upon each other. A wooden crucifix hung at one end, with a lectern beneath on which rested a large battered leather-bound Bible. High windows looked out on to an enclosed courtyard in which grew some dusty orange trees.

'A convent,' said Lucy. 'Of all places . . .'

199

Howard scrutinized the room more carefully and saw a green baize noticeboard peppered with drawing-pins, a large framed blackboard almost covering one wall, and a clutch of desks pushed together in one corner. 'A convent school, what's more. I suppose the nuns are going to see this as some sort of distorted answer to their prayers.'

She looked at him. 'At least you can joke.'

'Actually,' said Howard, 'I wasn't.'

As soon as they were assembled, clutching hand luggage, distressed, calm, noisy or quiet according to disposition, an officer entered the room. A different officer – a big burly fellow with a rather better command of English than his predecessor. He demanded silence and rattled out a series of instructions and informative points. No one might leave the building except to exercise in the courtyard. Both floors of the building were at their disposal; there was sleeping accommodation on the upper floor. Meals would be served here at eight o'clock, one o'clock and seven o'clock. There would be provision of essential medical equipment and sanitary necessities. Cameras and recording equipment must be surrendered now. A luggage search would be carried out shortly.

He finished, and barked an order to a subordinate, who began to tour the room collecting up cameras. Most of the group had received the spiel in glum resignation, but a few now tried to raise queries or objections, which were cursorily brushed aside or simply ignored as the officer stood at the door, tapping his thigh with a swagger stick and observing the confiscation of cameras.

And then Ted Wilmott flipped.

He had been standing apart, very white about the face and – as Howard vaguely noticed – shaking slightly. The soldier came up to him to demand the camera that was slung over his shoulder and he was pitched at once into hysteria. His voice, shrill and beyond control, rang around the room.

'You can't fucking do this! Leave me alone! Just bloody well leave me alone!'

The soldier hesitated. The officer walked over, contemplated Ted for an instant, and then hit him. His fist came up and smashed into Ted's face. Then he turned and walked back to the door.

Ted staggered. Blood poured from his nose and mouth. Someone screamed. Children were crying. People converged upon Ted. A chair was brought. The soldier finished collecting cameras and piled them on the refectory table. The officer conferred with him for a moment and then left the room. The soldier stood at the door, observing with detachment as people milled around the bleeding boy in the yellow T-shirt.

And Howard, watching mesmerized, saw in hideous bewildering juxtaposition the chalk-smeared blackboard, the ink-stained desks, the wooden crucifix and Ted Wilmott's scarlet glistening mask. He put his arm round Lucy's shoulders.

6

'He's lost a few teeth,' said Molly Wright. 'And his nose was like a fountain. But I don't think there's anything worse than bruising, we could have had a broken jaw to deal with.'

The incident had quenched any further resistance. Those who were not too demoralized set about exploring the building and assessing the facilities. Downstairs was the large room which had apparently served the convent school as refectory and classroom, and four further rooms, two of which were occupied by their guards. Upstairs were several dormitories equipped with rows of beds and half a dozen small cell-like bedrooms. There was a bathroom and lavatory and a further lavatory on the ground floor. The kitchens were locked off and out of use; food would be brought from elsewhere, evidently. And there was the courtyard, a rectangle bounded on three sides by the house and its ranges of outbuildings and on the fourth by a high wall topped with barbed wire. At one end were netball posts and at the other the battered orange trees and a wooden bench.

Ted was now in the care of the nuns, one of whom turned out to have nursing qualifications. Molly had taken charge of the inspection of the convent and proposed that the individual rooms on the upper floor should be allocated to families while everyone else disposed themselves in male and female dormitories. Lucy found herself putting her holdall down on an iron bedstead with a thin flock mattress and a couple of blankets. On the wall behind the bed a childish hand had drawn a face with pigtails and a grin, and the words *Marie-Hélène est ma copine*.

'It's hard luck, I'm afraid, splitting you two up like this,' said Molly. 'But I think it's only fair to give the rooms to the couples with kids.'

'We're not a couple. We only met here.'

'Oh, God! Putting my foot in it as usual. Sorry, my dear. I'd just assumed . . . Anyway, you see what I mean − like that they'll have more chance of quieting the children down, and the rest of us can muck in somehow. The bathroom's pretty basic but if we get some sort of rota system going we should all be able to make do.'

As though this were a Guide camp, thought Lucy. No, that's harsh. She's a decent well-meaning woman and probably this sort of hard-headed energy is exactly what's needed. The other way lies panic, and despair.

'I'm going down,' continued Molly. 'The idea is to have a general meeting in that refectory as soon as everyone's sorted out their sleeping arrangements. Talk things through and work out a plan of action. Hugh Calloway's going to take the chair, as it were − keep things as calm as possible.'

Lucy went to the window. The shutters were half closed but through the gap she looked down into the courtyard, where a soldier with a rifle wandered about. Beyond the high wall she could see only trees interrupted by rooftops. In the far distance was a line of hills. There were telephone wires, a television aerial on a rooftop, a street light visible between two palms. This must be a suburban area, and she was facing inland. The soldier halted, lit a cigarette and glanced up. She turned back into the room, where others were glumly inspecting the truckle beds and sorting out their belongings. The young teacher, Denise, was sitting on the bed next to Lucy's, with her head in her hands. Lucy said, 'Are you OK?'

'Not really. I've just been sick.'

'Come downstairs. There's going to be some sort of meeting. You'll feel better with something to think about.'

'I doubt if that would cut much ice,' said Hugh Calloway. 'But I'm prepared to discuss it if anyone else thinks it a useful course of action.'

No one did. The suggestion of a selective hunger strike had come from a middle-aged couple who had been on their way to a safari holiday. They wished to volunteer.

We're going round in circles, Lucy thought. Crackpot ideas like that, and the same things being said over and over again. Criminal behaviour . . . Callimbian politics not our affair . . . the United Nations . . . the Foreign Office . . . But it probably relieves people's feelings. And what else can we do?

Now the discussion was centred again on second-guessing the possible responses of their own government. 'They can't hand these people back,' Howard was saying. 'That's for sure.'

'Well, hold on . . .' said Calloway. 'In principle, no, they can't – I agree. But in practice – well, there'd be ways round it. Guarantees of fair trial. UN supervision . . .'

'If you believe that . . .' Howard exploded.

The computer salesman broke in. 'The way I see it, it's them or us, isn't it? And it's their bloody country, not ours. If these

204

guys have got themselves into some sort of political trouble, then they've got to face the music, haven't they?'

'Not music,' snapped Howard. 'A firing squad.'

'Well, you may be prepared to stand in for them, but I'm bloody well not, I can tell you that.'

'This sort of argument will get us nowhere,' said Calloway. 'I think we can take it as read that none of us feels inclined to face martyrdom in the interests of a situation that doesn't concern us. The point is that we are now involved, willy-nilly. We have to work out the most sensible way to react while those responsible for our safety find a way to get us out of here.'

At the outset of the discussion Calloway had invited Captain Soames of CAP 500 to give his account of events. There was a distinct aura of resentment as he began to speak. 'Right, mate,' said the computer salesman, not quite *sotto voce*. 'You got us here. There'd better be a good explanation.'

The pilot was a small gingery man with a neat moustache. Not, thought Lucy, the titan one imagines at the controls of those leviathan aircraft. But the group's palpable suspicion began to ebb as he spoke, matter-of-fact and direct. The technical problem had been such that a landing within half an hour was advisable. Marsopolis was the nearest airport with a suitable runway. The alternatives would have been Crete, and Cairo which was just beyond the range that he felt acceptable. The control tower at Marsopolis had agreed – after an initial hesitation – to his request for an emergency landing. He had radioed London to inform them of his predicament and intentions; they had raised no objection. He now felt that he should have paid closer attention to that hesitation in the Marsopolis control tower; there had been indications of some sort of calculated response, of conflicting instructions, which he had taken for the confusing signals of an unfamiliar airport. But at the time he had been preoccupied with getting the plane down. He had made what he thought to be the appropriate decision. Unfortunately, as they now knew, it was not.

And so, Lucy thought, by a whisker we are not hanging around complaining in a hotel in Crete. Or in Nairobi, dispersed, the flight and its attendant delay already out of our minds. And, by a whisker, whoever runs things here acquires this interesting opportunity for creative bargaining. She stared round the room, at the shabby anxious gathering, at the soldier lounging by the door, and felt for an instant quite incredulous.

The air crew had been held at what they took to be the army headquarters. They had been required to hand over the passenger list and the flight's documents, supplied with food and drink, and then left alone. There had been much coming and going in the building, an atmosphere of urgency. Their demands and protests were ignored. With wisdoms of hindsight, said Soames, one could now see their captors were waiting. For information. They were finding out to which country these chaps had fled in search of political asylum. They were waiting to know which national group they should hold, and which they should send on their way. Once they knew, they could move into action.

This sober and rational account somehow had the effect of both steadying nerves and lowering the emotional temperature. Soames became at once a respected figure rather than an object of suspicion. The discussion tailed off into a weary stalemate after some practical decisions had been made about how best to make use of the meagre resources offered by the convent. It was now past midday, and there was activity in the corridor beyond the room. Their guards were taking delivery of a consignment of food, which was presently brought into the refectory on trolleys. The meeting broke up, and the day inched onwards as the group melded gradually with the new environment, drifting from the refectory and the bedrooms into the sunstruck courtyard, where the children played in the dust and people conferred around the netball posts and on the slatted bench by the orange trees. They became one with the place in some accelerated process of forced identification, so that by evening their surroundings had taken on a timeless familiarity, as though they had always known these shuttered rooms with their creaking uncarpeted floors and flaking plaster walls, the echoing stone stairs and corridors, the sanitary smell and the assemblage of staring impervious icons, the Virgins, the Christs, the ascendant angels.

As it grew dark Lucy sat with Howard on the bench in the courtyard. They were all, now, hiving off into smaller enclaves when possible, into families or into like-minded gatherings, trying instinctively to find some sort of relief from the enforced proximity of so many others. The mood was volatile. There would be an outburst of frenetic merriment from somewhere, the ring of determined bravado, and then a pervasive edgy gloom. There were those who seemed anaesthetized by shock and those who were flung into ceaseless nervous activity, who endlessly paced the courtyard, talked, speculated, raged. Lucy had spent a good deal of time making up her notes and talking to others. She recorded opinions and reactions. As an objective activity, this was therapeutic; in other ways it was not.

Lucy said, 'One of the worst aspects of this is going to be other people.'

'Up to a point,' said Howard. His hand closed on hers.

'I didn't mean you.'

'I hoped you didn't.'

'Anyway, let's not talk about it. We've been talking about it all day. Everything that can be said has been said.'

'I quite agree. How do you feel?'

Lucy considered. 'Rather tired. Strung up. Frightened, I think. And my mum will know about this now, which bothers me. Will anyone be worrying about you?'

'My parents, certainly.' He paused. 'The person I lived with until recently will be taking a detached interest but I doubt if she's losing much sleep.'

'Why aren't you living with her any more?'

'Because we didn't really like each other. It took rather a long time to realize that.'

'Ah,' said Lucy. 'Well, that seems a good enough reason.'

They sat in silence. Howard's hand was folded over hers. A few yards away James Barrow was talking noisily with members of the air crew. Children ran about. The guard paced up and down.

'What about you?' said Howard. 'Just your mother?'

'And my brother and sister. And the odd friend, I suppose. That's about it. I've never lived with anyone.' She thought of Will, and added, 'At least not in a very positive way.'

'When this is over,' said Howard, 'I hope that you won't just feel that I'm part of it. I mean, I hope I won't be over as well.'

'Oh, I shouldn't think so. In fact I'm sure not. This is going to be over, isn't it? Eventually.'

'Yes,' said Howard firmly. 'It's going to be over and all right.' His thumb caressed the back of her hand; a finger slid between two of hers.

'Good. I feel a bit better. I'd been having doubts.'

'Then don't. We must concentrate on remaining sane and healthy. Are you getting cold? I could get my anorak.'

'I'm fine. It's a nice night. They have good stars here, if nothing else. Which is what, I wonder? Are you any good at stars?'

'Only the obvious ones,' said Howard. 'The Plough, which I don't see. That could be Orion – straight up from the TV aerial on that roof. I used to star-watch on field trips in British Columbia, but in an uninformed sort of way. Communing with nature more, that sort of stuff.'

'And you a scientist.'

'Quite. I should be ashamed.'

'It's supposed to be soothing. The permanence of it. I'm not sure that I'm finding the stars much help, right now. Are you?'

'No,' said Howard, after a moment. 'To be honest. On the other hand you are – a help, I mean.'

'Well, good.' And at this point Lucy found herself suddenly speechless, incapacitated by a turmoil of feeling, unable to think of anything to say that was not inappropriate or inept. Her emotions thrashed around, anxiety jostling something else quite indescribable and unnamable. Her hand lay inertly in Howard's. At last she said, 'You know, I think I'm going to go up and try to get some sleep.'

In the event, of course, she could not sleep. At two o'clock in the morning she lay flat on her back on the lumpy mattress, staring at the ceiling. Around her, others stirred and sighed and breathed. The room took on the same insistent intimacy as the rest of the building; she had always been here, in this fuggy twilight, amid these strangers, in this place which was alien, hostile and yet now appallingly inevitable.

She knew that she had to tether herself to a known world. She began to re-create, in her head, the landscape of her own bedroom in her flat in London. She toured it, summoning up the dressing-table with the woven mat from the Philippines, her brush and comb, the jars and bottles. The mirror on the wardrobe reflecting the yellow glow of the curtains. The white-ribbed curve of the paper lampshade. Her green dressing-gown slumped over the arm of the chair. An exercise in mnemonics. Reassuring, up to a point.

And then, as she began to shape the Pre-Raphaelite poster from the V & A, there swam into the centre not the luxuriant head of a Rossetti woman but the face of Howard Beamish. His nose, his lips, his beard, his gaze directed upon her. He too now seemed eternally familiar, but in a very different way. She thought: whatever happens to me, even if it is ghastly, at least I've known what it is to be in love.

Howard could not sleep either. His companions seemed to roam around all night. They made forays to the bathroom, or stood at the door, muttering to one another. Ted Wilmott had a nightmare and yelled out loud. Someone smoked incessantly.

He tried to concentrate upon rational assessment of the situation. He considered the various options available to those in London who were also, he sincerely hoped, spending a sleepless night. But this was an exercise of limited usefulness since you had no idea of the extent of their information. They must know things that he did not. Furthermore, there was no way of judging the accuracy of what the interpreter had said. They had been told that they were being held as bargaining counters against the repatriation of an unspecified number of Callimbian political refugees, and that these people were known to have fled to Britain. On the face of it, he felt inclined to accept this as genuine information. Why offer it, otherwise? They could have been kept in ignorance. Possibly at some point they would be used to put pressure upon those with whom the Callimbians were in negotiation, in which case they had to know what was at issue. But there must be a whole range of surrounding circumstances upon which one could only speculate. It was frustrating and ultimately fruitless to construct a sequence of moves and counter-moves when you were probably short of some crucial determining factor.

He gave up, and thought about Lucy. This relieved his feelings of tension and apprehension but soon became frustrating in a different way. He tried to think about his work. He conjured up the animal on which he had been working a few weeks ago, resurrected the intricate tangle of its anatomy and tried to make sense of it. He juggled with trunk segments, feeding appendages, mouth, gills and eyes. He saw them, quite clearly, and could summon up no interest. He thought of his parents, also possibly awake and anxious. He thought of his own innocent, ignorant *alter ego* of a few days ago, pondering which garments to pack, slamming the front door of the flat, swaying in the crowded Tube, checking in at the British Capricorn desk, drinking a coffee in the departure lounge cafeteria. And then his thoughts whipped away from these fixed points of existence to the other passengers in the plane and he saw them as they might be now, released to normal life, going about their business. The American mission-school teacher, chivvying small boys on a games pitch. The Indian paterfamilias, back behind the counter of his shop, ringing up a sale on the till. The Japanese, inspecting their rolls of developed film, some of which included shots of the interior of CAP 500, with perhaps a glimpse of Howard himself edging down the aisle. He pictured each and any of these people switching on a radio, picking up a newspaper, following with awe but also with benign detachment

211

the unfolding of a crisis in which they no longer played a part. They had had their brush with public events, had been sucked for an instant into the current and then allowed to fall aside. They, like Howard, knew now which was preferable.

When it was almost daylight he plummeted into heavy sleep and woke to find the room empty except for Ted Wilmott; harsh yellow sunshine poured through the gaps in the shutters. He was instantly and dreadfully aware of where he was, and why.

He said, 'Where's everyone?'

'Downstairs. There was some food brought.' Ted's speech was slurred in consequence of the missing teeth. He sat on the edge of his bed and looked as though he might be still in shock.

'Can't you eat?' Howard inquired sympathetically.

'I don't want anything, anyway.'

'You should try. Coffee, at least. I'll bring some up, shall I?'

Ted shook his head. He was a thin, sallow youth with an acne problem. Which had no doubt until now been the most stressful factor in his life. By rights he should at this moment be behind the counter of the bank for which he worked in Nairobi, cashing someone's cheque. Instead, he was minus several teeth and traumatized in a country of which he knew nothing.

Howard decided to report Ted's condition to the nuns or to Molly Wright, and left the room. He had a wash in the bathroom with its row of basins and rusty shower attachments. There was a tattered handwritten notice on one wall – injunctions about not wasting water and observing the correct *heures de silence*. In the lavatory cubicles were childish graffiti: *Zut pour les bonnes Soeurs!*, a palm tree, a dog, a game of noughts and crosses. He wondered fleetingly about the convent's previous occupants. Were they long gone? Or had they been hurriedly ejected in the last few days? He decided against this; the place had the feeling of having been abandoned over a considerable period.

He set off for the refectory. The walls, this morning, seemed to blaze with the building's totems: the pink-faced Virgin whose saccharine smile greeted him at the bend on the stairs, the resurrected Christ surging skywards from a pulsating saffron bonfire, the blood-spattered Crucifixions, the fleshy purple Sacred Heart, the smirking troupes of angels. He turned into the refectory and found Lucy sitting alone at the end of a trestle table.

'I have never been so close to iconoclasm. Did you get any sleep?'

'Oh,' she said. 'The pictures. Perhaps we'll get used to them. Not much. Did you? There's coffee in that urn. I kept a couple of rolls for you.'

He fetched himself coffee, had a word with Molly Wright about Ted, and returned to Lucy. The room was milling with people. The french windows into the courtyard had been opened; outside, clotheslines had been improvised and were festooned with drying washing: shirts, pants, children's garments.

Howard said, 'Mostly, I can take a more or less tolerant view of organized religion. Just occasionally, I become outraged. This is one of the occasions.'

'Did you feel like that before you became a scientist?'

'Long before.' He gulped down coffee, staring into the courtyard. 'It's getting very domestic out there. That washing. They'll think we're accepting this situation.'

'People need to wash their clothes,' said Lucy. 'There's no alternative.'

'I suppose not.' He dismissed the laundry. 'As far as I can remember I was about ten when I first felt uneasy about dogmatic belief, and fourteen or so when I got outraged. By then I knew a bit of history and I'd heard of evolution.'

'Which did the damage?'

'Both equally, I imagine. The malevolence of fate and the problem of creation – both. Then when I became a palaeontologist there was a further dimension – the manipulation of the discipline. Man has traditionally been seen as created in the image of God. So early palaeontologists had to see evolution as a progression to higher and higher forms of life until it achieves *Homo sapiens*.'

'Suppose,' said Lucy, 'that God is something else altogether. Supposing there were a God.'

'Precisely. I've often thought about that. He, she or it must be laughing, in that case. Watching it all veer off in the wrong direction.' He wiped a hand across his face. 'How can we sit here talking about that? In the midst of this.'

'Because it's entirely sensible to do so. That way we'll stay sane.'

He looked directly at her. 'Anyway . . . You're here.'

'I'm here,' said Lucy.

'I kept thinking of that in the night. It did wonders.'

She said nothing to this. Instead, her hand strayed across the grainy, ink-stained surface of the table and brushed for an instant against his. The feel of her lingered on his skin. But she did not look at him, continuing to stare into her empty cup.

He said, 'That poor bloke Ted is in a bit of a bad way. Mentally rather than physically.'

'Oh dear. I thought he might be. Denise is in a dodgy state, too – she keeps being sick. It may just be the food, I suppose.

Quite a lot of people have got stomach trouble. Molly Wright is dishing out Imodium right and left.'

'Well, it's hardly to be expected that we'll all survive this in the pink of condition. Can I fetch you some more coffee?'

'No, thanks. It's peculiarly nasty. I don't know how I've got through one cup. Sheer native grit.' She suddenly beamed at him.

'That's better,' said Howard. 'It's like the sun coming out, when you smile. Amazing. It makes me feel quite different. Could you do it again?'

'Not to order. And we're about to have company.'

James Barrow was coming from the other side of the room. He dumped himself opposite them. 'Hi there. How are you two bearing up?'

'Not too bad,' said Lucy. Howard grunted and went to get himself another roll. James had been one of the most disruptive elements of the night, perpetually smoking and conferring in a maddening undertone with anyone who would comply. When Howard returned to his seat, James was advocating a more aggressive attitude to their captors.

'We're just bloody accepting the situation, aren't we? God knows what's going on in London and in my experience the FO people are a bunch of dithering bureaucrats but we need to damn well take a bit of initiative ourselves, not just settle in here like a lot of shell-shocked refugees. Look out there!'

He pointed into the courtyard, where one of the guards was teaching the older children a version of hopscotch. The guard squatted in the dust, tracing out a system of squares with a stick. The children clustered about him. The guard cast a pebble into the system of squares; he hopped. Olive-skinned and curly-haired, he looked about twenty. The children clamoured for turns; they hopped, they shouted. The senior officer strolled into the courtyard, stood benignly watching for a few moments, and wandered off again.

'This is just the sort of thing one's read about. Identifying with the captors. Carry on like this and we'll be saying thank you to them when they bring the rations. We'll be rolling around with our paws in the air.'

'You can't very well forbid children to play,' said Lucy.

'Christ, no, I don't mean that. I just mean I think we're forgetting that we've been hijacked by a bunch of thugs, not rescued by some nice guys who've fixed up accommodation. We're developing an attitude problem.'

Howard stared at the man in irritation. 'What do you propose, then, mass insurrection? The first priority is to make sure that no one else gets hurt, I should have thought. There's such a thing as expedient behaviour.'

'Craven's another word for it.'

'That's absurd,' snapped Howard. 'Just look rationally at . . .'

Lucy broke in. 'Arguing won't help. We've got to get along somehow with these people. That doesn't mean we're condoning what's been done.'

James subsided. 'OK, OK. I take your point. I can't stand being made to feel so bloody helpless, that's all. I'm a hustler, by nature. Right now I should be talking my way through Kenya. Greasing the odd palm. Fixing the guys who look like making difficulties. I do it around the world. Go somewhere and suss out the system and set things up so we can go in and make the movie. I feel as though I've had my balls cut off, in this situation.'

We're none of us feeling so hot, Howard thought sourly. He

216

kept silent, eyeing Barrow. A stocky man, tight-packed like a punchball. Fast-talking and insistent, moving in upon people with the indiscriminate confidence of one immersed in his own concerns. He had switched topics entirely now and was giving Lucy a rattle-paced account of some current film project. Go away, pleaded Howard silently. Before I lose my temper again.

Eventually, James Barrow moved off. Lucy, turning to catch Howard's expression, said, 'Come on – he's not as bad as that. And you were raising doubts about the washing lines yourself, earlier.'

'True. He was beginning to feel like the last straw, though.'

'I'm afraid there may be further straws than him.'

It was ten o'clock. In the courtyard the children continued to play hopscotch. The air crew had found a quoit and were throwing it around half-heartedly. Someone was doing press-ups; someone else hung up a wet shirt and socks. Upstairs, a baby was screaming. From outside there came the rasp of insects and the continuous cheep of sparrows. Along the corridor a couple of the guards were shouting and laughing. Denise Sadler, whey-faced, sat staring into a coffee cup at another table.

'Day Five,' said Lucy. 'The fifth day. How many will there be?'

7

Time and space became the dual torments; the dragging hours, the claustrophobic familiarity of their surroundings. Shackled to the passage of the day, they were flung into an inescapable intimacy with each feature of the place. The rusty taste of the tap-water, the echo of footsteps on the stone stairs, the movement of shadow around the courtyard. Those pictures. They learned, too, more than they wished to know of each other: the needling note of a particular voice, someone's persistent gesture, the fads and neuroses of a bunch of strangers. Their guards became distinguishable, no longer a sequence of alien presences but the tall thin one and him with the squint and the curly-haired boy and the chain-smoker. There was nothing to do but wait, and the waiting itself became a further point of stress, exacerbating the crawl of the day, heightening the impact of everything seen or heard. They had moved imperceptibly into a different frame of reference – the confines of the building, its occupants and the progress of the hands on the clock at one end of the refectory. A round-faced clock, with roman numerals, its glass fly-blown, the manufacturer's name in slanting script at the base: *J. Bompierre et Cie, Lyon*.

Every incident swelled to the status of an event. Molly

Wright had an argument with the officer in charge about the non-arrival of promised supplies – nappies, soap, toilet paper. A child fell over in the courtyard and cut his knee. A midday meal was brought: rice, beans and a watery stew, with a tray of bananas and dates for afters. One of the air crew climbed the perimeter wall to look beyond and was vigorously reprimanded by the guard.

At times Lucy and Howard sat together in the refectory or against the courtyard wall. And then in a deliberate exercise of self-denial they would drift apart and fall in with someone else. Howard spent a while talking to the married couple who had been on their way to a safari holiday – a silver wedding treat, he learned, and now they quietly anguished not for themselves but for the pregnant daughter who would be worried out of her mind. 'All I can think of,' sighed the wife, 'is how nearly we didn't come. It was a toss-up between the wretched safari and the West Indies, right till the last moment.' The husband was a wry, stoical man; he played game after game of patience, slapping the cards down on the refectory table and whistling through his teeth as his hand hovered above them. 'We'll be out of this sooner or later,' he said. 'One way or another. I'd have liked to put a bit of pressure on these blighters, though. Fay and I are still game for a hunger strike stunt, but if no one's in favour that's OK by us.'

Lucy, in the midafternoon, went up to the dormitory to work on her notes and found Paula and Jill, two of the British Capricorn stewardesses. 'We're feeling glum,' said Paula. 'Jill has this bloody great boil on her neck and I've got the jitters. We're bad for morale, down there with the others. How's yours? Morale, I mean.'

'So-so.'

'It was that fellow getting his face smashed in did for me. I've been queasy ever since. You realized suddenly . . .' The girl flinched and looked away. She was sallow, with dark rings under her eyes. Lucy remembered her on the plane, trim and pert in the airline uniform, with that bright undiscriminating smile.

'Do you ever think of this kind of thing, doing your job?'

'Christ, no. I mean, you know it's on the cards – a crash, anything – but it's always going to be someone else, isn't it? Not you. I still can't believe this is for real, half of me can't, anyway.'

'What do you do?' asked Jill. 'In real life?'

'I'm a journalist.'

'I suppose you know about this place, then. Callimbia.'

'Not a lot. Not enough. I'm wishing now I'd paid it more attention.'

'What use would that be?' Jill shrugged. 'It's still none of our business, is it? Whatever's going on here. And we're having to suffer. To be quite honest, I think our government should hand back these people and the hell with it. What about us? They're involved. We're not.' Her hand strayed to her neck. 'This bloody thing hurts like mad now.'

'Don't touch it, you'll make it worse,' advised Paula. 'You know something? I've been all over the world, in the last few years. You name it – I've been there. And what that means is, you sit by swimming-pools and suss out the currency and the shopping facilities and you reckon you know everything. You're the expert. Sri Lanka? Oh, yes – been there. Mexico City, Johannesburg, Bangkok – know them all, inside out. And you don't know a damn thing, do you? And after this I don't ever want to. I'll stop in Ealing, thanks very much. If I ever get back to Ealing.'

'I'm sure you'll get back to Ealing,' said Lucy.

There had been the sound of booted feet on the stairs. One of the guards – him with the squint – stood now in the doorway. He jerked his head at them. 'Come!'

They stared. Paula got to her feet, uncertainly.

'Come where?' said Lucy.

'Come down.'

'Why?'

'Officer says come.'

He hustled them ahead of him down the stairs. In the corridor stood the interpreter, flanked by the officer on duty and another guard. The interpreter appeared agitated. As they approached he turned and pointed at once to Lucy, speaking to the officer. Then he addressed Lucy.

'You must come with me, please.'

'Why?'

'Miss Faulkner, yes?'

'Yes, but why must I come?'

'Where are you taking her?' demanded Paula, her voice rising shrilly. 'What's this about? You can't just . . .'

The interpreter cut her off. 'No one else is concerned. Please go. Miss Faulkner . . . This way. There is a car.' He began to move Lucy towards the convent doors, putting a hand on her arm.

Lucy shook him off. 'No.' She backed against the wall. 'Where are you taking me? Why me, anyway?'

'There is nothing to worry about.'

'That's for me to say,' said Lucy. 'And I am worried.'

'It is for a short time only. I bring you back here myself very soon.'

'Maybe. But I prefer not to go at all.'

Jill and Paula were no longer there. The interpreter hesitated. The officer said something sharply in an undertone and moved towards Lucy. The interpreter gestured him back. He lowered his voice. 'I am instructed to bring you to Samara Palace.'

Lucy gazed at him. 'Why?'

The interpreter cleared his throat. 'You will be received by His Excellency the President.'

'Why me?'

'His Excellency has expressed a wish to meet you. It is a very great honour.'

'Why does he want to meet me?'

'That is interesting,' said the interpreter. He coughed again, and fingered his tie. His glance fell upon Lucy's face before flickering away again. 'It appears that His Excellency happened to notice your passport photograph. It appears that you remind him of his mother.'

Howard was wandering morosely in the courtyard, wondering where Lucy had got to and if he could decently go to look for her, when suddenly the airline girls were at his side, both talking a blue streak. At first he couldn't make head or tail of what they were saying, and then all at once he could. He dashed through the refectory and into the corridor, and there were Lucy and the interpreter and the officer and one of the guards. Lucy was backed up against the wall. The interpreter was talking to her.

Howard broke in. 'What's the problem?'

'There is no problem,' said the interpreter. 'Please go. I am concerned only with Miss Faulkner.'

'Why? What about?'

'It is not your business. Please go.'

'What do you want her for?'

'If you do not go it will be necessary to . . .'

'He says he's got to take me to the President,' said Lucy.

'Why?'

'He says I remind the President of his mother.'

'This is ridiculous,' said Howard.

'That is not respectful,' said the interpreter angrily. 'Do not speak like that.'

'How on earth could your President have any idea . . .'

'Passport photo,' said Lucy.

The officer, evidently tiring of his marginal role, now began to shout at Howard. He clenched a fist; he took a step forward.

'Look,' said Lucy, 'if I must come then at least . . .'

'If you take her anywhere you take me too,' said Howard.

'It is not your business,' snapped the interpreter.

'It damn well is. She's my wife.' The words rose to his lips almost involuntarily, in a moment of pure inspiration.

The interpreter was silenced. He stared at Howard. Then he rallied. 'That is not so. Different name.'

'Of course we have different names,' said Howard. 'It's a common law marriage. I thought you'd lived in England. If you knew England at all well you'd know that common law marriage is general nowadays.'

The interpreter's expression became complicated. Doubt struggled with something else.

'In our country it is extremely offensive to separate a wife from a husband. I should have thought you would know that. I imagine your President would expect you to know that, in your professional capacity.'

The interpreter looked from one to the other of them. He conferred with the officer, in an undertone. They apparently argued. Then the officer suddenly shrugged. Have it your own way seemed to be his verdict. Be it upon your own head. The interpreter turned again to Howard and Lucy. He had recovered himself, more or less. The smack of authority was tempered only by a faint note of petulance.

'I will permit that you accompany your wife. I know very well English customs. I am living for many years in your country. Come with me now, please.'

The car was driven by a soldier. Another sat in the passenger seat. In the back were Howard, Lucy and the interpreter. They swung out of the convent driveway and into a suburban road. Villas, gardens with palms and casuarina trees. A line of oleanders. Travelling fast, they swept along similar roads for several minutes and then plunged into a cluttered district of narrow streets lined with shabby apartment buildings from which jutted poles of washing. Small shops brimmed fruit and vegetables on to the pavements. The driver, obliged to slow up, blasted his horn at pedestrians and traffic alike.

'These are not nice parts of the city,' said the interpreter. His fingers tapped impatiently on his knee. He leaned forward to remonstrate with the driver. A donkey and cart blocked the way. The driver slammed his hand on the horn. Under cover of the din Howard managed to speak to Lucy.

'Do you mind?'

'No,' she said indistinctly. 'I don't mind.'

'I feel awful about it now. But . . . I couldn't let him take you off alone like that.'

'It's fine. You were clever. Thanks.'

The driver surged up on to the pavement, forcing a clutch of pedestrians into a doorway. The interpreter sat back. 'I am sorry for the delay. I am telling the driver he should go a different way but he says there is a problem with obstructions.' He consulted his watch, shook his head irritably.

'Why are you in a hurry?' said Lucy.

'His Excellency is expecting you.'

'How can I possibly look like his mother?'

'That is interesting,' said the interpreter. 'His Excellency's mother was an English lady, I have been told.'

'Does he suppose that she would approve of his treatment of us?' demanded Howard.

'I understand that His Excellency's mother died many years ago.'

'So that makes it all right, does it?'

'I do not understand,' said the interpreter.

The car screeched around a tight corner, its rear end banging into a lamp-post, and forged down another alley, at the end of which they emerged into a wide road.

'Very soon now we reach Samara Palace. Please look on the right and you see the ruins of the Greek temple. Very famous antiquity. You are interested in antiquities, Miss Faulkner?'

'Not at the moment,' said Lucy.

There was hardly any traffic now. The car sped down a boulevard flanked with flowering tamarisks. On one side the broken columns of the temple rose abruptly between a petrol station and a used car lot.

They reached a roundabout and turned into another boulevard.

'Now you see Samara Palace,' said the interpreter. 'It is a most elegant building constructed in nineteen hundred and twenty-five, I think.'

The Palace was straight ahead of them, not so much a

building as an architectural flight of fancy in which Gothic windows were juxtaposed with Tudor casements and Moorish balconies beneath a roof-line where crenellation struggled with the intrusions of onion domes and minaret-like spires. The whole edifice appeared to sprawl without rhyme or reason in every direction.

The car drove to a side entrance. They were hustled into the building along corridors. The place bristled with military. At one point the interpreter dived into a room in which he could be heard conferring with unseen colleagues.

Lucy said, 'It looks as though he was telling the truth. We are going to see this man.'

'It does look like it.'

'What do we do?'

'Cash in.'

'How?'

'Talk. Ask questions. Reason with him.'

'I'm more likely to spit at him,' she said.

'I wouldn't do that.'

The interpreter rejoined them. 'His Excellency will receive you immediately.'

They sat side by side on a spindly gilt sofa. His Excellency Omar Latif, President of Callimbia, sat at an immense leather-topped desk. The interpreter was perched on a chair at his elbow. Periodically Omar lost interest in them and conducted a telephone conversation or received from a minion a heap of papers which he would shuffle through and then shove aside. They had been served Turkish coffee. People kept coming in and out of the room – soldiers, flunkeys. Telephones rang.

He was fat. He was flesh made manifest, flesh that strained

226

against the fabric of his military uniform, that swelled luxuriantly over his collar, flesh that pulsed with well-being, that blazed his presence. He seemed to fill the room, and the room was an acreage of oriental carpeting and gilt-encrusted walls against which were marshalled glass display cabinets and ranks of satin-upholstered chairs. He compelled attention. He was the incarnation of triumphant existence, like some thriving dominant animal bent exclusively upon self-perpetuation. His features seemed exaggerated: the bold nose, the wide mouth with very white teeth, the large very dark brown eyes which he fixed upon Howard and Lucy – especially Lucy – each time his attention focused once more upon them. He spoke at machine-gun speed and at length. The interpreter's version always appeared much curtailed.

'His Excellency is saying that now he sees you in person the resemblance to his mother is not so close. His Excellency asks if you have brothers and sisters.'

'No,' said Lucy after a moment.

The interpreter spoke to Omar.

'I didn't say all that,' said Lucy. 'I just said no.'

'It is not suitable to address His Excellency in that way.'

Howard said, 'Will you ask him again why we have not been allowed access to our embassy?'

'His Excellency has already said he cannot discuss these matters.'

'I don't care,' said Howard. 'I want you to ask him again. I insist that you ask him again.'

Omar looked up. He had been scrawling an ornate signature at the foot of some papers. He now grinned hugely in Howard's direction and said, 'I want doesn't get.'

'Sorry?' said Howard, startled. The words did not immediately take shape, disguised by the man's staccato delivery.

The grin was replaced by a scowl. Omar snapped something to the interpreter.

'His Excellency is saying that those who make categorical demands do not always receive satisfaction. He is saying also that he was under the impression you understood English.'

'I follow now,' said Howard coldly. 'The expression escaped me at first. I haven't heard it since I was a child.'

Omar's mood had changed once more. He tapped his front teeth with the nib of a gold fountain pen, apparently locked in thought. Then he pointed the pen triumphantly at Howard and spoke again.

'Don't care was made to care, Don't care was hung. Don't care was put in a pot and boiled till he was done.' He lay back in his chair and shook with laughter. The interpreter discreetly tittered.

Omar, still chuckling, contemplated Lucy and Howard. Then, apparently, a further thought struck him. He leaned forward, picked up the phone on the desk and rattled out some instructions. He appeared now mellifluous and expansive, a man all set for a bout of harmless pleasure. He swung towards the interpreter and held forth, laughing from time to time. The interpreter's expression was a struggle between discomfort and servile compliance; he addressed Howard and Lucy.

'His Excellency is saying that he remembers English people like to play games. He has in his possession some amusing games. He is telling them to bring these games.'

'What games?' asked Lucy after a moment.

The interpreter hesitated. 'I am not so sure.'

'For the third time,' said Howard, 'will you kindly ask him when we will be allowed access to our embassy.'

'That is not possible.'

'Why not?'

'His Excellency has already stated he does not wish to refer to these matters. This is a social occasion.'

'Look,' said Howard. 'We simply want to discuss, quite straightforwardly and without prejudice . . .'

'You must not talk like this. In His Excellency's presence it is permitted only to address His Excellency.'

'That's exactly what I'm trying to do.'

Omar was now having a telephone conversation. He broke off to wave a finger angrily at Howard.

Howard subsided. 'This is insane,' he muttered.

'Better keep calm. We may yet find a way in.'

'The man's crazy.'

'Yes,' said Lucy. 'But we're not. That's our only advantage.'

The interpreter was becoming agitated. 'It is not permitted to talk during the audience with His Excellency.'

Omar concluded his telephone conversation and became restless. He snapped his fingers, sent attendants scurrying from the room, conducted an irritable exchange with the interpreter. And then a soldier came into the room bearing a pile of shallow boxes, which he set upon the desk in front of Omar, who brightened up. He beckoned to Howard and Lucy.

'His Excellency wishes you to come over here.'

They rose. They approached the desk. They gazed, incredulous.

Snakes and Ladders . . . Monopoly . . . Ludo . . . The boxes were battered and faded. Some of them had been scribbled on. Omar sorted through the pile until he came to a box adorned with a coloured picture of what appeared to be trench warfare. ATTACK! Omar lifted the lid. Within was a board laid out in squares, and an assortment of small cardboard rectangles, blank on one side and with the picture of a uniformed and equipped soldier on the other – private, captain, colonel, general. These cards could be fitted into small metal holders to stand upright. Omar, smiling indulgently, began to assemble the pieces and range them on the desk, talking the while, pausing only for the interpreter to catch up.

'This is a very amusing game. The English army fights the French army. The armies are placed facing each other. The pieces are put so that each player does not know the arrangement of the other army – he sees only the blank side. The pieces are moved to challenge a member of the other army, and always the higher-ranking piece kills the lower-ranking. The general kills everybody. Only the spy can kill the general. But everybody is blown up if they challenge a mine. All pieces can be moved except the mines. The objective is to challenge the enemy's general with your spy, but the spy can be killed by anyone, even a private. So it is very skilful. Very amusing.'

Omar continued to sort out the pieces. He gestured to one of the attendants to bring up chairs for Lucy and Howard.

'No,' said Lucy.

'His Excellency wishes to play this game.'

'I don't want to. Tell him I'm a pacifist.'

The interpreter frowned and murmured to Omar, who shook his head dismissively.

'There is a translation difficulty,' said the interpreter. 'His Excellency is not familiar with the term.'

'This is grotesque,' said Howard.

Lucy suddenly stood up. 'All right. We may as well.'

Omar slapped the desk jovially. He finished assembling and sorting the pieces and pushed the English army over to Howard and Lucy, issuing instructions as he did so. He began thought-fully to set out his own array on the board.

'His Excellency says you will join to play as a single player. He allows that you should consult with each other concerning moves since you are novices at this game.' Omar glanced at them, evidently in high spirits. He placed a piece, then changed his mind and altered its position.

Howard began to set out their pieces.

'No,' said Lucy after a moment. 'Not like that. It would be better to put the low-ranking pieces at the front where they can be picked off first. And we can use them to test the water – find out what he's got in his front row. Put the general somewhere at the back. With mines near.'

'I thought you were a pacifist,' said Howard.

'If we're being made to play this stupid game, then we're damn well going to win.'

Omar advanced one of his pieces. 'Attack!' he announced.

'Ah,' said the interpreter. 'Your piece is only a scout and His Excellency has challenged with a captain, so you are dead. You must take your piece from the board. Now it is your turn to move.'

Howard advanced a colonel, thus disposing of Omar's captain. The colonel's next encounter, though, was with a mine. Omar laughed loudly.

'This game is most amusing,' said the interpreter.

After a few minutes their front line had been polished off. Omar sat with folded arms, a watchful expression on his face. He lost a couple of privates and a lieutenant to an advancing captain of the opposition, and the watchful look changed to a scowl.

'We know where three of his mines are now,' muttered Lucy. 'And I think his spy's in that top right corner – he never shifts those pieces. Move the colonel up that way.'

231

Omar rapped out an objection.

'Ah,' said the interpreter. 'Unfortunately it is not permitted to move a colonel by four paces, only three. Therefore you lose your turn.'

'That's the first time we've heard that rule,' said Lucy.

'Unfortunately it is so.'

Omar advanced his general, with considerable carnage. 'His Excellency is most skilful in this game,' said the interpreter.

'It's a curious concept of skill,' said Howard.

'I beg your pardon?'

'Never mind.'

'I think perhaps soon all your personnel will be killed,' said the interpreter complacently.

'We'll see about that,' said Lucy. 'Attack!'

Omar sulkily removed his second colonel from the board.

'Now he knows where our general is,' Howard pointed out.

'Yes. That should flush out his spy.'

'To say my heart isn't in this would be the understatement of all time.'

'Probably. But we're not just going to let him walk all over us.'

The interpreter broke in.

'It is permitted only to discuss the next move.'

'That's what we're doing,' said Lucy.

'Excuse me. I could not hear.'

The two armies were now considerably reduced. Omar stared intently at the board. He reached for a cigarette from the silver box by his elbow, lit it, took a swig of coffee. He spoke, chuckling.

'His Excellency says he is enjoying this amusing game. His Excellency had forgotten these games and was reminded by your arrival. He learned these games from his mother, you understand.'

'Fine,' said Howard. 'Will you tell His Excellency that we are glad he is enjoying the game, and we would appreciate it if when the game is finished he could answer the questions we have been trying to put to him.'

'I do not think so.'

'You do not think what?' snapped Howard in barely suppressed rage.

The phone rang. Omar snatched it up irritably, rapped out an interrogative. He listened. His expression darkened. He turned away, hunched over the receiver. From time to time he grunted a query. The interpreter shifted apprehensively in his seat. Omar spoke, angrily and at length. The interpreter's glance slid uneasily to Howard and Lucy. Omar listened again, fired some terse instruction and slammed down the receiver. He stared again at the board, but it was clear that there had been a profound and dramatic change of emphasis. He swept the telephone towards him again, knocking over several pieces as he did so. They noted his spy, upended, exactly where Lucy had foreseen. Omar picked up the receiver and began to talk simultaneously down the line and at the interpreter. He gestured dismissively at Lucy and Howard. The interpreter leapt to his feet. 'His Excellency is called away on urgent matters. The audience is finished.'

'I insist that we are given an opportunity to . . .'

'It is not possible. The audience is finished.' The interpreter had his hand on Howard's arm, hustling.

'There hasn't been an audience, this is . . .'

'Come. We leave now.'

'Look,' said Howard. 'At the very least we must be allowed to . . .'

233

Two of the attendant military had now stepped forward and began, with the interpreter, to herd them towards the door. Behind them, Omar could be heard roaring into the telephone. In the corridor, people scurried to and fro.

'His Excellency has heard some very bad things,' said the interpreter, in an accusatory tone. He looked sternly at Howard. 'Your government is very foolish and uncooperative.'

'What has he heard?'

'I am not able to say.'

'Why?'

They were chivvied down a flight of stairs, at the trot.

'What has our government said?'

'I cannot discuss these things.'

'If the President would give us an opportunity to . . .'

The interpreter halted. He was infused, it seemed, with righteous indignation. 'Your government is most arrogant and unreasonable. I think the consequence will not be good.' He glared at them.

'If we are to be told nothing,' Lucy began, 'how can we . . .'

'I cannot discuss further. Come now, quickly.' Tight-lipped, the interpreter turned away. He hurried on. The escorting military closed in behind Howard and Lucy, and the group proceeded in a rush down further stairs, along further corridors and out into the waiting car. The interpreter sat in hostile isolation in the passenger seat as they hurtled once more through the streets of Marsopolis in the direction of the convent.

8

'He's mad,' said Lucy wearily. 'That's all we can tell you.'

They had given their story to the entire group, at a hurriedly convened meeting in the refectory. Now they mulled it over once more with the smaller cabal of James Barrow, Calloway and Molly Wright.

Howard said, 'I've led a sheltered life so far as political leaders are concerned. Indeed, this is the first time I've come face to face with one. But frankly I would not imagine that a session with an American president, say, or a German chancellor or a French what have you, or indeed the large majority of rulers around the world, could be anything like what we've just experienced.'

'What's he *like*, then, this man?' persisted Molly Wright.

'Mad,' said Lucy again. And then, 'No, not that, exactly. That's a simplification.' She thought of the room at Samara Palace, charged with that volatile and torrential presence. More like a climatic condition than a human being. Like something elemental and unstoppable. 'You can't describe him,' she concluded. 'It's like coming across some entirely new kind of individual.'

'For you, maybe,' said Calloway. 'Not for our Foreign Office people, we must assume.'

'I hope you're right,' said Howard bleakly.

There was a silence, broken at last by Molly, determinedly striking a note of cheer. 'Anyway, thank heaven poor Lucy didn't have to go through it on her own. That was an inspired move of yours, Howard.'

James Barrow grinned. 'Good grief! In the middle of all this we've never got around to congratulating the pair of you. All joy and prosperity! When can we look forward to the patter of little footsteps?'

Howard got to his feet. He said, 'Shut up, you stupid fool.' Then he walked out of the refectory into the courtyard.

He dumped himself down on the ground against the wall under one of those desiccated orange trees. He fended off the conversational overtures of the airline girls, of various others. Then Lucy was beside him. He said, 'I shouldn't have behaved like that. I'm sorry.'

'You were fully entitled. He was very irritating.'

'The point is that I have not yet had a chance to apologize to you. For putting you in this position. It was an appalling thing to do, I now see. In one sense. But at the time all I could think of was that no way was I going to let them take you off alone. Absolutely no way. It came into my head, and it worked, rather surprisingly, and now I feel appalled. I'm extremely sorry.'

'Are you?' said Lucy. 'I'm not.'

He looked at her. 'You don't mind too much, then?'

'I don't mind in the least.'

She was sitting in the dust beside him, with her arms clasped round her knees. Sunshine fell strongly on the side of her face and he could see a faint down of golden hairs. He saw also the neat curve of her nostril, the line of her foot, the sheen of her

236

fingernails. He could smell her, he could feel the warmth of her. The words she had just spoken hung still in his head. It came to him that possibly this was the most significant moment of his life.

He said, 'I love you, you know.'

'Yes. I thought perhaps you did.'

'And . . . is there any chance that . . .'

'Yes,' she said. 'I do too.'

Howard sighed. He felt now as though he hung suspended, free of time and place, connected only to this exquisite sensation of delight. Whatever happens, he thought, there will have been this.

He said, 'I should very much like to kiss you.'

'I'd like that too,' said Lucy.

'But if I do there will be twenty people looking on.'

'Yes.'

'And there is absolutely nowhere we can go.'

'No,' she said. 'There isn't.'

'It will have to wait, then,' said Howard. 'I shall think about it a lot. I'm not sure if that will make things better or worse.'

'Both, I think.'

'Does that mean you'll be thinking about it too?'

'Yes. It does.'

'I shall be thinking about a lot of things,' said Howard. 'Not just kissing you. I shall be constructing whole scenarios. I love you, Lucy. Will you get tired of me saying that?'

I doubt it. Oh, I very much doubt it. Say it again. And again.

Howard's hand lay on his knee. She saw that, and the crease-lines of dirt on his trousers, and a very small ant of which he was presumably unaware which tracked doggedly across his fingers. I shall always see that ant, she thought, and the scratch on his thumb. Like I'll always smell orange leaves and cigarette smoke and sweat. And I'll always hear what he's just said.

'What sort of scenarios?'

'I don't think I'll go into that,' said Howard. 'Not now, anyway.'

She said, 'Something most odd is happening. I don't feel as though we were where we are any more. I feel as though we had escaped it all somehow. As though we were on another level.'

'Oddly enough, I know exactly what you mean.'

'An illusion is a very peculiar thing to be sharing.'

'It's a good start, though, I should think, wouldn't you?'

'It's the perfect start,' she said. 'In the circumstances. I'd like to hang on to it. Stay inside it. Wouldn't you?'

'Yes and no. I also have a compelling urge to get on with things. The rest of life has never seemed so enticing.'

'Getting on with things is just what we can't do.'

'Someone, I trust, is getting on with them for us.'

'Men in dark suits,' said Lucy. 'In offices in Whitehall. I can't imagine them. They are more incredible than the guard there. The one who smokes all the time. Or the President.'

He swivelled to face her. He took her hand and pulled it down to lie in his within the little dusty area of privacy between them. Two yards away, the guard finished his desultory patrol of the perimeter wall, ground out a cigarette butt and turned to go back the other way. A child threw a quoit. A group near by were talking, every word audible, intelligible but somehow unheard. She saw the blaze of Howard's eyes and the configuration of his face, both infinitely familiar and constantly amazing.

He said, 'Don't give any of them a thought, just at this moment. They don't exist. Right?'

238

'Right,' she said.

At 3.20 the next morning she swarmed up from some brilliant confusing landscape in which jack-booted military figures streamed to and fro down avenues of flowering trees. Arriving on the hard mattress in the convent dormitory, she was aware at once, before identifying her surroundings, that there was something very bad and something else that was wonderful. She lay for an instant helplessly in the grip of these schizophrenic sensations, and then her mind cleared and she knew where she was and everything that had happened. Emotion was fused with hard perception; she saw the dim outlines of the other beds, heard the stirrings of her companions, the shuffle of feet in the passage outside, the sound of a toilet flushing. In her head, there flickered the violently contrasting images of Samara Palace, that room, Omar's frenetic presence, his ranting voice . . . and Howard.

Beyond a couple of walls, a dozen yards away, he too was lying awake perhaps. She concentrated upon this thought, while in some other part of her panic churned. What will happen? What will they do to us? How much longer?

Waking again, much later, to broad daylight and the clamour of the convent's rising, she found the panic subsumed once more into that chronic state of unease. But in some exotic emotional feat the unease was overlaid now by precarious joy. She got up, dressed, and took her turn in the washroom, and then went down to the refectory, where the first of the day's perfunctory meals had already been delivered. She saw Howard across the room, and stood still, savouring the moment.

As the day progressed the feeling of tension in the convent

239

increased. People had had time to digest and consider the implications of what they had heard from Howard and Lucy. They were in the hands of some capricious lunatic. The thought was both chilling and disorienting. Morale sank to a new low, with varying effect; some sat about in catatonic misery, others gathered in groups, endlessly discussing possible options and eventualities. To compound the discomfort, there was now a high proportion of physical ailments. Several people had some kind of bronchitic infection. There were many cases of diarrhoea; the toilets stank. The man with a heart condition was displaying signs of stress. Ted Wilmott was still badly shocked, and the young teacher Denise seemed to be on the edge of breakdown. Some of the women were in need of tampons and sanitary towels, but when Molly Wright put in a request for these along with other supplies she was subjected to an outburst of abuse from the officer in charge. There seemed to have been some ominous shift in the attitude of their captors. The previous stance of indifference tempered with occasional displays of friendliness became one of unconcealed hostility. The hopscotch-playing curly-haired youth lashed out angrily when a child threw a ball at him. One of the airline girls was deliberately jostled and manhandled by another guard.

'So what does this mean?' said Hugh Callow. 'Instructions from above?'

'They've been told something. They know something we don't about what's going on behind the scenes, or they think they do, and they've been told we're to be made the fall guys.' This was James Barrow's view. Whatever the diagnosis, everyone was dismayed and disturbed by this new evidence of volatility. The guards were treated with circumspection. There was nothing to do but sit it out, and hope that perhaps the spasm of aggression would pass.

The midday distribution of food was even more unpalatable than usual. Someone who inadvertently dropped and broke a plate was harangued by the officer in charge and banished from the refectory for the duration of the meal.

In the midafternoon Howard and Lucy sat again in the courtyard. Those bent upon exercise were determinedly circling, as usual; the place seemed an uncomfortable parody of a prison yard.

'All right?' he asked.

'Half of me is very much all right. The other half . . . surviving.'

'Me too. Emotional fission. I wouldn't have believed it possible. I thought of you all night. I had improper thoughts, Lucy.'

'Ah. You did?'

'If these were normal circumstances,' said Howard, 'I would be trying to make love to you by now.'

'Would you . . . I see.'

'How would you react, I wonder?'

'I'll have to think about that. I'd . . . Well, I rather think I'd react quite favourably.'

Howard sighed.

'I suppose I'd be taking my clothes off,' she went on after a moment.

He looked at her.

'T-shirt first.'

'The T-shirt. Yes. And then . . .'

Lucy glanced down at herself, considering. 'The jeans next, I imagine.'

'The jeans.'

'No, wait. Shoes, I've forgotten. Back to the beginning. Scrub that. Shoes first. Then T-shirt. Then jeans.'

'Yes. I see.'

'Then bra, I suppose.'

'Bra . . .' said Howard.

'It's white, Marks and Spencer. At least it was white – it's rather grubby now, I'm afraid.'

'I don't think I'd mind very much about that.'

'That just leaves the pants. So it has to be them next.'

'Yes,' said Howard. 'It does.'

'They're red,' said Lucy.

Howard groaned. 'I don't think I can stand much more of this.'

'We have to stop there anyway. We'll talk about something quite different now. Something tranquillizing. Such as . . .'

'There isn't anything that would be entirely tranquillizing,' said Howard.

'Weather. Weather is always a surrogate. Actually it is much hotter.'

'Is it? I hadn't noticed.'

'Distinctly hotter. This sun is burning. Ironic, to get a tan.'

Howard gazed at her. 'Now you mention it, your nose has gone slightly pink.'

'Bother. And then it will peel, which is uncomfortable.'

'I have some sun-tan cream in my haversack. Why don't I go up and get it?'

'Good idea,' she said. 'Thanks.'

She watched him cross the courtyard in the direction of the refectory door. As he was doing so, she noticed that there seemed to be some sort of activity inside. A clutch of soldiers. Another figure. She took a few steps in that direction, and saw that it was the interpreter. Others were now also paying attention. James Barrow, who had been sitting near by, rose and moved towards the refectory entrance. Ted Wilmott had just come out into the courtyard; he stood and looked back uncertainly. Howard arrived at the door.

The interpreter was in a heightened state. He seemed almost frenzied. Flanked by attendant soldiers, he pushed through the bottleneck of the refectory door and stood at the foot of the steps down into the courtyard. The officer on duty was just behind. The interpreter talked, fast. The officer nodded. The interpreter gestured. He pointed, with little stabbing movements of his forefinger, at those nearest to him. A random, fortuitous selection: James Barrow, Ted Wilmott, the father of one of the young families, one of the airline stewards. Howard.

The soldiers closed in. They grabbed each of those selected. Ted Wilmott tried to duck aside. The soldier twisted his arm backward till he yelped.

It happened with mesmerizing speed. James Barrow was protesting, asking questions, and was dragged through the refectory door and out of sight as he did so. The soldiers were shouting to each other. Later, Lucy thought she had heard Howard say something, and strove desperately to pick up the words. At the time, she stood appalled for moments, and then hurried into the refectory and out into the corridor beyond. Others were milling about in dismay. She cried, 'What's happening? What are they doing with them?' The girl married to the young father was crying hysterically. The officer was standing at the convent's open entrance doors, shouting at people to keep away. Beyond, in the forecourt, Lucy could just see a vehicle like a large police van, into which a stumbling figure was being shoved by a soldier.

The officer now slammed the convent doors. People clustered round, asking questions. He shouted. Guards appeared. Lucy said, 'Where are they taking them? What's going on?' Or she may have said something quite different. Afterwards, she could no longer hear her own voice, only the man bawling at her. One of the guards stepped forward and pushed her violently away, so that she fell sideways on to the stone floor and sat for a minute or so leaning up against the wall, dazed, while Hugh Calloway bent over her and the officer strode off to his headquarters at the end of the corridor.

And now it was as though she had stepped into some new, nightmarish existence. Three minutes had passed since Howard turned to her out there in the courtyard, talking of sun-tan cream. That was now some unreachable haven of normality, of security. Even her body had reacted – gone light, unreliable, so that her legs wavered, she seemed filled with some unstable substance. She moved from one to another of the anxiously speculating groups, and nothing that was said was of any help. Indeed, she hardly heard, and if she contributed it was in some mechanical process. Periodically she glanced at her watch – for some reason the passage of time seemed of great importance – and whenever she did so the hands had barely moved.

She went out into the courtyard and sat under the orange trees, where she had been with Howard yesterday. She felt as though she were floating, so frail with anxiety that she seemed to have become just a feverish intensified consciousness tethered in some way to a body which had lost all stability. She saw Howard, over and over again – his face, his hair, the way he stood, the way he moved. She heard his voice, saying what he had said. She looked at her watch. 3.41. She observed an ant which crawled across a fallen leaf, disappeared over the edge, came up again the other side. She saw that other ant, yesterday,

244

back in that other existence. Someone stood beside her, saying something, and she said something back. They went away. She looked at her watch. 3.43.

They will kill him, she thought. They are killing him at this moment. They have already killed him. He is dead, and I am not.

3.44.

Everything that had happened up till now had been endurable, she saw. It had been a question of keeping calm and rational and taking each day as it came. This was of another order. This was a further dimension. The rest was a warm-up.

You have known this man for five days.

She got up and walked around the courtyard. She stood talking to Molly Wright. Molly Wright said, 'That poor girl is frantic about her husband. She's trying to keep a stiff upper lip but she's in a bad way. She's pregnant, you know. I hadn't realized that.'

Lucy went into the refectory. The nuns, clustered together in one corner, gave off a gentle murmur. Praying. Lucy passed them, out into the corridor and up the stairs.

She used the evil-smelling lavatory. She lay on her bed. She lay on her bed for a long time, but when she stood up again, checked her watch, it had been twelve minutes only.

So long as nothing positive is known, then nothing positive has happened to them. So long as we do not hear anything bad, then nothing bad has happened.

Five days. Out of twenty-nine years, ten months and a couple of weeks. During all of which time you never missed him.

She sat down on the bed, took out her notebook and began to write. She recorded what had happened. She wrote tersely in language that seemed such a mocking representation of those heightened minutes that it made her impatient. 'Talking to Howard B. in the courtyard at about 3.30. He got up to go into the building to fetch something. As he was about to enter the refectory, soldiers appeared. Also the interpreter. The following were seized and taken off: Howard Beamish, James Barrow, Ted Wilmott, Paul Morrison, Clive Stirling.' She paused, staring at the paper, and saw the whole process unreel again: the men pushed and shoved by the soldiers, the interpreter shouting and pointing, Howard turning to look back at her. She completed the account. Then she turned back the pages of her notes and determinedly reread her entry for the day before. She made a correction, and expanded in a couple of places. Then she put away the notebook and checked the time: 4.15.

She came down again, past the simpering Virgin on the bend of the stairs, past the bleeding Christ and the radiant rising Christ and the smirking angels. I have never been so close to iconoclasm. Nor I, thought Lucy. Nor I.

She reached the foot of the stairs at the same moment as the officer in charge emerged from the room used by the guards as their headquarters.

She confronted him. 'Where are Mr Barrow and Mr Beamish and the others?'

He shook his head dismissively.

'Where have they been taken? When will they be brought back?'

He went to pass her and she nipped in front of him. He was a big man. She looked up into the black bush of his moustache and smelled his lunch on his breath.

'Where . . . are . . . they?'

He roared at her. 'Is not your business! These men are taken away.'

246

He started to push past her. She sidestepped so that she was in front of him still. All rationality was gone; she was caught up in a gust of anger and fear. 'You're a bunch of shits, you and your masters – that's what you are. Shits!'

He put out a huge hand and batted her aside. She staggered against the wall. He paused, and for a moment she thought he was going to hit her. And then he spat. A jet of saliva hit her cheek and trickled down on to her T-shirt. He roared at her again – words she could not understand. Then he stamped off down the passage.

She turned and ran up the stairs. In the dormitory she ripped off the T-shirt, put on her spare one, and took the other to the bathroom. She held it under the tap, wrung it out, and spread it over the end of her bed. She was shaking now, and near to tears. She sat down until the shaking grew less. She ground her teeth against the tears.

Molly Wright came in. 'Are you all right, Lucy? Someone said one of them was bawling you out.'

'I'm OK. I tried to find out what's going on.'

'Hugh's had a go. I've had a go. Lots of us have. They won't give an inch.'

'They're shits,' said Lucy. 'Bastards.'

Molly put a hand on her shoulder. 'Come downstairs. Don't sit up here festering on your own. It won't help.'

'In a minute.'

Presently she came down. She saw the officer through the open door of the guards' room, and stalked past.

She walked again in the courtyard. She sat in the refectory. Sometimes she was alone; sometimes she was with others. She saw the sun inch down the sky, through the branches of the casuarina tree in someone's garden, into a mesh of television aerials. She saw its rim touch the roofline of a low apartment building. 5.30.

Perhaps he is seeing the sun go down, too. Perhaps he is not seeing anything, any more.

Five days.

The sun fell behind the apartment block. Presently the sky took on that fragile, bruised look of early evening. The place was very quiet. People talked in low voices, or not at all. 6.20.

Lucy went back into the building, yet again. Yet again she wandered upstairs, came down. And as she did so she heard a commotion in the forecourt. A vehicle door was slammed. She froze, standing at the angle of the staircase.

The front door opened. A soldier came in. He stood aside. James Barrow came ... the airline steward ... the young father. Ted Wilmott.

Howard.

People converged upon them. Howard said, 'I think someone should look after Ted – he's had a rough time.'

'He threw up, that's all. Poor little sod. And they clobbered him a bit for it. Well, more than that ... I'll tell you. In a straight line, though, when I can think straight again.'

'Wait a bit,' she said. 'Don't try right away ...'

'I'm OK. A bit punch drunk. Christ ... Is that really the time? It felt like days, not a couple of hours.'

'There's a slight bruise on the side of your face,' she said.

'Is there? That happened when they chucked us into the van, I expect. There was nothing to sit on and they were pretty ... unceremonious. I fell over. There were a couple of them in with us – peculiarly nasty types – and they jabbed the end of a rifle into anybody who uttered. So we shut up. And they seemed to

248

be taking us for miles – God knows how long that bit of it went on. There was plenty of time to speculate about things, anyway, I can tell you. Not comfortable at all. I thought . . . Well, I thought of course that they were going to dispose of us, to show they meant business. Or something along those lines. It would have been a fairly standard move.'

Lucy said, 'I think a lot of us thought that, too.'

'Then in odd moments of optimism I thought no, they're going to use us to put pressure on London, in some way. That didn't feel very encouraging either, though, thinking about it. I think I sort of stopped thinking and tried just to go along with it. And then suddenly we'd arrived somewhere. The van stopped and there was a lot of shouting and milling about and they bundled us out and into some long low building. An army barracks, I'd say. It all happened so quickly there wasn't any chance to get one's bearings but I feel as though it may have been outside the city. There was a sense of space. Anyway, they hustled us into a room with bars on the window that was very definitely some sort of guard room, or prison cell. Just concrete floor and a bench and a bucket in the corner. That was a pretty grim moment. And one of them standing outside the door glaring through the peep-hole and threatening to give us another jab if we talked. So we just muttered to each other a bit, feeling pretty glum. I mean, for all we knew we were going to be in there for days, weeks. But then after half an hour or so the door opened and we were off again – hustled off into another place, a big bare room with a desk. Pictures of our friend His Excellency on the wall. And a military bloke behind the desk, high-ranking evidently, much by way of brass buttons and gold braid. And the interpreter.'

'Him,' said Lucy.

'Him. The arch apparatchik. Because that's all he is. I'm convinced of that, after today. I'd been wondering if he didn't have some more influential role. But now I'm sure. He's the ultimate yes-man. There he was, dancing attendance on this big shot. Doing his stuff. Because the big shot set about haranguing us, right away. A stream of abuse about how our government was an enemy of Callimbia and London would learn that it could not act with such arrogance and we had been brought here to see that the government of Callimbia was strong and determined. And so forth and so on . . . the interpreter was hard put to it to keep up. It made pretty worrying listening. We deduced that the negotiations weren't going too well. So anyway, when he paused for breath I tried to say that it would be useful if we could be told the state of play, that if we were better informed we could be more helpful, that sort of thing. But he just roared back and the interpreter said, "You are not here to take part in discussions, you are here to understand that this is a serious situation." Barrow then started trying to say that in the circumstances we'd never for a moment thought otherwise but the interpreter cut him off. "Nobody is to speak, it is not permitted that you speak." And the big shot harangued a bit more and then suddenly broke off and walked out of the room. The interpreter said, "Now you will be taken to a place that you will find interesting." And he went too.' Howard broke off. He blinked, shook his head.

'Don't go on if you don't want to,' said Lucy. 'Have a rest. You look pretty shattered, you know.'

He ignored this. 'So then soldiers closed in on us – several of them, and some sort of officer – and it was back in the van again. They didn't take us very far this time. Just a few minutes. And then we were at some other sort of barrack or

250

prison or something. A lot of concrete passages, that was the impression one got. Unpleasant smells. Being marched past a lot of closed iron doors. Once we heard someone groaning. At least I think we did. And then they pushed us through a door and there was a big enclosed compound, with a very high wall topped off with barbed wire. We just stood there. We didn't understand at first what it was all about. There was this rectangular space and high walls, nothing else. The soldiers sort of watched us. And we went on standing there, vaguely looking round, and then we began to see. The surface of the compound had been scattered with sand, and the sand was an odd colour. It was soaked with blood. It had been put down to cover it, and the blood had soaked up through.'

After a moment Lucy said, 'Perhaps it was animals. A slaughterhouse or something . . . to make you think . . .'

'Possibly,' said Howard bleakly.

After a few moments he went on. 'When they were sure we'd registered – taken in what we'd seen – they started to herd us off again. That was when Ted Wilmott threw up. He threw up on the floor where we were standing, and one of them whacked him with a rifle butt and then they made him get down on his hands and knees and eat his vomit. We protested, and Barrow got whacked too. Then they let Ted get up and moved us on. I was pretty dazed by then, I can tell you. I was only taking things in at half cock. I remember they took us to a room where there were these dark stains on the floor and the walls. And once we passed a man just lying on the floor in a passage with his hands tied behind him. I think he was dead. To be honest by then I thought I was going to throw up too. Or pee myself. And then suddenly time was up, or they'd got bored with us, or something, and they were taking us outside again and shoving

251

us back in the van. I was beyond having any idea what to expect next by then. It could have been anything. I just sat there being rattled to bits – the driver was going hell for leather – and then we stopped again and they hauled us out and I saw we were back here. I think it's only now that I've completely taken that in. We're back here. I'm seeing you again. That was one thing I do remember quite clearly – the only clear thought I had at one point. I thought – if they're going to do something ghastly to us, I'll never see Lucy again. And then I thought that I'd only known you for five days, and that didn't seem possible.'

9

'This was to put the frighteners on,' said Hugh Calloway. 'But to what end?'

For, twenty-four hours later, nothing further had happened. Nothing, that is, by way of information or any hint as to what might be going on. Things happened in the claustrophobic world of the convent. Ted Wilmott was in a state of near-collapse, and requiring constant ministrations from the nuns and Molly Wright. His demoralization was contagious; several others now clung precariously to their balance of mind. There had not been any collective account of what the group of five had seen and heard, but everyone knew, either at first hand from one of those concerned, or through others. A chill ran through the entire group.

Lucy thought: it is as though a door opened a crack and you saw for a moment into a room where something hideous is going on.

Those able to remain reasonably level-headed went over and over recent events in search of clues.

'One thing I can tell you,' said Howard. 'It's only us they've locked up. This military big-shot let that drop at one point, when he was going on generally about British iniquities. People from your country are not wanted here. All are now told to leave. More along those lines . . . the impression was that other Brits, whoever there may have been, were given immediate notice to clear out on day one.'

'I suppose we should be relieved,' said Calloway.

'In the abstract, yes. In a practical sense, one can't help feeling that the more people they held the more difficult it would be for them to keep on hanging on to them.'

James Barrow had a livid bruise across one cheekbone, where he had been punched. It seemed to have knocked the stuffing out of him. He slumped gloomily on the bench in the courtyard, as a small group stood around in the early evening. The only mildly cheering factor was that the attitude of their guards appeared to have undergone yet another adjustment during the course of the day. There had been no further abuse. A delivery of soap, nappies and sanitary towels arrived.

'But why aren't they pressuring us in some way?' pondered Calloway. 'What you would expect, is that yesterday's exercise was a warm-up for something. They were putting the frighteners on, and then we were going to be told to . . . make some sort of plea to London, I should imagine. Something along those lines.'

'It may yet happen,' said Howard.

But the day ended without further event. The convent fell silent and into that suspended state which passed for night, when people slept, or did not, when movement diminished to the passage of footsteps to and from the toilets, and the restless shifting of those for whom sleep was out of the question.

Lucy was in a state of emotional fragmentation. Relief and apprehension alternated with gusts of pure fear. Sometimes optimism came padding out: it has been ultimately all right so far, none of us has been seriously hurt, Howard came back, it will be all right in the end. And then the fear stalked. She heard Howard again, and saw what he had conjured up. The door opened; she glimpsed horrors. Somewhere out there, no great distance from us, other people are going through worse yet. Callimbians. People for whom last week is now some unreachable paradise of normality, just as it is for us. People who have been pitched into nightmare.

She lay thinking of this. Out there in the night, unknown people screamed. Died. Not the grey remote figures of catastrophe in newspaper pictures nor yet the vivid cinematic characters of television film but real conceivable people with whom she shared time and space. She could give them features – iconic, Byzantine, negroid, light, dark, the whole significant freighted range she had seen around her over these last days. People who were themselves the legacy of everything that had happened in this country, and who were now paying the price for being present, and in the wrong circumstances, at another climactic moment. It was possible, she found with surprise, even feeling the way she did – the mind spinning, the body aching – to experience some community with these invisible strangers. You felt subtly strengthened, by empathy and outrage.

These thoughts were still uppermost when she joined Howard the next day. They sat opposite one another at a table in the refectory. He took her hands for a moment: 'Hello.'

She said, 'I keep thinking about what you saw.'

'Maybe I shouldn't have told you.'

'You had to tell me.'

'I've thought about it too – for most of the night,' he said. 'There wasn't much alternative. And of whatever may have happened there. In that place ... Poor sods, whoever they were. Anyone with the wrong credentials, I suppose.'

Lucy said, 'It's as though something hideous and primeval came crawling out. You've always known it was there, but you don't think about it. You don't really believe in it.'

'The depraved regime. The mad ruler. One had hoped to go through life without coming up against them. In so far as one had considered the matter. It's the privilege of having spent one's life in a relatively stable political climate.'

'I used to write heated pieces about abuse of the planning laws. I'd get indignant about dog registration.'

'We have lived luxuriously,' said Howard. 'Compared with most.'

'This man is half English. People like him can happen anywhere.'

'Of course. When the time is ripe.'

'One thing,' said Lucy. 'At the beginning of all this I felt that this place wasn't really anything to do with me. It was interesting but ultimately not quite relevant, like most of the rest of the world. I don't feel that any more.'

'To that extent we're older and wiser. One could have wished to become so rather less traumatically.'

'I'm so tired,' she said. 'Suddenly, I want to go home. I'm not going to go under, am I?'

He took her hands again. 'No, you're not.'

In the late morning a small child stricken with a bronchial infection took a turn for the worse. Molly Wright argued with the duty officer for the provision of a doctor. The initial scowling intransigence gave way, rather unexpectedly, to grudging agreement and some hours later a taciturn but apparently efficient man arrived, equipped with antibiotics and a further range of medication. He attended to the child and took a look at other ailing members of the group. His demeanour was of brisk professional competence tinged with unease; conversational overtures of any kind were rejected. It was clear that he would have preferred not to be saddled with this duty, and wished to be done with it as quickly as possible.

'Anyway,' said Molly. 'That child should recover now. Them allowing the man to come has to be a good sign, doesn't it?'

'All it means is that they don't want us to expire of our own accord,' said James Barrow. 'They have something else in mind for us, maybe.'

Molly exploded, uncharacteristically. 'Don't bloody well talk like that! It's irresponsible and defeatist!'

Such flare-ups were quite common now. The indifference or superficial politeness due to transient strangers had given way to the charged attention bestowed upon associates. There were sudden rows, and equally sudden reconciliations. Everyone seemed to regress in their behaviour: the convent was like some grotesque allegory of the workplace, the school playground. Even those who had barely spoken to one another knew each other intimately, it seemed. There were undefined alliances, irrational hostilities. Lucy knew that, come what may, she would remember each of these people, always: this woman's speech pattern, that man's gesture, a child's expression.

In the afternoon one of the flight crew devised a game for the children involving a predatory hunter and hectic flights to safe bases in the four corners of the courtyard. A number of the adults were drawn in, and there was a brief period of febrile gaiety. The guards observed, impassive. And then the thing had run its course and a kind of reactionary gloom descended. The evening meal was delivered. Darkness fell. There would be another night, with all its implications by way of insomnia and solitary contemplation. For most people this was the grimmest period of the day, and they would fight it by postponing for as long as possible the moment of going up to the dormitories. The courtyard would fill up with drifting figures and groups making desultory conversation. Sometimes the guards would become impatient and take a hand, driving people within and up the stairs.

And thus it was that when the soldiers first erupted among them, shouting incomprehensible orders, no one at first sensed anything out of the ordinary. Hugh Calloway said, 'They're imposing the curfew. All right, you bastards, all right . . .' Lucy steeled herself to go up to that bed, that room, those interminable hours. And then she saw suddenly that this was not normal, not routine.

She said to Howard, 'These aren't the usual guys. They're a different lot.'

'So they are. A new shift, I suppose.'

'I don't think so. Look, they're making everybody come outside, not go in.'

For this, they now saw, was the purpose of the shouted orders. Those still in the refectory were being hustled out into the courtyard. There was further shouting from within. People who had already gone upstairs reappeared, half-dressed and anxious, carrying bleary-eyed children.

'Oh, God . . .' said Molly. 'Now what? At this hour . . .'

Others were speculating excitedly that this was it, this was the end, they're sending us home. One of the soldiers had spoken of buses waiting. But this optimism was soon quenched as a further intention became apparent. People were being directed to go into the refectory or remain outside in the courtyard. There was a system.

'They're separating men and women,' said Lucy. 'I don't like this.'

There was a soldier heading for them as she spoke.

'Go, go . . . Women go that way.'

'No,' she said. 'Why? Where are we going?'

Howard had taken her arm. He addressed the soldier. 'Look,' he began, propitiating, reasonable. 'Look, please tell us why it's necessary to . . .'

'Go, go . . .' The man shoved him back, herding Lucy away. Elsewhere there was a thwack, a thump, a sharp cry, shouts. A child screaming. Lucy heard Howard say, 'Don't worry . . . I'll see you soon.' She looked back and saw him being pushed towards the wall by another soldier. She saw his face, over the man's shoulder, looking after her, his features caught in a shaft of light from the windows of the convent. The moment seemed to hang there – Howard gazing across at her, everyone milling about, a confusion on the edges of her vision where a person was on the ground, someone was crying out hysterically . . . And then she was at the doors of the refectory, with Denise, with the airline girls, they were being swept within, and she couldn't see Howard any more. Just dark figures moving about out there.

Paula was saying, 'They knocked that fellow down, did you see? He was trying to go with his wife and they just knocked him down.' There was an officer standing at the door, guards and soldiers everywhere. Molly Wright was talking to the officer, then she was coming round telling everyone that they were to get their belongings, evidently they were being taken somewhere else. The girl whose husband had been hit was in tears. Molly was trying to calm people down: 'The assumption is that they're bringing the men along separately. Heaven knows why. The best thing to do is to go along with it, rather than anyone else get hurt.'

She went up to the dormitory and pushed her things into her flight bag. Everyone else was doing the same. There was little talk. Someone said, 'At least we're seeing the back of this place . . .' One of the nuns muttered continuously: 'Dear Lord . . .' Lucy heard, 'Blessed Father . . .' She pulled back the shutter and looked into the courtyard. She could see nothing except for a dark mass of figures at one end, and soldiers moving about. No faces. No Howard. She turned away and went downstairs with the others.

There were two minibuses. They got into them. Then the officer came round with a list, checking names.

Lucy said, 'Where are we going?'

'Soon will be information.'

'When are the men coming?'

'Soon.'

His face was unfamiliar – this was not one of the regular guards. He looked blankly at her as he ticked her name on the list.

'That won't do,' she said. Loudly, violently. Along the coach, heads swung round. The man ignored her, turning to Molly, in the seat behind. 'Name?'

Lucy stood up. She blocked his way. 'You know where we're going. You must do. You know where they've taken the others. Tell us.'

'Information later.'

'Information *now*!'

He pushed past her, treading on her foot as he did so. She sat down. When he came back along the aisle, his register completed, she shouted at him. 'Why are we being split up like this? *Why?*' He took no notice, hurrying for the exit.

The buses plunged off into the night. The windows were

uncovered. Lucy thought, this time they don't care if we are seen, or what we see. What does that imply, if anything?

'It's bloody unnerving,' said Molly. 'Losing half the party like this.' She glanced at Lucy. 'Wretched for you, my dear. I realize you two . . . Sorry – enough said.'

'It's all right.' Lucy rubbed the window, watched darkness and street lights rushing past. Which way were they going? Back into Marsopolis, it seemed: the buildings closed in, the streets grew brighter. There were a few people about. A café was still open.

'It could be straightforward,' said Molly. 'It could be that we're on our way home. Just some sort of administrative sort-out – nothing sinister.'

They came round a corner. Space. Greenery. Lights. Now I know where we are, thought Lucy. There she is again – Cleopatra's sister.

White marble breast in profile against a midnight-blue sky. A marble palm in her marble hand. Please look – it is the work of a very famous French sculptor. Greek lady. French sculptor. Italian marble, no doubt. Interesting. Keep thinking along these lines, she told herself, it concentrates the mind. What was her name? Queen Berenice – that's it.

I feel sick.

Berenice. Until a few days ago I'd never heard of her. I didn't know Cleopatra had a sister. Maybe that was a problem at the time. She was overshadowed. Sibling rivalry.

Howard.

Now we shall see her from the other side, as the bus turns. We are being given a tour of Cleopatra's sister. Her marble cloak is fastened with a vast marble brooch. She has marble flowers in her marble hair. If she ever existed – if – she had feelings and thoughts like anyone else. Like all of us in this bus, like that man walking there, like everyone who has been here, back and back in time.

Like the people in that place they showed Howard.

Molly said, 'Well, it's not the airport we're heading for, I fear.'

Howard, Lucy thought. Howard.

The buses sped away from the square, down a wide street, on to the corniche road.

'We've been along here before, haven't we?' said Molly. 'Right back at the beginning.'

'Yes.'

'Oh, God . . . I wonder if . . .'

'Yes,' said Lucy. 'I'm wondering that too.'

Within five minutes they knew, as the buses swung sharply off the road. That barrack-like building. The compound empty but for heaps of oil drums. Someone exclaimed, 'Oh, no . . . It's the place we were in at the start.'

They were shepherded out of the buses and into the building, glum, despairing and in some cases mutinous. Lucy accosted the officer again: 'How long are we going to be here? When are the men coming?' She heard her own voice – pitched high with anger and anxiety.

'No information now. Tomorrow.'

'You're a swine,' she said coldly.

There was the room. The same room. The same mattresses heaped in a pile in one corner.

It was now past midnight. Wearily, they established themselves. The mattresses were laid out. Lucy took her turn visiting the dirty toilet at the end of the corridor. She looked out of the window and saw just darkness punctured by a sodium light on the perimeter fence. There had been a donkey trotting along the path in a field, she remembered; she had watched it, six days ago.

They settled, at last, after a fashion. The light was turned out. Children cried, ceased, began again. Lucy took out her notebook and forced herself to write. Then she lay on her side, her jacket folded under her head as a pillow. She was cold. He had put his anorak over her, then. She had woken in this same place, that other day, to find him looking at her. In between there lay some vast tract of time, it seemed. A tract of time and of experience. I am someone else now, she thought. I am different. I can never go back to being who I was then. It is always like that, of course, but more now. More than I would have thought possible.

She lay alone in that crowded room. Occasionally she dipped into a hectic form of sleep. Then she would surge up again on to a switchback of faith, foreboding, hope, despair.

They were made to stand in a group at one end of the courtyard. The soldiers prowled, threatening anyone who made a move. The man who had been knocked down had injured a knee. He tried to sit on the bench and was ordered to his feet. He leaned against the wall, wincing and cursing.

Howard watched the windows of the building. The lights were on and figures moved about within. And then a shutter was opened and he saw Lucy's face, looking out. He saw her turn her head from side to side, searching the darkness. He raised his arm, waved. And then she was gone. He went on watching the building, and presently it seemed to go still. There was no more movement. Hugh Calloway, standing beside him, said, 'I think they've taken them away, you know. The women. I don't think there's anyone inside any more.'

They stood there for a long time. When Howard looked at his watch it was past midnight, but he did not know when it had all begun. The officer came out of the convent with a list in his hand. They were required to identify themselves. The barrage of questions and objections was ignored: 'Information later.' Anyone too persistent or vociferous was threatened with a rifle butt. The officer vanished again and they continued to stand there. Several times the telephone rang within the convent.

'Fuck this,' said James Barrow. 'This is the worst yet. They're up to something.'

And then the interpreter arrived. He was suddenly there, stepping quickly across the courtyard towards them with an entourage of military, fussing over a sheaf of papers in his hand. He halted. He exchanged sharp words with the officer. He sent a soldier scurrying for a further piece of paper. He emanated importance and irascible purpose. At last he turned his attention to the group of standing men.

'I will check all names now. Anderson?'

'This has already been done,' said Hugh Calloway.. 'We are all present and correct. Would you please tell us why we are being treated like this and what is happening to the rest of our group.'

'You must not interrupt. Barrow?'

'I'm here. There's not a hell of a lot of alternative, is there?'

'Beamish?'

'Where have they taken the rest of our group?' demanded Howard.

'I cannot give this information at the moment. You must answer to your name, please.'

'Oh, sod off . . .'

'Calloway? Davies?. . .' Laboriously, the interpreter completed his register. He conferred with the officer. The officer turned away and hurried into the convent.

The interpreter now confronted the group. He raised his voice. 'You will give me your attention now. I have very important instructions.'

'Get on with it . . .'

'Who is speaking there? Anyone speaking will be severely punished. I have very important instructions on the part of the government of this country. I am instructed to inform you that your government continues to be most arrogant and uncooperative. This is very unfortunate for you. In order that your government understands that the Callimbian government will not tolerate this behaviour it is necessary to take certain steps.'

The group went still. 'Oh, Christ . . .' muttered James Barrow.

'The women group is removed to other accommodation. Men group will remain here but there will be exception.' He paused. They watched him.

'There will be exception of one person. In order that your government understands that it must be more co-operative it is necessary to make example of one person. One person must receive punishment.' He paused again. He eyed them. No one spoke.

'One person will be selected for punishment. Selection will be by fair process.'

'This is barbaric,' said Hugh Calloway. 'What punishment?'

'Severe punishment. This is the fault of your government. The Callimbian government regrets. Unfortunately there is no alternative. Now I will explain method of selection.'

Barrow said, 'I knew there would be something like this, sooner or later. The bastards.'

The officer now came hurrying from the convent. The interpreter turned aside. The two men bent over an object supplied by the officer. They became absorbed in some process requiring meticulous attention. There were terse exchanges. The interpreter became tetchy. Then he was satisfied. He turned back to the group. 'For making of selection you will each pick from straws that I will hold out. All straws are long straws except one. The man picking short straw is man selected for punishment.'

'For God's sake,' said Captain Soames. 'You just can't do this.'

Calloway said, 'This is appalling. I can't believe you're serious.'

I can, thought Howard. Unfortunately I can. He saw now what the officer was holding. A bible. The large black bible from the lectern in the refectory.

'This is very fair system of selection. Very traditional. Each man has equal chance and selection is question of fate. That is most fair and there is no injustice. We will now make selection. There are five straws placed in this book. I will hold out the book and the first five men will each take straw. Then if no man has taken the short straw the next five men will choose straw.' He snapped an order. Soldiers leaped forward. Five men at the front of the group were cordoned off and pushed forward. Soames. James Barrow. Three others.

'I refuse to take part in this,' said Soames.

'This is very stupid,' said the interpreter. 'Take straw, please.'

'No.'

The interpreter spoke to one of the soldiers. The soldier took a pistol from his belt and slammed the barrel against Soames's jaw. Soames staggered backwards. The interpreter said, 'That

266

man will take straw later. Now you . . .' He nodded to James Barrow.

Barrow hesitated. The interpreter held out the bible. The bible had a battered black cloth binding. From the gilt-edged pages there protruded the ends of five plastic drinking straws, spirally striped in candy pink.

Barrow reached forward and took a straw. Howard heard his exhalation of breath. He fell back.

'Next person, please.'

The group was now absolutely silent.

The interpreter said, 'None of these people have taken short straw, so we continue.' He turned aside. The officer leaped forward to assist. Captain Soames was sitting down on the tarmac, holding his face in his hands.

The interpreter was now ready again. 'Next five men will now choose straw.'

The soldiers closed in once more. The one who pushed Howard forward did so with such violence that he nearly fell. The proffered bible was almost in his face.

'Take straw, please.'

He knew it was the one as soon as he had hold of it, began to pull. It came too easily.

Of course, he thought. Of course. It was always going to be me. He looked down at the straw. A spiral stripe in candy pink. Short. Very short.

The interpreter said, 'There is no need to continue further. Unfortunately Mr Beamish has taken the short straw, so the selection is now finished.'

10

Howard sat at one end of the back seat, the interpreter at the other. The car careered through the night.

Initially, Howard thought only in obscenities. He was not a man given to foul language, but now a torrent of obscene verbiage poured through his head. He had not realized he knew such words. Then occasional rafts of clarity and reason joined the flow. Why didn't they do it there and then, in front of the others? Where are they taking me? What will they do, and how quickly?

The interpreter did not address him. Once or twice he had a brief exchange with the driver or the soldier in the passenger seat.

Howard felt a surge of nausea. He decided to speak, if only to distract his own attention from this discomfort. 'Do you happen to know what your employers have in mind for me?'

'Excuse me?'

'Oh, for Christ's sake, man . . . What are they going to do with me?'

'I am not so sure. Perhaps it is better we do not discuss this. It is most unfortunate. You should feel very angry that your government is so stupid and forces the Callimbian authorities to take these steps.'

Howard said, 'Whatever step they have in mind is perfectly avoidable. At least I must be allowed an opportunity to speak to a representative of my government.'

The interpreter was silent. Howard stared at the back of the driver's head. He saw the nape of his neck, the glint of his hair, the intimate detail of an insect bite. He was aware of the darkened landscape rushing past the car windows: the outline of a tree etched against the sky, a building packed with light.

He said, 'I wonder if you have any idea of the atrocity of the things with which you are so complacently involved.' He spoke quietly, perhaps to himself.

'Excuse me?'

'Never mind.'

'I am obliged to carry out instructions,' said the interpreter. 'That is all.'

'A familiar plea,' said Howard.

'It is a pity for your wife,' said the interpreter. His tone was quite dispassionate. He smoothed his tie. He glanced at his watch.

Howard turned to look out of the window more intently. He had barely heard the man. They seemed to be going away from the city: the street lights and glimmering buildings had given way to darkness. His nausea had ebbed now and he felt just a cold sinking gloom, a black depth that he would not have thought possible. It occurred to him that if he was going to be shot, then the actual process would be, one assumed, painless. He would die. At once. The pain, the torment, was the anticipatory process. It was what was happening now, in fact. With, presumably, worse to come. The sentence. The physical preparations.

He thought of Lucy. He summoned her, placed her alongside

him on the seat of the car, took her hand in his. We were going to have such an extraordinarily good time together, you and I, he told her. And then this thought became unendurable; he let her go.

He thought of his parents, decent harmless people who did not deserve this anguish. He thought of his work. He thought for an instant of the unattainable and now almost inconceivable pleasure of gazing down into the tranquil elegant world of *Hallucigenia*, of *Marrella*, of *Aysheaia*. He experienced a flood of wild anger. No, he thought. No, no, no.

And suddenly there came floating forth an alien voice, from somewhere far within, far back, an echo of childhood maybe, of the time before enlightenment. 'Please God . . .' it said. 'Please God look after me. Please God may this not be happening.'

He quenched the voice, silenced it. Rather the obscenities.

The car fled now along a wide highway. There was no other traffic. Its lights forged a channel in the darkness, flooding the shining metal studs in the centre of the road and the trees at the side. Then suddenly it wheeled to the right. Howard saw a high wire fence, a barrier across the road, a concrete guardhouse from which soldiers emerged.

That place. Of course, he thought again. Of course. I always knew we were coming here. But he could go no deeper in despair. The black hole engulfed him now, a kind of anaesthesia. He stepped from the car, was led across tarmac towards an entrance. He was aware of sky above him, glittering with stars, the icy brilliance of space. Suddenly he wanted above all to stay out here, where he could see that. He hung back, and hands pushed him violently onwards.

They went into the building. Lights. Soldiers. He was hustled down a passage. A door was opened. He saw a room, windowless, with a bench. He clawed up out of the black hole of his despair and said, 'Let me speak to a representative of my government.' He heard his own voice, loud and angry, and was surprised; it sounded like someone else's.

The interpreter was just turning away. He paused. He said, 'That is not possible, I think.' One of the soldiers pushed Howard into the room and closed the door. He heard a bolt slam shut.

He stood there for a moment. Then he sat down on the bench, largely because he felt unsteady. There was a bucket in one corner, which stank. He saw the contents. Someone else had sat here, waiting. And another person, or that person, had made a small drawing on the dirty plaster of the wall. He stared at this for a while, not really seeing it except as an abstract shape, a circle from which sprang a girdle of spikes. The sun. Oh, yes, the sun.

He inched again out of the black hole. All the time that I am waiting, he thought, nothing has yet happened. And so long as nothing has happened it may not happen. There is still hope. We sat in this room before, or this cell or whatever it is, or if not this one then one very like it, the five of us sat here, and we came out and went back to the convent and I saw Lucy again.

That was different. They had not said then what has been said this time.

Nothing that they say is to be relied on.

Why, in that case, bring me here?

He got up and paced the room, to test his legs. Four paces one way, four the other. There seemed to be a lot of coming and going outside the door. People hurrying to and fro, urgent exchanges. What are they saying?

He sat down again. The black hole swarmed up and sucked

him in. He supposed that they would come to fetch him, soon. Or possibly not soon. But they would come. And then they would take him somewhere else and whatever they were going to do to him would be done. Punishment.

A word capable of wide interpretation.

Logically, it must be supposed that they intended to show that they meant business. They intended to present London with a dead body in order to put on the pressure.

Or possibly not a dead body, but a severely damaged one.

At this point he began to panic. His heart raced; he felt weak, dizzy. He made himself get up and walk again, counting the steps. Thirty-six paces for his age. Now nine paces for the month, September. Now sixteen for the date, or was it seventeen? Make it seventeen. Now another hundred for good measure.

Better. Just a little better. Sit down again.

He told himself that he must not accede to this. Nobody is entirely powerless. He had a voice. He must continue to protest, to demand contact with London, to remind these people that their actions were criminal.

For what that was worth.

And he must remember all the time, every moment, that while to wait was torment, to wait was also to hope. He came surging from the black hole in a fit of indignant disbelief. This could not be happening, not to him, not to anyone.

Footsteps beyond the door, again. Going past, once more.

What have they done with the rest of them? What have they done with Lucy?

And now, somehow, he began to drift. In exhaustion, perhaps, or shock. He stopped hearing the noises beyond the door, and entered a state of suspension, in which there crowded into his head images of familiar places – his flat, his office in the college, the lab, the lecture room. He was in each of these places, simultaneously, their furnishings shimmered above the walls and the floor of the room in which he sat. He saw faces, too. His parents. Colleagues. Vivien. Lucy. Lucy above all. It was as though some benign faculty of the brain had come into play, submerging reality, distancing him from what was taking place, or was about to take place, or might take place. He seemed to float asunder; his body continued to sit on that bench, nauseous and shivering, but his mind roamed free, intent upon these definitions of identity. Every now and then panic threatened, he could feel it start to well up and he fought it, he tamped it down, forced himself back to this reassuring parade of references. He felt grimly proud of himself, as though he had succeeded in some crippling rite of passage.

He lost sense of time, focused entirely upon this exercise of will and of endurance. He threw himself into the pursuit of trivia. What was his father's birthplace? What had been his grandmother's given names? In what subjects had he received A's at O level? How many drawers were there to the filing cabinet in his office?

What colour were Lucy's eyes?

Hours might be passing, or perhaps only minutes. Occasionally he would hear the footsteps and the voices in the passage outside and some part of him would respond, his stomach lurching or his eyes anxiously trained upon the door.

And then, when he was not looking at it, when he was staring at the floor, constructing the outline of an imaginary *Opabinia*, it opened. The door sprang open and a soldier stood there.

He held a tray. A tray of food. An arrangement of meat and

rice on a plate. A cup of coffee. A paper napkin folded in a triangle. He held the tray out to Howard.

Howard stared, numbed. He said, 'I don't want it.'

The soldier continued to proffer the tray. Howard shook his head. The soldier shrugged, set the tray down on the bench alongside him and left. The bolt banged shut once more.

Howard looked at the food. The sight of it made him feel even more nauseated than he had been before. He pushed the tray further from him. He looked now, for the first time, at his watch and saw that it was a quarter past five. He was astonished.

So what the hell did this mean? Food. Do you feed a person if you are about to execute him? Well, yes, traditionally you do. But not, Howard felt, in these circles. So what then did this imply? He looked again at the food. It would make sense to eat it, he supposed. That, though, was quite impossible.

And now there was definitely even more activity beyond the door. Boots thudding past. Someone shouting orders. He listened, with gathering unease. Minutes passed. Five. Ten. Time was on the move once more. Erratically. Twelve minutes. Twenty.

The door opened. Another soldier. An officer, this, Howard noted queasily.

The man held open the door. He indicated that Howard should come. Howard got slowly to his feet. He stepped forward. Outside there was a little phalanx of soldiers. Three of them. They moved off down the corridor. Howard and the officer in front, the soldiers close behind.

Lucy saw the day begin. She saw, quite clearly, the precise moment at which light started to suffuse the dark rectangle of sky framed by the window. She watched it seep upwards: midnight-blue mutated to grey stained with yellow. It was now 5.15.

She stood up and went to look outside, moving cautiously. A few people were asleep. She was still standing there when she heard the sound of a large vehicle manoeuvring in the compound, somewhere out of sight. She heard, registered, but did not respond – stupid with sleeplessness and gloom. She watched a bird wing slowly across the apricot sky, moving exactly parallel with the top of the wire fence. Behind her, a baby was crying; people shifted and murmured.

And then everything happened very quickly. There were soldiers suddenly in the room, urging everyone to their feet. 'Go,' they said. 'Go now. Go in bus.' Weary and confused, the women stumbled around gathering up their things. They trailed out of the room, into the passage, out into the cool fresh morning. There stood a coach. They trooped on board, still dazed, not knowing how to react. Was this good or bad? Nothing, surely, could be worse than the place from which they had come? It had all been so quick. 'Go . . . Go now.' Go where?

The coach moved off. Deserted, early morning roads. The corniche. They stared out of the windows, not saying much. Lucy tried to get a sense of direction. This, she thought, this is surely the way we came. At the beginning. I've seen these buildings before. This roundabout. Is it conceivably possible that we are going to the airport?

Howard gazed incredulously at the interpreter. 'Say that again?'

They were in the back of the car. The same car. The car was pulling out on to the highway along which they had come, when it was still dark. It was light now. Howard saw scrubby fields, a petrol station, a line of hills in the distance.

'Say that again. Say where we're going.'

'I take you now to the airport. There has been a very interesting development. The Callimbian government is now able to make arrangements that you return to your own country. All the group. I am very pleased to tell you this.'

'Why should I believe you?' demanded Howard, after a moment.

The interpreter looked petulant. 'Why is it necessary that I tell you lies? I have instructions from the highest authority. This is a very recent happening. There is very recent news from London.'

'What do you mean?' said Howard. 'Do you mean that our government has handed over these people?' He was shaking; it was an effort to speak steadily.

'I think that is not the case. I think it is the case that these people in question are no longer a problem.'

'I don't understand.'

'The Callimbian government has been able to make arrangements that these people will not be a threat to the internal security of this country. Certain measures have been taken. In your country. There are people friendly and co-operative with the Callimbian authorities who have taken certain measures. This is very satisfactory. You should be very pleased. Now it is possible that you go home.'

Howard was silent. 'I take it that you're saying that they've been assassinated, these people. In England.'

The interpreter winced slightly, as though Howard had committed a social solecism. 'This is some very dangerous people. It was necessary for the security of this country to make them no longer able to operate.'

276

Howard's head was spinning. He was so divided by emotions that he felt as though he might fly apart. Elation. Compunction (we may have got through this, but others have not). Relief. Doubt (is there any truth in this?). He tried to sort it out and think rationally. There is a strong possibility that it is true: it makes sense, and why otherwise take me from that place and drive me off somewhere else? But there will be no certainty until I see the airport.

He tried to contain the elation, the relief, and concentrated on the landscape, searching for clues. The hills to the left now, so they were going parallel, between hills and sea. The rising sun ahead, so they were going east. But he had never made any note of directions on their previous travels, so this was not much help.

'I am sure that your wife will be most pleased to see you,' said the interpreter benignly.

Howard ignored him. Indeed he barely heard the man, who seemed now like some irritating and repellant insect. He was focused entirely upon controlling his own brimming feelings, upon stopping himself from getting too excited, too hopeful. Not yet. Not yet. It may be another cruel device. Grimly he fought optimism and stared out of the car windows. Now the car turned off the highway, on to a lesser but still purposeful road. And there was a road sign: 7 kilometres to a place whose name meant nothing to him.

The soldier in the passenger seat turned his head and made some remarks. The interpreter responded, in a desultory tone. He seemed preoccupied, as though something had occurred to him. He fished in his pocket, took out a thick black leather gold-tooled notebook and appeared to hunt for an entry. He delved in another pocket, brought out a note pad and wrote on it. He turned to Howard. 'Perhaps I ask you a small favour, Mr Beamish?'

Howard leaned forward, staring between the heads of the driver and the soldier. He had caught sight of another sign ahead. A sign bearing that ubiquitous, global logo: a small stylized aircraft. His heart thumped; he became lightheaded. Left, said the sign, left takes you to the airport.

The car turned left.

'Mr Beamish, perhaps I ask you a favour?'

Howard gave a great involuntary sigh. He felt suddenly quite calm, quite balanced, almost dispassionate. He said, 'Tell me something, if things hadn't worked out as you say they have, what exactly would have been done with me?'

The interpreter became obtuse. 'Excuse me?'

'Come on,' said Howard. 'You know damn well what I mean. Were they going to shoot me? Or something along those lines?'

The interpreter was patently embarrassed. He cleared his throat, ostentatiously examined the face of his watch. 'Very soon now we arrive . . .'

'Well, were they?'

The man avoided Howard's eye. 'I am not so sure. I think perhaps unfortunately that would have been necessary. Personally I am very happy that is avoided. This is very good news.'

The car swung off on to another slip road. There was another airport sign. And another. In the distance Howard saw the long low line of a hangar.

'Mr Beamish, I ask you perhaps . . .'

'That's all I wanted to know,' said Howard. 'Just shut up now, could you?' He gazed in ecstasy at the mundane and beautiful equipment of the airport: the empty approach road sweeping towards a clutter of buildings, trucks, trailers, a line of small aircraft, neatly roosting. A big jet, burning silver-gilt in the sun.

The interpreter was peeved. 'I think you do not understand, Mr Beamish. I am personally liking your country very much. I act on instructions of my government. It is not a personal matter.'

The car sped down the approach road, through an entrance, round a corner. It drew up in front of the main airport building. Howard was out of it first. The interpreter was hurrying behind him, saying something. Howard headed into the building.

They were at the far side of the central concourse. He saw James Barrow, Molly, the airline girls. Someone spotted him and shouted out. And then he saw Lucy. She had her back to him. She turned. She saw him. She stood stock-still. And he began the long walk towards her.

They were scattered throughout the plane, a 747 and inappropriately large. Some people had stretched out over a row of seats and were sleeping. Most were too euphoric. They roamed the aisles, chatted, laughed, visited the luggage lockers. Some of the lockers contained boxed and wrapped lap-top computers and instamatic zoom-lens cameras. These items had appeared loaded on to several trolleys, just as they were moving towards the gate which would lead them to the aircraft. The interpreter had come hurrying forward to explain that the Callimbian government wished to make a present to each member of the group. It wished to make a small compensation for the inconvenience caused. Here were very nice lap-top computers, and autofocus superzoom cameras for the ladies. The group had at first been too stunned to respond. Then some people laughed. Others became interested.

The computer salesman said, 'That's the LS 386. Lovely job. We can't get enough of them.'

There were those who hesitated for a moment, and then helped themselves. Paula took a camera, defiantly. 'I always wanted a decent camera, and those cost an arm and a leg. I may as well get something out of this.'

The interpreter had been perplexed that not everyone followed suit. He said to James Barrow, 'Take. Please take. This is very exceptional computer.'

James said, 'Look, just bugger off, would you?'

As Howard and Lucy passed the interpreter stepped quickly forward. 'You do not want?'

'No,' said Howard. 'We do not want.'

'Mr Beamish, I ask you then small favour . . .' He reached into his pocket, pulled out a slip of paper with a name and address written on it. 'I ask you if you very kindly take camera to my landlady in Cambridge. She will like this very much.'

Howard stared at him in blank amazement. Then he put his hand under Lucy's elbow and moved on, towards the plane. When he glanced back, the man was still proffering electronic equipment, with an air of offended benevolence.

And now Howard sat with Lucy at his side. She had fallen asleep. She had started to write in that notebook and then, as he covertly watched, he had seen the pencil slide from her fingers. She was in the window seat, with her head turned towards him, her chin slumped upon her shoulder. When her elbow slid from the armrest he wedged an airline pillow to make her more comfortable. He watched over her, luxuriating. He learned her features: an interesting irregularity about the nostrils, one wider than the other, a small mole high on the left cheek, those freckles.

From time to time he looked beyond her, out of the window. The plane was cruising now, embarked on its tranquil path between the quilt of cloud beneath and the blue heights above. Earlier, he had watched Callimbia drop away below, its features diminishing by the minute. Buildings went out of focus and became areas of geometrical patterning, cars melted into roads and roads became delicate scribblings on a counterpane of green and brown. He saw the coast, an undulating band of yellow frilled with white. The place began to recede into unreality – it became a geographical expression, a lavish illustration, something to gaze down upon with detached interest. Marsopolis fell away, and with it the furnishings of the previous days – the Excelsior Hotel, the convent, that cell, the execution ground. Omar. The interpreter. They mutated. They lost the crucial hard edge of immediacy and became a sequence in the head, almost as though they were fictions, a disturbing exercise of the imagination.

He leapt ahead. He thought of the weeks to come. Should he go yet to Nairobi? Would Lucy go to Nairobi? Might they go together to Nairobi? But Lucy now would be caught up in more pressing concerns, given her trade. He contemplated the immediate future, to which he had not until now given a thought. To which in fact he had not dared to give a thought. The fuss. The newspapers. He did not want any of this. He did not want to hear the reverse account of everything – the explanations, the justifications, the complementary facts which would illuminate their own experience in Marsopolis. Which would show why the Callimbians had done this at that point, why they had behaved thus at another. He preferred to leave it as it was: irrational and inexplicable. He knew that this attitude was perverse, and also that it was inconsistent with his habits of mind, was intellectually offensive, indeed. All he could feel, right now, was that explanations and revelations had nothing to do with what had happened and could not be undone, with the whole contingent sequence. He considered this sequence: he dismantled it and looked at its component parts, at moments which could have flown off in some other direction, at the whole precarious narrative. The narrative which had dealt him Lucy and which, by the same token, might yet remove her, in which perhaps there lurked already some fatal twist, some malevolent disposition of events. He stared for an instant at capricious fate, and then turned away, because that is all that anyone can do. He looked at Lucy. She woke. She smiled.